CLANS OF THE ALPHANE MOON

Philip K. Dick was born in Chicago 1928 and lived in California for most of life. He attended college for a year at Berkeley. Apart from writing, his main interest was music. He won the Hugo Award for his classic novel of alternative history, *The Man in the High Castle* (1962). He was married five times and had three children. He died in March 1982. His novel *Do Androids Dream of Electric Sheep?* was adapted into the world famous film *Blade Runner* in the same year.

'One of the most original practitioners writing any kind of fiction'

Sunday Times

BY THE SAME AUTHOR

Novels

Solar Lottery
Eye in the Sky
Vulcan's Hammer
The Man Who Japed
The Cosmic Puppets
The World Jones Made
Time Out of Joint
Dr Futurity
The Man in the High Castle
The Game Players of Titan
Clans of the Alphane Moon
Flow My Tears, the Policeman Said
The Penultimate Truth
The Simulacra
Martian Time-Slip
Dr Bloodmoney, or How We Got Along After The Bomb
The Zap Gun
Now Wait for Last Year
Counter-Clock World
Blade Runner (also published as *Do Androids Dream of Electric Sheep?*)
Ubik
Our Friends from Frolix 8
Galactic Pot-Healer
The Three Stigmata of Palmer Eldritch
A Scanner Darkly
Valis
The Divine Invasion
The Transmigration of Timothy Archer
Confessions of a Crap Artist
The Ganymede Takeover (with Ray Nelson)
Deus Irae (with Roger Zelazny)
A Maze of Death
Lies, Inc. (The Unteleported Man)
The Man Whose Teeth Were All Exactly Alike
In Milton Lumky Territory
Puttering About in a Small Land
Humpty Dumpty in Oakland
Radio Free Albemuth
We Can Build You
The Broken Bubble

Short Stories

A Handful of Darkness
I Hope I Shall Arrive Soon
The Variable Man
The Book of Philip K. Dick
The Golden Man
The Preserving Machine
Collected Stories 1: Beyond Lies the Web
Collected Stories 2: Second Variety
Collected Stories 3: The Father-Thing
Collected Stories 4: The Days of Perky Pat
Collected Stories 5: We Can Remember It For You Wholesale

PHILIP K. DICK

Clans of the Alphane Moon

HARPER
Voyager

HarperVoyager
An imprint of HarperCollins*Publishers*
77–85 Fulham Palace Road,
Hammersmith, London W6 8JB

www.harpercollins.co.uk

This paperback edition 2008
1

Previously published in paperback by Voyager 1996

First published in Great Britain
by Panther Books 1975

A catalogue record for this book is
available from the British Library

ISBN-13: 978 0 00 648248 2

Set in Times

Printed in Great Britain by
Clays Ltd, St Ives plc

ONE

Before entering the supreme council room, Gabriel Baines sent his Mans-made simulacrum clacking ahead to see if by chance it might be attacked. The simulacrum – artfully constructed to resemble Baines in every detail – did many things, since it had been made by the inventive clan of Manses, but Baines only cared to employ it in its manoeuvring for defence; defending himself was his sole orientation in life, his claim to membership in the Pare enclave of Adolfville at the north end of the moon.

Baines had of course been outside Adolfville many times, but he felt safe – or rather relatively safe – only here, within the stout walls of this, the Pare city. Which proved that his claim to membership in the Pare clan was not contrived, a mere simulated technique by which he could gain entry into the most solidly-built, sturdy and enduring urban area anywhere. Baines beyond doubt was sincere ... as if there could be any doubt of *him*.

For example, there was his visit to the incredibly degrading hovels of the Heebs. Recently he had been in search of escaped members of a work brigade; being Heebs they had perhaps straggled back to Gandhitown. The difficulty, however, was that all Heebs, to him at least, looked alike: dirty, stooped creatures in soiled clothing who giggled and could not concentrate on any complicated procedure. They were useful for mere manual labour, nothing more. But with the constant need for tinkering improvement of Adolfville's fortifications against the predations of the Manses, manual labour was currently at a premium. And no Pare would dirty his hands. Anyhow, among the dilapidated shacks of the Heeb he had felt pure terror, a sense of almost infinitely vast exposure among the most flimsy of human constructs; it was an inhabited garbage dump of cardboard dwellings. The Heebs however did not object. They dwelt among their own refuse in tranquil equilibrium.

Here today, at the twice yearly council meeting representing all the clans, the Heebs would of course have a spokesman; speaking for the Pares he would find himself seated in the same room with an odious – literally so – Heeb. And this scarcely dignified his task. Probably it would be straggle-haired, fat Sarah Apostoles again this year.

But more ominous would be the Mans representative. Because, like every Pare, Baines was terrified of each and every Mans. Their reckless violence shocked him; he could not comprehend it, so purposeless was it. For years he had put Manses down as simply hostile. But that did not explain them. They *enjoyed* violence; it was a perverse delight in breaking things and intimidating others, especially Pares such as himself.

But knowing this did not fully help him; he still quailed at the anticipated confrontation with Howard Straw, the Mans delegate.

Wheezing asthmatically his simulacrum returned, a fixed smile on its Baines-like artificial countenance. 'All in order, sir. No deadly gas, no electrical discharge of a dangerous degree, no poison in the water pitcher, no peepholes for laser rifles, no concealed infernal machines. I would offer the suggestion that you can safely enter.' It clacked to a halt, became silent.

'No one approached you?' Baines asked cautiously.

The simulacrum said, 'No one is there yet. Except, of course, for the Heeb sweeping the floor.'

Baines, out of a lifetime of protective cunning, opened the door a crack for that which was essential: a momentary glimpse of the Heeb.

The Heeb, a male, swept in his slow, monotonous way, the usual silly Heeb expression on his face, as if his work amused him. He could probably keep it up for months without becoming bored; Heebs could not tire of a task because they could not comprehend even the concept of diversity. Of course, Baines reflected, there was some virtue in simplicity. He had for instance been impressed by the famous Heeb saint, Ignatz Ledebur, who radiated spirituality as he wandered from town to town, spreading the warmth of his harmless Heeb personality. This one certainly looked devoid of dangerousness....

And the Heebs, at least, even their saints, did not try to convert people, as did the Skitz mystics. All the Heebs asked was to be let alone; they simply did not want to be bothered by life, and each year they shed more and more of the complexities of living. Returned, Baines reflected, to the mere vegetable, which, to a Heeb, was ideal.

Checking his laser pistol – it was in order – Baines decided that he could enter. So step by step he walked into the council room, took a chair, then abruptly changed to another; that one had been too close to the window: he presented too good a target to anyone outdoors.

To amuse himself while he waited for the others to arrive, he decided to bait the Heeb. 'What's your name?' he demanded.

'J-Jacob Simion,' the Heeb said, sweeping with his standard silly grin unchanged; a Heeb never knew when he was being baited. Or if he did he did not care. Apathy toward everything: that was the Heeb way.

'You like your work. Jacob?' Baines asked, lighting a cigarette.

'Sure,' the Heeb said, and then giggled.

'You've always spent your time sweeping floors?'

'Huh?' The Heeb did not appear able to comprehend the question.

The door opened and plump, pretty Annette Golding, the Poly delegate, appeared, purse under her arm, her round face flushed, her green eyes shining as she panted for breath. 'I thought I was late.'

'No,' Baines said, rising to offer her a chair. He glanced professionally over her; no sign that she had brought her weapon. But she could be carrying feral spores in capsules secreted in a gum-pocket within her mouth; he made it a point, when he reseated himself, to select a chair at the far end of the big table. Distance ... a highly valuable factor.

'It's warm in here,' Annette said, still perspiring. 'I ran all the way up the stairs,' She smiled at him in the artless way that some Polys had. She did seem attractive to him ... if only she could lose a little weight. None the less he liked Annette and he took this opportunity to engage in light banter with her, tinged with overtones of the erotic.

'Annette,' he said, 'you're such a pleasant, comfortable person. A shame you don't marry. If you married me —'

'Yes, Gabe,' Annette said, smiling. 'I'd be protected. Litmus paper in every corner of the room, atmosphere analysers throbbing away, grounding equipment in case influence machines radiating —'

'Be serious,' Baines said, crossly. He wondered how old she was; certainly no more than twenty. And, like all Polys, she was childlike. The Polys hadn't grown up; they remained unfixed, and what was Polyism if not the lingering of plastic childhood? After all, their children, from every clan on the moon, were born Polys, went to their common, central school as Polys, did not become differentiated until perhaps their tenth or eleventh year. And some, like Annette, never became differentiated.

Opening her purse Annette got out a package of candy; she began to eat rapidly. 'I feel nervous,' she explained. 'So I have to eat.' She offered the bag to Baines, but he declined – after all, one never knew. Baines had preserved his life for thirty-five years now, and he did not intend to lose it due to a trivial impulse; everything had to be calculated, thought out in advance if he expected to live another thirty-five.

Annette said, 'I suppose Louis Manfreti will represent the Skitz clan again this year. I always enjoy him; he has such interesting things to tell, the visions he sees of primordial things. Beasts from the earth and the sky, monsters that battle under the ground ...' She sucked on a piece of hard candy thoughtfully. 'Do you think the visions that Skitzes see are real, Gabe?'

'No,' Baines said, truthfully.

'Why do they ponder and talk about them all the time, then? They're real to them, anyhow.'

'Mysticism,' Baines said scornfully. He sniffed, now;

some unnatural odour had come to him, something sweet. It was, he realized, the scent of Annette's hair and he relaxed. Or was it supposed to make him think that? he thought suddenly, again alert. 'Nice perfume you have on,' he said disingenuously. 'What's it called?'

'*Night of Wildness,*' Annette said. 'I bought it from a pedlar here from Alpha II; it cost me ninety skins but it does smell wonderful, don't you think? A whole month's salary.' Her dark eyes looked sad.

'Marry me,' Baines began again, and then broke off.

The Dep representative had appeared; he stood in the doorway and his fear-haunted, concave face with its staring eyes seemed to pierce Baines to the heart. Good lord, he groaned, not knowing whether to feel compassion for the poor Dep or just outright contempt. After all, the man could buck up; all the Deps could buck up, if they had any courage. But courage was totally lacking in the Dep settlement to the south. This one palpably showed this lack; he hesitated at the door, afraid to come in, and yet so resigned to his fate that in a moment he would do so anyhow, would do the very thing he feared ... whereas an Ob-Com of course would simply count to twenty by twos, turn his back and flee.

'Please enter,' Annette coaxed pleasantly, indicating a chair.

'What's the use of this conversation?' the Dep said, and entered slowly, sagging with despair. 'We'll just tear each other apart; I see no point in convening for these fracases.' However, resignedly, he seated himself, sat with bowed head, hands clenched futilely together.

'I'm Annette Golding,' Annette said, 'and this is Gabriel Baines, the Pare. I'm the Poly. You're Dep, aren't you? I can tell by the way you stare at the floor.' She laughed, but with sympathy.

The Dep said nothing; he did not even give his name. Talking for a Dep, Baines knew, was difficult; it was hard for them to summon the energy. This Dep had probably come early out of a fear of being late; over-compensation, typical of them. Baines did not like them. They were useless to themselves and the other clans; why didn't they die? And, unlike the Heebs, they could not even function as labourers; they lay down on the ground and stared sightlessly up at the sky, devoid of hope.

Leaning toward Baines, Annette said softly, 'Cheer him up.'

'The hell I will,' Baines said. 'What do I care? It's his own fault he's the way he is; he could change if he wanted. He could believe good things if he made the effort. His lot's no worse than the rest of ours, maybe even better; after all, they work at a snail's pace . . . I wish I could get away with doing as little work in a year as the average Dep.'

Now, through the open door, walked a tall, middle-aged woman in a long grey coat. This was Ingred Hibbler, the Ob-Com; counting silently to herself she passed around and around the table, tapping each chair in turn. Baines and Annette waited; the Heeb sweeping the floor glanced up and giggled. The Dep continued to stare sightlessly down. At last Miss Hibbler found a chair whose numerology satisfied her; she drew it back, seated herself rigidly, her hands pressed tightly together, fingers working at great speed, as if knitting an invisible garment of protectiveness.

'I ran into Straw on the parking lot,' she said, and counted silently to herself. 'Our Mans. Ugh, he's an awful person; he almost ran over me with his wheel. I had to—'

She broke off. 'Never mind. But it's hard to rid yourself of his aura, once it infects you.' She shivered.

Annette said, to no one in particular, 'This year if Manfreti is the Skitz again he'll probably come in through the window instead of by the door.' She laughed merrily. The Heeb, sweeping, joined her. 'And of course we're waiting for the Heeb,' Annette said.

'I'm the d-delegate from Gandhitown,' the Heeb, Jacob Simion, said, pushing his broom in his monotonous way. 'I j-just thought I'd do this while I w-waited.' He smiled guilelessly around at all of them.

Baines sighed. The Heeb representative, a janitor. But of course; they *all* were, potentially if not actually. Then that left only the Skitz and the Mans, Howard Straw, who would be in as soon as he finished darting about the parking lot, scaring the other delegates as they arrived. Baines thought. He better not try to intimidate me. Because the laser pistol at Baines' waist was not simulated. And there was always his sim, waiting outside in the hall, to call on.

'What's this meeting about?' Miss Hibbler the Ob-Com asked, and counted rapidly, her eyes shut, fingers danging. 'One, two. One, two.'

Annette said, 'There's a rumour. A strange ship has been sighted and it's not traders from Alpha II; we're reasonably sure of that.' She went on eating candy; Baines saw, with grim amusement, that she had devoured almost the entire bagful by now. Annette, as he well knew, had a dienecephalic disturbance, an overvalent idea in the gluttony-syndrome area. And whenever she became tense or worried it became worse.

'A ship,' the Dep said, stirring into life. 'Maybe it can get us out of our mess.'

'What mess?' Miss Hibbler asked.

Stirring, the Dep said, 'You know.' That was all he could summon up; he became inarticulate once more, lapsed into his coma of gloom. To a Dep things were always a mess. And yet, of course, the Deps feared change, too. Baines' contempt grew as he pondered this. But – a ship. His contempt for the Dep turned to alarm. Was this true?

Straw, the Mans, would know. At Da Vinci Heights the Manses had elaborate technical devices for sighting incoming traffic; probably the original word had come from Da Vinci Heights ... unless of course a Skitz mystic had foreseen it in a vision.

'It's probably a trick,' Baines said aloud.

Everyone in the room, including the gloomy Dep, gazed at him; the Heeb momentarily even ceased sweeping.

'Those Manses,' Baines explained, 'they'll try anything. This is their way of getting an advantage over the rest of us, paying us back.'

'For what?' Miss Hibbler said.

'You know the Manses hate all of us,' Baines said. 'Because they're crude, barbaric roughnecks, unwashed stormtroopers who reach for their gun when they hear the word "culture." It's in their metabolism; it's the old Gothic.' And yet that did not really state it; to be perfectly honest he did not know why the Manses were so intent on hurting everyone else, unless, as his theory went, it was out of sheer delight in inflicting pain. No, he thought, *there must be more than that*. Malice and envy; they must envy us, know we're culturally superior. As diverse as Da Vinci Heights is, there's no order, no aesthetic unity to it; it's a hodgepodge of incomplete so-called 'creative' projects, started out but never finished.

Annette said slowly, 'Straw is a little unpolished, I admit. Even typically the reckless sort. But why would he report a foreign ship if one hadn't been sighted? You haven't given any clear reason.'

'But I know,' Baines said stubbornly, 'that the Manses and especially Howard Straw are against us; we should act to protect ourselves from —' He ceased, because the door had opened and Straw strode brusquely into the room.

Red-haired, big and brawny, he was grinning. The appearance of an alien ship on their minute moon did not bother *him*.

It remained now only for the Skitz to arrive and, as usual he might be an hour late; he would be wandering in a trance somewhere, lost in his clouded visions of an archetypal reality, of cosmic proto-forces underlying the temporal universe, his perpetual view of the so-called *Urwelt*.

We might as well make ourselves comfortable, Baines decided. As much so as possible, given Straw's presence among us. And Miss Hibbler's; he did not much care for her either. In fact, he did not care for any of them with perhaps the exception of Annette: she of the inordinate, conspicuous bosom. And he was getting nowhere with her. As usual.

But that was not his fault; all the Polys were like that – no one ever knew which way they'd jump. They were contrary on purpose, opposed to the dictates of logic. And yet they were not moths, as were the Skitzes, nor debrained machines like the Heebs. They were abundantly *alive*; that was what he enjoyed so about Annette – her quality of animation, freshness.

In fact she made him feel rigid and metallic, encased in thick steel like some archaic weapon of a useless, ancient war. She was twenty, he was thirty-five, perhaps that explained it. But he did not believe so. And then he thought, I'll bet she wants me to feel this way; she's deliberately trying to make me feel bad.

And, in response, all at once he felt icy, carefully-reasoned Pare hatred for her.

Annette, simulating obliviousness, continued to devour the remnants of her bag of candy.

The Skitz delegate to the bi-annual get-together at Adolfville, Omar Diamond, gazed over the landscape of the world and saw, beneath it and upon it, the twin dragons, red and white, of death and life; the dragons, locked in battle, made the plain tremble, and, overhead, the sky split and a wizened decaying grey sun cast little if any comfort in a world fast losing its meagre store of the vital.

'Halt,' Omar said, rasing his hand and addressing the dragons.

A man and wavy-haired girl, walking along the sidewalk of Adolfville's downtown district toward him, halted. The girl said, 'What's the matter with him? He's doing something.' Repugnance.

'Just a Skitz,' the man said, amused. 'Lost in visions.'

Omar said, 'The eternal war has broken out afresh. The powers of life are on the wane. Can no man make the fatal decision, renounce his own life in an act of sacrifice to restore them?'

The man, with a wink at his wife, said, 'You know, sometimes you can ask these fellows a question and get an interesting answer. Go ahead, ask him something – make it big and general, like, "What is the meaning of existence?" Not, "Where's the scissors I lost yesterday?"' He urged her forward.

With caution the woman addressed Omar. 'Excuse me, but I've always wondered – *is* there life after death?'

Omar said, 'There is no death.' He was amazed at the question; it was based on enormous ignorance. 'What you see that you call "death" is only the stage of germination in which the new life form lies dormant, awaiting the call to assume its next incarnation.' He lifted his arms, pointing. 'See? The dragon of life cannot be slain; even as his blood runs red in the meadow, new versions of him spring up at all sides. The seed buried in the earth rises again.' He passed on, then, leaving the man and woman behind.

I must go to the six-storey stone building, Omar said to himself. They wait there, the council. Howard Straw the barbarian. Miss Hibbler the crabbed one, beset by numbers. Annette Golding, the embodiment of life itself, plunging into everything that lets her *become*. Gabriel Baines, the one who is compelled to think up ways of defending himself against that which does not attack. The simple one with the broom who is nearer to God than any of us. And the sad one who never looks up, the man even without a name. What shall I cal him? Perhaps Otto. No, I think I'll make it Dino. Dino Watters. He awaits death, not knowing that he lives in anticipation of an empty phantom; even death cannot protect him from his own self.

Standing at the base of the great six-storey building, the largest in the Pare settlement of Adolfville, he levitated; he bobbed against the proper window, scratched at the glass with his fingernail until at last a person within came to open it for him.

'Mr. Manfreti isn't coming?' Annette asked.

'He cannot be reached this year,' Omar explained. 'He has passed into another realm and simply sits; he must be force-fed through the nose.'

'Ugh,' Annette said, and shuddered. 'Catatonia.'

'Kill him,' Straw said harshly, 'and be done with it. Those cat-Skitzes are worse than useless; they're a drain on Joan d'Arc's resources. No wonder your settlement's so poor.'

'Poor materially,' Omar agreed, 'but rich in eternal values.'

He kept far away from Straw; he did not care for him at

all. Straw, despite his name, was a breaker. He enjoyed smashing and grinding; he was cruel for the love of it, not the need of it. Evil was gratuitous with Straw.

On the other hand, there sat Gabe Baines. Baines, like all Pares, could be cruel, too, but he was compelled to, in his own defence; he was so committed to protecting himself from harm that he naturally did wrong. One could not castigate him, as one could Straw.

Taking his seat Omar said, 'Bless this assembly. And let's hear news of life-giving properties, rather than of the activities of the dragon of harm.' He turned to Straw. 'What is the information, Howard?'

'An armed ship,' Straw said, with a wide, leering grim smile; he was enjoying their collective anxiety. 'Not a trader from Alpha II but from another system entirely; we used a teep to pick up their thoughts. Not on any sort of trading mission but here to —' He broke off, deliberately not finishing his sentence. He wanted to see them squirm.

'We'll have to defend ourselves,' Baines said. Miss Hibbler nodded and so, with reluctance, did Annette. Even the Heeb had ceased to giggle and now looked uneasy. 'We at Adolfville,' Baines said, 'will of course organize the defence. We'll look to your people, Straw, for the technological devices; we expect a lot from you. This is one time we expect you to throw in your lot for the common good.'

'The "common good,"' Straw mimicked. 'You mean for *our* good.'

'My god,' Annette said, 'do you always have to be so irresponsible, Straw? Can't you take note of the consequences for once? At least think of our children. We *must* protect them, if not ourselves.'

To himself, Omar Diamond prayed. 'Let the forces of life rise up and triumph on the plain of battle. Let the white dragon escape the red stain of seeming death; let the womb of protection descend on this small land and guard it from those who stand in the camp of the unholy.' And, all at once, he remembered a sight he had seen on his trip here, by foot, a harbinger of the arrival of the enemy. A stream of water had turned to blood as he stepped over it. Now he knew what the sign meant. War and death, and perhaps the destruction of the Seven Clans and their seven cities – six, if you did not count the garbage dump which was the living space of the Heebs.

Dino Watters, the Dep, muttered hoarsely, 'We're doomed.'

Everyone glared at him, even Jacob Simion the Heeb. How like a Dep.

'Forgive him,' Omar whispered. And somewhere, in the invisible empery, the spirit of life heard, responded, forgave the half-dying creature who was Dino Watters of the Dep settlement, Cotton Mather Estates.

TWO

With scarcely a glance around the old conapt with its cracked sheet-rock walls, recessed lighting that probably no longer worked, archaic picture window and shabby, out-of-date pre-Korean War tile floors, Chuck Rittersdorf said, 'It'll do.' He got out his chequebook, wincing at the sight of the central wrought-iron fireplace; he had not seen one of these since 1970, since his childhood.

The owner of this deteriorating building, however, frowned in suspicion as she received Chuck's identification papers. 'According to this you're married, Mr. Rittersdorf, and you have children. You're not going to bring in a wife and children to this conapt; this was listed in the homeopape ad as "for bachelor, employed, nondrinker," and —'

Wearily Chuck said, 'That's the point.' The fat, middle-aged landlady in her Venusian whistle-cricket hide dress and wubfur slippers repelled him; already this had become a grim experience. 'I've separated from my wife. She's keeping the children. That's why I need this conapt.'

'But they'll be visiting.' Her purple-tinted eyebrows rose.

Chuck said, 'You don't know my wife.'

'Oh they will; I know these new Federal divorce laws. Not like the old days of state divorces. Been to court, yet? Got your first papers?'

'No,' he admitted. It was just beginning for him. Late last night he had gone to a hotel and the night before that – it had been his final night of struggling to achieve the impossible, to keep on living with Mary.

He gave the landlady the cheque; she returned his ID form and departed; at once he shut the door, walked to the window of the conapt and gazed out at the street below, the wheels, jet-hoppers, ramps and runnels of footers. Soon he would have to call his attorney, Nat Wilder. Very soon.

The irony of their marital breakup was too much. For his wife's profession – and she was good at it – was marriage counselling. In fact she had a reputation here in Marin County, California, where she maintained her office, as being the best. God knew how many fracturing human relationships she had healed. And yet, by a masterstroke of injustice, this very talent and skill on her part had helped drive him to this dismal conapt. Because, by being so successful in her own career, Mary could not resist feeling contempt, which had grown over the years, for him.

The fact was – and he had to face it – that in his career he had not been nearly as successful as Mary.

His job, and he personally enjoyed it very much, was the programming of simulacra from the Cheyenne government's intelligence agency for its unending propaganda programmes, its agitation against the ring of Communist states which surrounded the USA. He personally believed deeply in his work, but by no rationalization could it be called either a high-paying calling or a noble one; the programming which he concocted – to say the least – was infantile, spurious and biased. The main appeal was to schoolchildren both in the USA and in the neighbouring Communist states, and to the great masses of adults of low educational background. He was, in fact, a hack. And Mary had pointed this out many, many times.

Hack or not, he continued in this job, although others had been offered him during the six-year course of his marriage. Perhaps it was because he enjoyed hearing his words uttered by the human-like simulacra; perhaps it was because he felt the overall cause was vital: the US was on the defensive, politically and economically, and had to protect itself. It needed persons to work for the government at admittedly low salaries, and at jobs lacking heroic or splendid qualities. *Someone* had to programme the propaganda simulacra, who were deposited all over the world to do their job as reps of the Counter Intelligence Authority, to agitate, convince, influence. But —

Three years ago the crisis had come. One of Mary's

clients – who had been involved in incredibly complex marital difficulties including three mistresses at once – was a TV producer; Gerald Feld had produced the famous, the one and only Bunny Hentman TV show, and owned a major piece of the popular TV comic. In a little side-dealing Mary had passed on to Feld several of the programming scripts which Chuck had written for the CIA's local branch in San Francisco. Feld had read them with interest because these – and this explained Mary's selection – contained a good deal of humour. That was Chuck's talent; he programmed something other than the usual pompous, solemn stuff ... it was said to be alive with wit; it sparkled. And – Feld agreed. And had asked Mary to arrange a meeting between him and Chuck.

Now, standing at the window of the small, drab, old conapt, into which he had not moved so much as one article of clothing, gazing down at the street below, Chuck recalled the conversation with Mary which had erupted. It had been an especially vicious one, certainly classic; it had epitomized the breach between the two of them.

To Mary the issue had been clear: here was a job possibility; it had to be poked thoroughly into. Feld would pay well and the job would carry enormous prestige; each week, at the end of the Bunny Hentman show, Chuck's name, as one of the scriptwriters would appear on the screen for all the nonCom world to see. Mary would – and here was the key phrase – take *pride* in his work; it was conspicuously creative. And to Mary creativity was the open sesame to life; working for the CIA, programming propaganda simulacra who gabbled a message for uneducated Africans and Latin Americans and Asians, was not creative; the messages tended always to be the same and anyhow the CIA was in bad repute in the liberal, monied, sophisticated circles which Mary inhabited.

'You're like a – leaf-raker in a satellite park,' Mary had said, infuriated, 'on some kind of civil service deal. It's easy security; it's the way out of having to struggle. Here you are thirty-three years old and already you've given up trying. Given up wanting to make something of yourself.'

'Listen,' he said futilely. 'Are you my mother or just my wife? I mean, is it your job to keep goading me on? Do I have to keep rising? Is it becoming TERPLAN President, is that what you want?' Outside of the prestige and money *there was something more involved.* Evidently Mary wanted him to be another person. She, the one who knew him best in all the world, was ashamed of him. If he took the job writing for Bunny Hentman he would become different – or so her logic went.

He could not deny the logic. And yet he persisted; he did not quit his job, did not change. Something in him was just too inertial. For better or worse. There was a hysteresis to one's essence; he did not put by that essence easily.

Outside, on the street, a white Chevrolet de luxe wheel, a shiny new six-door model, dropped to the curb and landed. He watched idly and then he realized with a start of incredulity that – impossible but true – it was his ex-own; here was Mary. She had already found him.

His wife, Dr. Mary Rittersdorf, was about to pay him a visit.

He felt fright, and a sense of increased failure; he had not even been able to pull this off – find a conapt in which to live where Mary couldn't locate him. In a few more days, Nat Wilder could arrange legal protection, but now, at this point, he was helpless; he had to admit her.

It was easy to see how she had traced him; moderate detection devices were available and cheap. Mary had probably gone to a pry-vye, a robot detection agency, obtained use of a *sniffer*, presented it his cephalic pattern; it had gone to work, followed him to every place he had been since leaving her. Nowadays, finding someone was an exact science.

So a woman determined to locate you, he reflected, can. There probably was a law governing it; perhaps he could call it Rittersdorf's Law. In proportion to one's desire to escape, to hide, detection devices —

A rap sounded on the hollow-core door of the conapt.

As he walked stiff-legged, unwillingly, to the door he

thought, She will make a speech which will embody every known reasonable appeal. I, of course, will have no argument, just my feeling that we can't go on, that her contempt for me indicates a failure between us too profound to admit any future intimacy.

He opened the door. There she stood, dark-haired, wispy, in her expensive (her best) natural-wool coat, without make-up; a calm, competent, educated woman who was his superior in a flock of ways. 'Listen, Chuck,' she said, 'I won't stand for this. I've arranged for a moving company to pick up all your things and put them in storage. What I'm here for is a cheque; I want all the money in your current account. I need it for bills.'

So he had been wrong; there was no speech of sweet reasonability. On the contrary; his wife was making this final. He was absolutely stunned and all he could do was gape at her.

'I've talked to Bob Alfson, my attorney,' Mary said. 'I've had him file for a quit-claim deed on the house.'

'What?' he said. 'Why?'

'So you can sign over your share of the house to me.'

'Why?'

'So I can put it on the market. I've decided I don't need such a large house and I can use the money. I'm putting Debby in that boarding school back East we were discussing.' Deborah was their oldest, but still only six, years too young to be sent away from home. Good grief.

'Let me talk to Nat Wilder first,' he said feebly.

'I want the cheque now.' Mary made no move to come in; she simply stood there. And he felt desperate, despairing panic, the panic of defeat and suffering; he had lost already: she could make him do anything.

As he went to get his chequebook, Mary walked a few steps into the conapt. Her aversion for it was beyond words; she said nothing. He shrank from it, could not face it; he busied himself scratching out the cheque.

'By the way,' Mary said in a conversational tone of voice, 'now that you've left for good I'm free to accept that government offer.'

'What government offer?'

'They want consulting psychologists for an interplan project; I told you about it.' She did not intend to burden herself with enlightening him.

'Oh yes.' He had a dim memory. 'Charity work.' An outgrowth of the Terran-Alphane clash of ten years ago. An isolated moon in the Alphane system settled by Terrans which had been cut off two generations ago because of the war; a rookery of such meagre enclaves existed in the Alph' system, which had dozens of moons as well as twenty-two planets.

She accepted the cheque, put it folded into her coat pocket.

'Would you get paid?' he asked.

'No,' Mary said, remotely.

Then she would live – support the children as well – on his salary alone. It came to him: she expected a court settlement which would force him to do the very thing his refusal of which had pulled down their six-year marriage. She would, through her vast influence in Marin County courts, obtain such a judgment that he would have to give up his job with the San Francisco branch of the CIA and seek other work entirely.

'How – long will you be gone?' he asked. It was obvious that she intended to make good use of this interval of reorganization of their lives; she would do all the things denied her – allegedly, anyhow – by his presence.

'About six months. It depends. Don't expect me to keep in touch. I'll be represented in court by Alfson; I won't appear.' She added, 'I've started the suit for separate maintenance so you won't have to do that.'

The initiative, even there, was gone from his hands. He had as always been too slow.

'You can have everything,' he told Mary, all at once.

Her look said, But what you can give isn't enough. 'Everything' was merely nothing, as far as his achievments were concerned.

'I can't give you what I don't have,' he said quietly.

'Yes you can,' Mary said, without a smile. 'Because the

judge is going to recognize what I've always recognized about you. If you have to, if someone makes you, you can meet the customary standards applied to grown men with the responsibility of a wife and children.'

He said, 'But – I have to retain some kind of life of my own.'

'Your first obligation is to us,' Mary said.

For that he had no answer; he could only nod.

Later, after Mary had left with the cheque, he looked for and found a stack of old homeopapes in the closet of the apt; he sat on the ancient Danish-style sofa in the living-room, rooting through them for the articles on the interplan project which Mary intended to become involved in. Her new life, he said to himself, to replace that of being married.

In a 'pape one week old he found a more or less complete article; he lit a cigarette and read carefully.

Psychologists were needed, it was anticipated by the US Interplan Health & Welfare Service, because the moon had originally been a hospital area, a psychiatric care-centre for Terran immigrants to the Alphane system who had cracked under the abnormal, excessive pressures of inter-system colonization. The Alphanes had left it alone, except for their traders.

What was known of the moon's current status came from these Alphane traders. According to them a civilization of sorts had arisen during the decades in which the hospital had been severed from Terra's authority. However, they could not evaluate it because their knowledge of Terran mores was inadequate. In any case local commodities were produced, traded; domestic industry existed, too, and he wondered why the Terran government felt the necessity of meddling. He could imagine Mary there so well; she was precisely the sort which TERPLAN, the international agency, would select. People of Mary's type would always succeed.

Going to the ancient picture window he stood for a time once more, gazing down. And then, stealthily, he felt rise up within him the familiar urge. The sense that it was pointless to go on; suicide, whatever the law and the church said, was for him the only real answer at this instant.

He found a smaller side window that opened; raising it, he listened to the buzz of a jet-hopper as it landed on a rooftop on the far side of the street. Its sound died. He waited, and then he climbed part way over the edge of the window, dangling above the traffic which moved below....

From inside him a voice, but not his own, said, 'Please tell me your name. Regardless of whether you intend or do not intend to jump.'

Turning, Chuck saw a yellow Ganymedean slime mould that had silently flowed under the door of the conapt and was gathering itself into the heap of small globes which comprised its physical being.

'I rent the conapt across the hall,' the slime mould declared.

Chuck said, 'Among Terrans it's customary to knock.'

'I possess nothing to knock with. In any case I wished to enter before you – departed.'

'It's my personal business whether I jump or not.'

'"No Terran is an island,"' the slime mould more or less quoted. 'Welcome to the building which we who rent apts here have humourously dubbed "Discarded Arms Conapts." There are others here whom you should meet. Several Terrans – like yourself – plus a number of non-Ts of assorted physiognomy, some which will repel you, some which no doubt will attract. I had planned to borrow a cup of yogurt culture from you, but in view of your preoccupation it seems an insulting request.'

'I haven't moved in anything. As yet.' He swung his leg back over the sill, stepped back into the room, away from the window. He was not surprised to see the Ganymedean slime mould; a ghetto situation existed with non-Ts: no matter how influential and highly-placed in their own societies on Terra they were forced to inhabit substandard housing such as this.

'Could I carry a business card,' the slime mould said, 'I would now present it to you. I am an importer of uncut gems, a dealer in secondhand gold, and, under the right circumstances, a fanatic buyer of philatelic collections. As a matter of fact I have in my apt at the moment a choice collection of early US, with special emphasis on *mint blocks of four* of the Columbus set; would you —' It broke off. 'I see you would not. In any case the desire to destroy yourself has at least temporarily abated from your mind. That is good. In addition to my announced commercial—'

'Aren't you required by law to curb your telepathic ability while on Terra?' Chuck said.

'Yes, but your situation seemed to be exceptional. Mr. Rittersdorf, I cannot personally employ you, since I require no propagandistic services. But I have a number of contacts among the nine moons; given time —'

'No thanks,' Chuck said roughly. 'I just want to be left alone.' He had already endured enough assistance in job-acquisition to last him a lifetime.

'But, on my part, quite unlike your wife, I have no ulterior motive.' The slime mould ebbed closer. 'Like most Terran males your sense of self-respect is bound up in your wage-earning capabilities, an area in which you have grave doubts as well as extreme guilts. I can do something for you ... but it will take time. Presently I leave Terra and start back to my own moon. Suppose I pay you five hundred skins – US, of course – to come with me. Consider it a loan, if you want.'

'What would I do on Ganymede?' Irritably, Chuck said, 'Don't you believe me either? I have a job; one I consider adequate – I don't want to leave it.'

'Subconsciously —'

'Don't read my subconscious back to me. And get out of here and leave me alone.' He turned his back on the slime mould.

'I am afraid your suicidal drive will return – perhaps even before tonight.'

'Let it.'

The slime mould said, 'There is only one thing that can help you, and my miserable job-offer is not it.'

'What is it, then?'

'A woman to replace your wife.'

'Now you're acting as a—'

'Not at all. This is neither physically base nor ethereal; it is simply practical. You must find a woman who can accept you, love you, as you are; otherwise you'll perish. Let me ponder this. And in the meantime, control yourself. Give me five hours. And remain here.' The slime mould flowed slowly under the door, through the crack and outside into the hall. Its thoughts dimmed. 'As an importer, buyer and dealer I have many contacts with Terrans of all walks of life...' Then it was gone.

Shakily, Chuck lit a cigarette. And walked away – a long distance away – from the window, to seat himself on the ancient Danish-style sofa. And wait.

It was hard to know how to react to the slime mould's charitable offer; he was both angered and touched – and, in addition, puzzled. Could the slime mould actually help him? It seemed impossible.

He waited one hour.

A knock sounded on the door of the conapt. It could not be the Ganymedean returning because a slime mould did not – could not – knock. Rising, Chuck went to the door and opened it.

A Terran girl stood there.

THREE

Although she had a thousand matters to attend to, all pertaining to her new non-paying job with the US Interplan Health & Welfare Department, Dr. Mary Rittersdorf took time off for a personal item. Once more she rode by jet cab to New York and the Fifth Avenue office of Jerry Feld, the producer of the Bunny Hentman show. A week ago she had given him a batch of the very latest – and best – CIA scripts which Chuck had written; it was now time to find out if her husband, or ex-husband, had a chance at the job.

If Chuck wouldn't seek better employment on his own she would. It was her duty, if for no other reason than that she and the children, for the next year at least, would be totally dependent on Chuck's earnings.

Let off on the roof field Mary descended by in-ramp to floor ninety, came to the glass door, hesitated, then allowed it to open and entered the outer office in which Mr. Feld's receptionist – very pretty, with much make-up and a rather tight spider-silk sweater – sat. Mary felt annoyed at the girl; just because bras had become passé, did a girl with so pronounced a bosom have to cater to fashion? In this case practicality dictated a bra, and Mary stood at the desk feeling herself flushing with disapproval. And artificial nipple-dilation; it was just too much.

'Yes?' the receptionist said, glancing up through an ornate, stylish monocle. As she met Mary's coldness her nipples deburgeoned slightly, as if scared into submission, frightened away.

'I'd like to see Mr. Feld. I'm Dr. Mary Rittersdorf and I don't have much time; I have to leave for the TERPLAN lunar base at three p.m. New York time.' She made her voice as efficient – and demanding – as she knew how.

After a series of bureaucratic actions on the receptionist's part Mary was sent on in.

At his imitation oak desk – no genuine oak had existed for a decade – Jerry Feld sat with a videotape projector, deep in his business tasks. 'Just a moment, Dr. Rittersdorf.' He pointed to a chair; she seated herself, crossed her legs and lit a cigarette.

On the miniature TV screen Bunny Hentman was doing an act in which he played a German industrialist; wearing a blue, double-breasted suit, he was explaining to his board of directors how the new autonomic ploughs which their cartel was producing could be used for war. Four ploughs would guide themselves, at news of hostilities, into a single unit; the unit was not a larger plough but a missile-launcher. In his heavy accent Bunny explained this, putting it as if it were a great achievement, and Feld chuckled.

'I don't have much time, Mr. Feld,' Mary said crisply.

Reluctantly, Feld stopped the videotape and turned toward her. 'I showed Bunny the scripts. He's interested. Your husband's wit is dry, moribund, but it's authentic. It's what once was —'

'I know all this,' Mary said. 'I've had to hear his programming scripts for years; he always tried them out on me.' She smoked rapidly, feeling tense. 'Well, do you think Bunny could use them?'

'We're nowhere,' Feld said, 'until your husband sees Bunny; there's no use your —'

The office door opened and Bunny Hentman entered.

This was the first time Mary had seen the famous TV comic in person and she felt curious; how did he differ from his public image? He was, she decided, a little shorter, quite a bit older, than on TV; he had a large bald area and he looked tired. In fact, in real life Bunny looked like a worried Central European junk dealer, in a rumpled suit, not quite well-shaved, thinning hair disarrayed, and – to cap the impression – smoking the shortened remains of a cigar. But his eyes. He had an alert and yet warm quality; she rose and stood facing him. Over TV the strength of his gaze did not register. This was not mere intelligence on

Bunny's part; this was more, a perception of – she did not know what. And —

All about Bunny an aura hung, an aura of suffering. His face, his body, seemed sopped with it. Yes, she thought, that's what shows in his eyes. Memory of pain. Pain that took place long ago, but which he has never forgotten – nor will he. He was made, put on this planet, to suffer; no wonder he's a great comic. For Bunny comedy was a struggle, a fighting back against the reality of literal physical pain; it was a reaction formation of gigantic – and effective – stature.

'Bun,' Jerry Feld said, 'This is Dr. Mary Rittersdorf; her husband wrote those CIA robot programmes I showed you last Thursday.'

The comic held out his hand; Mary shook hands with him and said, 'Mr. Hentman —'

'Please,' the comic said. 'That's just my professional name. My real name, the one I was born with, is Lionsblood Regal. Naturally I had to change it; who goes into show biz calling himself Lionsblood Regal? You call me Lionsblood or just Blood; Jer here calls me Li-Reg – it's a mark of intimacy.' He added, still holding on to her hand, 'And if there is anything I like about a woman it's intimacy.'

'Li-Reg,' Feld said, 'is your cable address; you've got it mixed up again.'

'That's so.' Hentman released Mary's hand. 'Well, Frau Doktor Rattenfänger —'

'Rittersdorf,' Mary corrected.

'Rattenfänger.' Feld said, 'is German for rat-catcher. Look, Bun, don't make a mistake like that again.'

'Sorry,' the comic said. 'Listen, Frau Doktor Rittelsdof. Please call me something nice ; I can use it. I crave affection from pretty women; it's the small boy in me.' He smiled, and yet his face – and especially his eyes – still contained the world-weary pain, the weight of an ancient burden. 'I'll hire your husband if I get to see you now and then. If he understands the *real* reason for the deal, what diplomats call the "secret protocols."' To Jerry Feld he said, 'And you know how my protocols have been bothering me, lately.'

'Chuck is in a run-down conapt on the West Coast,' Mary said. 'I'll write the address down.' Quickly she took pen and paper and jotted. 'Tell him you need him; tell him —'

'But I don't need him,' Bunny Hentman said quietly.

Mary said, with caution, 'Couldn't you see him, Mr. Hentman? Chuck has a unique talent. I'm afraid if no one pushes him —'

Plucking at his lower lip Hentman said, 'You're afraid he won't make use of it, that it'll go abegging.'

'Yes.' She nodded.

'But it's *his* talent. It's for him to decide.'

'My husband,' Mary said, 'needs help.' And I ought to know, she thought. It's my job to understand people. Chuck is a dependent infantile type; he must be pushed and led if he's to move at all. Otherwise, he'll rot in that awful little old conapt he's rented. Or – throw himself out the window. This, she decided, is the only thing that will save him. Although he would be the last to admit it.

Eyeing her intently Hentman said, 'Can I make a side-deal with you, Mrs. Rittersdorf?'

'W-what kind of side-deal?' She glanced at Feld; his face was impassive as if he had withdrawn, turtle-like, from the situation.

'Just to see you now and then,' Hentman said. 'Not on business.'

'I won't be here. I'm going to work for TERPLAN; I'll be in the Alph' system for months if not years.' She felt panic.

'Then no job for your hubby,' Hentman said.

Feld spoke up. 'When are you leaving, Dr. Rittersdorf?'

'Right away,' Mary said. 'In four days. I have to pack my things, arrange for the children to —'

'Four days,' Hentman said meditatively. He continued to eye her up and down. 'You and your husband are separated? Jerry said —'

'Yes,' Mary said. 'Chuck's already moved out.'

'Have dinner with me tonight,' Hentman said. 'And meanwhile I'll either drop by your husband's conapt, or send someone from my staff. We'll give him a six-weeks' try ... get him started doing scripts. Is it a deal?'

'I don't mind having dinner with you,' Mary said. 'But—'

'That's all,' Hentman said, 'just dinner. Any restaurant you want, anywhere in the United States. But, if more develops ...' He smiled.

After flying back to the West Coast by jet cab, she travelled on the urban monorail into downtown San Francisco and TERPLAN's branch office, the agency with whom she had dealt regarding her highly desirable new job.

Shortly she found herself ascending by elevator; beside her stood a trim-cut young man, well-dressed, a P.R. official of TERPLAN whose name, as she had got it, was Lawrence McRae.

McRae said, 'There's a gang of homeopape reporters waiting, and here's what they'll throw at you. They'll imply, and try to get you to confirm, that this therapeutic project is a coverup for Terra's acquisition of the moon Alpha III M2. That fundamentally we're there to re-establish a colony, claim it, develop it, then send settlers to it.'

'But it was ours before the war,' Mary said. 'Otherwise how could it have been used as a hospital base?'

'True,' McRae said. They left the elevator, walked down a hall. 'But no Terran ship has visited it for twenty-five years and legally speaking that terminates our land-claim. The moon reverted five years ago to political and legal autonomy. However, if we land and re-establish a hospital base, with technicians, doctors, therapists, whatever else is needed, we can assert a fresh claim – if the Alphanes haven't and evidently they haven't. They're still recovering from the war, of course; that may be it. Or they may have scouted the moon and decided it's not what they want, that the ecology is too foreign to their biology. Here.' He held a door open and she entered, finding herself facing seated homeopape reporters, fifteen or sixteen of them, some with pic-cameras.

Taking a deep breath she walked to the lectern which McRae pointed out; it was equipped with a microphone.

McRae, speaking into the mike, said, 'Ladies and gentlemen, this is Dr. Mary Rittersdorf, the renowned marriage counsellor from Marin County who as you know has volunteered her services for this project.'

A reporter at once said, lazily, 'Dr. Rittersdorf, what is this project called? Project Psychotic?' The other reporters laughed.

It was McRae who answered. '*Operation Fifty-minutes* is the working name we've applied to it.'

'Where do the sickies on the moon go when you catch them?' another reporter asked. 'So maybe you sweep them under the rug, is that it?'

Mary, speaking into the mike, said, 'At first we will be involved in research, in order to fathom the situation. We know already that the original patients – at least some of them – and their progeny are alive. How viable the society they've formed is we don't pretend to know. I would guess it's not viable at all, except in the bare, literal sense that they do live. We will attempt corrective therapy with those we can. It's the children, of course, that we're most concerned with.'

'When do you expect to be on Alpha III M2, Doctor?' a reporter asked. The pic-cameras ground away, whirring like distant flights of birds.

'I'd say within two weeks,' Mary said.

'You're not being paid for this, are you, Doctor?' a reporter asked.

'No.'

'You're convinced, then, that this is in the public good? It's a Cause?'

'Well,' Mary said, hesitantly. 'It —'

'Terra then, will benefit by our meddling with this culture of ex-mental hospital patients?' The reporter's voice was sleek.

Turning to McRae, Mary said, 'What should I say?'

McRae, into the mike, said, 'This is not Dr. Rittersdorf's area; she's a trained psychologist, not a politician. She declines to answer.'

A reporter, tall, lean, experienced, rose to his feet and said drawingly, 'Has it occurred to TERPLAN just to leave this moon alone? To treat its culture as you would any other culture, respecting its values and customs?'

Haltingly, Mary said, 'We don't know enough yet. Perhaps when we know more —' She broke off, floundering. 'But it's not a subculture,' she said. 'It has no tradition. It's a society of mentally ill individuals and their offspring that came into existence only twenty-five years ago ... you can't dignify that by comparing it with, say, the Ganymedean or Ionian cultures. What values could mentally ill people develop? And in such a short time.'

'But you said yourself,' the reporter purred, 'that at this point you know nothing about them. For all you know —'

McRae, speaking into the microphone, said sharply, 'If they've developed any kind of a stable, viable culture, we'll leave them alone. But that determination is up to experts such as Dr. Rittersdorf, not to you or to me or the American public. Frankly, we feel there's nothing more potentially explosive then a society in which psychotics dominate, define the values, control the means of communication. Almost anything you want to name can come out of it – a new, fanatical religious cult, a paranoiac nationalistic state-concept, barbaric destructiveness of a manic sort – these possibilities alone justify our investigation of Apha III M2. This project is in defence of our own lives and values.'

The homeopape reporters were silent, evidently convinced by what McRae had said. And certainly Mary agreed.

Later, as she and McRae left the room, Mary said, 'Was that actually the reason?'

Glancing at her McRae said, 'You mean, are we going into Alpha III M2 because we fear the consequences *to us* of a mentally deranged social enclave, because a deranged society, as such, makes us uneasy? I think either reason is sufficient; certainly for you it ought to be.'

'I'm not supposed to ask?' She stared at the young clean-cut TERPLAN official. 'I'm just supposed to —'

'You're supposed to do your therapeutic task and that's it. I don't tell you how to cure sick people; why should you tell me how to handle a political situation?' He faced her coolly. 'However, I'll give you one further purpose for *Operation Fifty-minutes* that you might not have thought of. It's entirely possible that in twenty-five years a society of mentally ill people may have come up with technological ideas we can use, especially the manics – that most active class.' He pressed the elevator button. 'I understand they're inventive. As are the paranoids.'

Mary said, *'Does this explain why Terra hasn't sent anyone in there sooner?* You wanted to see how their ideas developed?'

Smiling, McRae waited for the elevator; he did not answer. He looked, she decided, absolutely sure of himself. And that, as far as the knowledge of psychotics went, was a mistake. Possibly a grave one.

It was almost an hour later, as she was returning to her house in Marin County to resume packing her things, that she realized the basic contradiction in the government's position. First, they were probing into the culture of Alpha III M2 because they feared it might be lethal, and then they were probing to see if it had developed something of use. Almost a century ago Freud had showed how spurious such double logic was; in actual fact each proposition cancelled the other. The government simply could not have it both ways.

Psychoanalysis had shown that generally, when two mutually contradicting reasons for an act were given, the genuine underlying motive was neither, was a third drive which the person – or in this case a body of governing officials – was unaware of.

She wondered what, in this case, the real motive was.

In any event the project for which she had volunteered her services no longer seemed so idealistic, so free of ulterior purpose.

Whatever the government's actual motive, she had one clear intuition about it: the motive was a good, hard, selfish one.

And, in addition, she had one more intuition.
She would probably never know what that motive was.

She was absorbed in the task of packing her drawerful of sweaters when all at once she realized that she was no longer alone. Two men stood in the doorway; swiftly she turned, hopped to her feet.

'Where is Mr. Rittersdorf?' the older man said. He held out a flat black ID packet; the two men, she saw, were from her husband's office, from the San Francisco branch of the CIA.

'He moved out,' she said. 'I'll give you his address.'

'We got a tip,' the older man said, 'from an unidentified informant, that your husband might be planning suicide.'

'He always is,' she said as she wrote down the address of the miserable hovel in which Chuck now lived. 'I wouldn't worry about him; he's chronically ill but never quite dead.'

The older CIA man regarded her with bleak hostility. 'I understand you and Mr. Rittersdorf are separating.'

'That's right. If it's any of your business.' She gave him a brief, professional smile. 'Now, may I continue packing?'

'Our office,' the CIA man said, 'tends to extend a certain protection to its employees. If your husband turns up a suicide there'll be an investigation – to determine to what extent you're involved.' He added, 'And in view of your status as marital counsellor, it might prove embarrassing, don't you agree?'

After a pause Mary said, 'Yes, I suppose so.'

The younger crew-cut CIA man said, 'Just consider this an informal warning. Go slow, Mrs. Rittersdorf; don't put the pressure on your husband. You understand?' His eyes were lifeless, frigid.

She nodded. And shivered.

'Meanwhile,' the older man said, 'if he should show up here, have him call in. He's on a three-day leave of absence but we'd like to talk to him. Both men moved from the room, to the front door of the house.

She returned to her packing, gasping in relief, now that the two CIA men had gone.

The CIA isn't going to tell me what to do, she said to herself. I'll say anything I want to my husband, do anything I want. They're not going to protect you, Chuck, she said to herself as she packed sweater after sweater, pressing them down savagely into the suitcase. In fact, she said to herself, it's going to be worse on you because you involved them; so be prepared.

Laughing, she thought, You poor frightened snink. Thinking you had a good idea in intimidating me by sending your co-workers around. *You* may be frightened of them, but I'm not. They're just stupid, fatheaded cops.

As she packed she toyed with the idea of calling her attorney to tell him of the CIA's pressure-tactics. No, she decided, I won't do that now; I'll wait until the divorce action comes up before Judge Erizzolara. And then I'll give that as evidence; it'll show the sort of life I've been forced to lead, married to such a man. Exposed to police harassment, constantly. And, in helping find him a job, propositioned.

Gleefully she placed the last sweater on the suitcase, closed it, and with a rapid turn of her fingers, locked it tight.

Poor Chuck, she said to herself, you don't stand a chance, once I get you into court. You'll never know what hit you; you'll be paying out for the rest of your life. As long as you live, darling, you'll never really be free of me; it'll always cost you something.

She began, with care, to fold her many dresses, packing them into the large trunk with the special hangers.

It will cost you, she said to herself, *more than you can afford to pay.*

FOUR

The girl in the doorway said in a soft, hesitant voice, 'Um, I'm Joan Trieste. Lord Running Clam said you just moved in here.' Her eyes roved; she was looking past Chuck Rittersdorf at the apt. 'You don't have any of your things moved in yet, do you? Can I help? I can put up curtains and clean the shelves in the kitchen, if you want.'

Chuck said, 'Thanks. But I'm okay.' It touched him that the slime mould had done this, rounded up this girl.

She was, he decided, not even twenty; she wore her hair in one large massive braid down her back, and it was brown hair, without particular colour, really just ordinary hair. And quite white, much too pale. And, it seemed to him, her neck was a trifle too long. She had no figure at all to speak of, although she was at least slender. Joan Trieste wore skin-tight dark pants and slippers and a cotton man's-style shirt; as far as he could tell, she had on no bra, as fashion dictated, but her nipples were merely flat dark circles beneath the white cotton fabric of her shirt: she could not afford or did not care to have the currently-popular dilation operation. It came to him then that she was poor. Possibly a student.

'Lord Running Clam,' she explained, 'is from Ganymede; he lives across the hall.' She smiled slightly; she had, he saw, very fine small even white teeth, quite regular, well-formed. Almost perfect, in fact.

'Yes,' Chuck said. 'He flowed in here under the door an hour or so ago.' He added, 'He said he was sending someone. Apparently he thought —'

'Did you really try to kill yourself?'

After a pause he shrugged. 'The slime mould thought so.'

'You did. I can tell even now; I can see it about you.' She walked past him and into the apt. 'I'm a – you know. A Psi.'

'What kind of Psi?' He left the hall door open, went to get his pack of Pall Malls to light up. 'There're all kinds. From those who can move mountains to those who can only —'

Joan broke in, 'I have a very meagre power, but look.' Turning, she raised the lapel of her shirt. 'See my button? Bona fide member of Psi-men, Incorporated, of America.' She explained, 'What I can do is, I can make time flow backward. In a limited area, say twelve by nine, about the size of your living-room. Up to a period of five minutes.' She smiled, and once again he marvelled at her teeth; they transformed her face, made it beautiful; as long as she smiled and she was delightful to behold, and it seemed to Chuck that this told something about her. The quality of beauty arose from within; inside, she was lovely, and he realized that over the years, as she aged, it would gradually work its way outward, influence the surface. By the time she was thirty or thirty-five she would be radiant. Right now she was still a child.

'Is that a useful talent?' he asked.

'It has a limited use.' Perching on the arm of his archaic Danish-style sofa she stuck her fingers in the pockets of her tight pants and explained, 'I work for the Ross Police Department; they rush me to bad traffic accidents and – you'll laugh, but it really works – I turn time back to before the accident, or if I'm too late, if more than five minutes has gone by, sometimes instead I can bring back a person who's just died. See?'

'I see,' he said.

'It doesn't pay much. And worse than that, I have to be on call twenty-four hours of the day. They notify me at my conapt and I go by high-speed jet hopper to the spot. See?' She turned her head, pointed to her right ear; he saw a small stubby cylinder embedded in her ear and realized that it was a police receiver. 'I'm always tuned in. That means I can't be more than a few seconds run from transportation, of course; I can go to restaurants the theatres and other people's houses, but—'

'Well,' he said, 'maybe you can save my life sometime.' He thought, If I had jumped you could have forced me back into existence again. What a great service....

'I've saved many lives,' Joan held out her hand. 'May I have a cigarette, too?'

He gave her one, lit it, feeling – as usual – guilty of his lapse.

'What do *you* do?' Joan asked.

With reluctance – not because it was classified but because it held so low a status in the ladder of public esteem – he described his job with the CIA. Joan Trieste listened intently.

'Then you help keep our government from falling,' she said, with a smile of delight. 'How wonderful!'

Charmed, he said, 'Thanks.'

'But you do! Just think – right this moment hundreds of simulacra all over the Communist world are saying your words, halting people at street corners and in jungles...' Her eyes shone. 'And all I do is help the Ross Police Department.'

'There's a law,' Chuck said, 'which I call Rittersdorf's Third Law of Diminished Returns, which states that proportional to how long you hold a job you imagine that it has progressively less and less importance in the scheme of things.' He smiled back at her; the glow in her eyes, the sparkle of white teeth, made smiling easy. He was beginning to forget his burdening, despairing mood of a short while ago.

Joan roamed about the conapt. 'Are you going to move a lot of personal things in? Or are you going to live just like this? I'll help decorate it for you, and Lord Running Clam will, too, to the extent he can. And down the hall there's a molten metal life form from Jupiter called Edgar; he's hibernating these days, but when he comes back to life he'll want to pitch in. And in the apt to your left there's a wizbird from Mars; you know, with the multicoloured headdress ... it has no hands but it can move objects by psychokinesis; it'll want to help, except that for today it's hatching; it's on an egg.'

'God,' Chuck said. 'What a polygenetic building.' He was a little stunned to hear all this.

'And,' Joan said, 'on the floor below you is a greeb-sloth from Callisto; it's all wound around a three-way floor lamp that's standard equipment in these conapts ... circa 1960. It'll wake up as soon as the sun sets; then it goes out and shops for food. And you already met the slime mould.' She puffed vigorously – and a trifle inexpertly – on her cigarette. 'I like this place; you meet all sorts of life forms. Before you a Venusian moss inhabited this apt. I saved its life once; it had dried out ... they've got to keep moist, you know. In the end this climate here in Marin County was too dry for it; finally it moved north to Oregon where it rains all the time,' Turing, she halted and surveyed him. 'You look like you've had a lot of trouble.'

'No real trouble. Just the imaginary kind. The avoidable kind.' He thought, Trouble that if I had used my head I never would have become involved with; I never would have married her.

'What's your wife's name?'

Startled, he said, 'Mary.'

'Don't kill yourself because you've left her,' Joan said. 'In a few months or even weeks you'll feel whole again. Now you feel like one half of an organism that's split apart. Binary fission always hurts; I know because of a protoplasm that used to live here ... it suffered every time it split, but it had to split, it had to grow.'

'I guess growth hurts.' Going to the picture window he once more looked down at the footer runnels and the wheels and jet hoppers below. He had come so close ...

'This isn't a bad place to live,' Joan said. 'I know; I've lived a lot of places. Of course everybody in the Ross Police Department knows The Discarded Arms,' she added candidly. 'There's been a lot of trouble here, petty thefts, fights, even one homicide. It's not a clean place ... you can see that.'

'And yet —'

'And yet I believe you ought to stay. You'll have company. Especially at night the non-T life forms that live here begin to circulate, as you'll find out. And Lord Running Clam is a very good friend to have made; he's helped a lot of people. Ganymedeans possess what St. Paul called *caritas* ... and remember, Paul said caritas was the greatest of all the virtues.' She added, 'The modern word for it would be empathy, I guess.'

The conapt door opened; Chuck turned instantly. And saw two men whom he knew quite well. His boss, Jack Elwood and his co-worker in scriptwriting, Pete Petri. At the sight of him both men looked relieved.

'Darn it,' Elwood said, 'we thought we were too late. We stopped by your house, thinking you might be there.'

Joan Trieste said, speaking to Elwood, 'I'm from the Ross Police Department. May I see your ID papers, please?' Her voice was cool.

Elwood and Petri showed her their CIA identification, briefly, then strolled over to Chuck. 'What's the city police doing here?' Elwood asked.

'A friend,' Chuck said.

Elwood shrugged; obviously he did not intend to press for details. 'Couldn't you've found a better apt for yourself?' He surveyed the room. 'This place literally smells.'

'It's only temporary,' Chuck said, uncomfortably.

'Don't deteriorate,' Pete Petri said. 'And your leave; they cancelled it. They think you ought to be at work. For your own good. You shouldn't be alone where you can brood.' He eyed Joan Trieste, clearly wondering if she had interfered with a suicide attempt. No one, however, enlightened him. 'So will you come back to the office with us? There's a hell of a lot to do; you'll be there all night, the way it looks.'

'Thanks,' Chuck said. 'But I've got to start moving my things. I need to decorate this apt, to some extent anyhow.' He still wanted to be alone, as much as he appreciated their intentions. It was an instinct, to crawl away, to hide himself; it came from the blood.

To the two CIA men Joan Trieste said, 'I can stay with

him for a while, at least. Unless I get an emergency call. There's usually one at around five o'clock, when the heavy commuter traffic starts. But until —'

'Listen,' Chuck said brusquely.

The three of them turned questioningly toward him.

'If someone wants to kill himself,' Chuck said, '*you can't stop him.* Maybe you can delay it. Maybe a Psi like Joan here can drag him back. But even if he's delayed he'll do it, and even if he's brought back he'll find a way to do it again. So leave me alone.' He felt tired. 'I've got a four o'clock appointment with my attorney – I've got many things to do. I can't stand around talking.'

Looking at his watch Elwood said, 'I'll drive you to your lawyer's. We can just make it.' He curtly motioned to Petri.

To Joan, Chuck said, 'Maybe I'll see you again. Sometime.' He felt too weary to care one way or another. 'Thanks,' he said, vaguely; he did not know precisely what he was thanking her for.

With careful emphasis Joan said, 'Lord Running Clam is in his room and he can pick up your thoughts; it you try to kill yourself again he'll hear and interfere. So if you intend to do it —'

'Okay,' Chuck said. 'I won't try it here.' He went to the door with Elwood and Petri, one of them on each side of him; Joan followed.

As they passed out into the corridor he saw that the slime mould's door was open; the huge yellow mound undulated slightly in greeting.

'Thank you, too,' Chuck said, half-ironically, and then passed on with his two co-workers from the CIA.

As they drove by wheel to Nat Wilder's office in San Francisco, Jack Elwood said, 'This *Operation Fifty-minutes* – we've asked to be allowed to include a man in the initial landing party; a routine request which of course has been honoured.' He glanced thoughtfully at Chuck. 'I think we'll use a simulacrum in this case.'

Chuck Rittersdorf nodded vacantly. It was standard procedure to use a simulacrum in projects involving potentially hostile factions; the CIA had a low operating budget and did not like to lose its men.

'In fact,' Elwood said, 'the simulacrum – it was made for us by G. D. down in Palo Alto – is finished and at our office. If you'd care to view it.' He examined a small note pad which he brought from his coat pocket. 'Name is Daniel Mageboom. Twenty-six years old. Anglo-Saxon. Graduated from Stanford with a master's in poly sci. Taught for one year at San Jose State, then joined the CIA. That's what we'll tell the others in the project; only ourselves will know it's a sim gathering data for us.' He concluded, 'As yet we have not decided who to put in as determining guide for Dan Mageboom. Maybe Johnstone.'

'That fool,' Chuck said. A sim could operate autonomously to some extent, but in an operation of this type too many decisions were required; left to itself Dan Mageboom would quickly reveal itself as a construct. It would walk and talk, but when time arrived for it to decide policy – then a good operator, seated in complete safety in Level One of the CIA building in San Francisco, took control.

As they parked the wheel on the roof-field of Nat Wilder's office building Elwood said reflectively, 'I was thinking, Chuck, that you might like to handle Danny. Johnstone, as you say, isn't the best.'

Chuck glanced at him, taken by surprise. 'Why? It's not my job.' The CIA had a corps of men trained for simulacra animation.

'As a favour to you,' Elwood said slowly, gazing off into the heavy afternoon airborne traffic that hung like a layer of smoke over the city. 'So you could be with your wife, so to speak.'

After a time Chuck said, 'Absolutely no.'

'Watch her, then.'

'What for?' He felt baffled anger. And outrage.

'Let's be realistic,' Elwood said. 'It's obvious to CIA's psych-men that you're still in love with her. And we need a full-time operator for Dan Mageboom. Petri can do your scripts for a few weeks; take this on, see how you like it, if you don't, then drop it and go back to your scripts. Lord, you've programmed simulacra for years; you ought to be a natural at remote – I'd make book on it. And you'd be going on the same ship with Mary, landing on Alpha III M2 at the same time —'

'No,' Chuck repeated. He opened the door of the wheel, stepped out on the surface of the field. 'I'll see you later; thanks for the ride.'

'You know,' Elwood said, 'I could order you to take this remote. I would, if I thought it would be in your interest. Which it might well be. Here's what I think I'll do; I'll get out your wife's folder – from the FBI – and go over it. Depending on the kind of person she is —' He gestured. 'I'll decide on that basis.'

'What kind of person should she be,' Chuck said, 'for me to spy on her out of a CIA simulacrum?'

Elwood said, 'A woman worth your going back to.' He shut the door of the wheel; Petri started up the motor and the wheel shot up into the late-afternoon sky. Chuck stood watching it go.

CIA thinking, he said to himself caustically. Well, I ought to be used to it by now.

But Elwood was right about one thing. He had indeed programmed many simulacra – and with calculatedly persuasive rhetoric. If he took over the remote, he could not only successfully manage Dan Mageboom or whatever it was called; he could – and this did make him pause – he could transform the simulacrum into a delicately-tuned instrument, a machine that guided, beguiled, and, yes, even corrupted, those around him. He, himself, could not be that articulate; only in his craft was he masterful.

Dan Mageboom, in Chuck's hands, could accomplish a great deal vis-á-vis Mary Rittersdorf. And no one knew that better than his boss Jack Elwood. No wonder Elwood had suggested it.

But it had a potentially sinister quality. It repelled him; he shrank back from it, intuiting its odiousness.

And yet he could not simply turn it down out of hand; things – life itself, existence on Earth – were not that candid.

The solution, perhaps, lay in having someone he could rely on do the remote. Petri, for instance. Someone who could watch out for his interests.

And then he thought, Just what are my interests?

Reflexively, he descended by in-ramp, deep in thought. Because a new idea, not one suggested by his boss Jack Elwood, had slipped without notice into his mind.

He thought, There is one thing that might be accomplished under such circumstances. A CIA simulacrum with Mary on a distant moon in another star-system entirely ... among the psychotic members of a deranged society. Something which might pass, given such exceptional circumstances.

It was not an idea which he could discuss with anyone; in fact, he found it difficult to express it even to himself. However, it had its advantages over suicide, and he had almost achieved that.

Under such circumstances I could actually manage to kill her, he said to himself. Through the CIA construct, or rather General Dynamic's construct. Legally I'd stand a reasonable chance of acquittal, since a simulacrum operated at that distance often functions on its own; its autonomic circuits often take precedence over the long-range instructions from the remote. Anyhow it's worth a try. In court I'll plead that the simulacrum acted on its own; and I can sequester countless technical papers proving that simulacra often do such things ... the history of CIA's operations is full of such bunglings at crucial points.

And it will be the burden of the prosecution to prove that I gave the instructions to the simulacrum.

He came to Nat Wilder's door; it opened and he passed on in, still deep in thought.

It might or might not be a good idea; certainly its merits were open to debate – on moral grounds alone, if not on merely practical grounds. But in any case it was the sort of idea that once entertained did not tend to go away; like an *idée fixe* it had entered his mind and once there it stayed, could not be reversed.

It was not by any means even theoretically a 'perfect

crime.' Great suspicion would at once fall on him; the county or state prosecutor – whoever it was who handled such matters as this – would accurately guess very quickly what had transpired. So would the homeopape reporters, among whom were some of the shrewdest minds in the US. But suspecting it and proving it were totally different matters.

And to some extent he could conceal himself behind the top-secret curtain which continually obscured the activities of the CIA.

Between Terra and the Alphane system it was over three light years, an immense distance. Certainly far too great a distance, under ordinary circumstances, over which to commit a capital crime. Many a slip of the electromagnetic signal, as it passed into and out of hyperspace, could in any case reasonably be assumed to exist as a constant factor. A defence attorney, if he were any good, could make a damn good case on that point alone.

And Nat Wilder was such an attorney.

FIVE

That evening, after he had eaten dinner at the Blue Fox restaurant, he called his boss Jack Elwood at his home.

'I'd like to see the creature you call Dan Mageboom,' he stated cautiously.

On the small vidscreen his boss's face writhed into a smile. 'Okay. Easy enough – go home to that rundown conapt you're stuck in, and I'll have Dan hop on over. He's here at my house. Doing dishes in the kitchen. What made you decide?'

'No particular reason,' Chuck said, and rang off.

He returned to his conapt – at night, with the faulty old recessed lighting turned on, the room was even more depressing than ever and seated himself to wait for Dan.

He heard, almost at once, a voice in the hall, a man's voice asking for him. And then the Ganymedean slime mould's thoughts formed in his brain. 'Mr. Rittersdorf, there's a gentleman in the corridor searching for you; please open your door and greet him.'

Going to the door Chuck opened it.

In the hall stood a middle-aged man, short, with protruding belly, wearing an old-fashioned suit. 'Are you Rittersdorf?' the man demanded sullenly. 'Jeez, what a dump. And it's filled with weird non-Ts – what's a Terran doing living here?' He wiped his red, perspiring face with a pocket handkerchief. 'I'm Bunny Hentman. You're the scriptwriter, aren't you? Or is this a complete foul-up?'

'I'm a simulacrum scriptwriter,' Chuck said. This was, of course, Mary's doing; she wanted to be sure he had a good income to support her in the post-marital situation.

'How come you didn't recognize me?' Hentman said crossly. 'Aren't I world-famous? Or maybe you don't watch TV.' He puffed on his cigar in irritation. 'So I'm here, I'm here. You want to work for me or not? Listen, Rittersdorf – I'm not used to coming around begging. But your stuff is good; I got to admit it. Where's your room? Or do we have to stand out here in the hall?' He saw the half-open door of Chuck's conapt; at once he strode toward it, passed through and disappeared.

Thinking rapidly, Chuck followed after him. Obviously there was no easy way to get rid of Hentman. But, as a matter of fact, he had nothing to lose by Hentman's presence; it would be a good test of the effectiveness of the Dan Mageboom simulacrum.

'You understand,' he said to Hentman as he shut the apt door, 'that I'm not actively seeking this job.'

'Sure, sure,' Hentman said, nodding. 'I know; you're a patriot – you like working for the I-spy outfit. Listen.' He waved a finger at Chuck. 'I can pay you three times what they pay. And you'll have a lot more latitude to write in. Although naturally I have a final say-so as to what's used and exactly how it's phrased.' He gazed around the living-room of the conapt with horror. 'Cripes. Reminds me of my childhood in the Bronx. I mean, this is real poverty. What happened, did your wife wipe you out in the divorce settlement?' His eyes, wise and full of compassion, flickered. 'Yeah, it can be bad; I know. I been divorced three times, and each time it's cost like hell. The law's with the woman. That wife of yours; she's attractive, but—' He gestured. 'I don't know. She's sort of cold; you know what I mean? Sort of – deliberate. I don't envy you. A woman like that, you want to be sure there's no legal entanglement with them when you get involved. Make sure it's extralegal; you know, limited to an affair.' He studied Chuck. 'But you're the marrying kind; I can see that. You play fair. A woman like that can run over you with both treads. And leave you flatter than a worm's ass.'

A knock sounded on the door. And at the same time the thoughts of the Ganymedean slime mould, Lord Running Clam, formed in Chuck's mind. 'A second visitor. Mr. Rittersdorf. A younger man this time.'

'Excuse me,' Chuck said to Bunny Hentman; he walked to the door and opened it.

'Who's doing the mind-talking act?' Hentman mumbled behind him.

An eager-faced young man, good-looking and extremely well-dressed in the most fashionable Harding Brothers clothes, said as he faced Chuck, 'Mr. Rittersdorf? I'm Daniel Mageboom. Mr. Elwood asked me to drop by.'

It was a good job; he would never have guessed. And realizing this Chuck felt elation. 'Sure,' he said, 'come on in,' and led the simulacrum into the shabby conapt. 'Mr. Mageboom,' he said, 'this the the famous TV comic Bunny Hentman. You know – ya-ya, boom-boom Hentman who runs out in a big rabbit suit with crossed eyes and flapping ears.'

'What an honour,' Mageboom said, extending his hand; the two of them shook, measuring one another. 'I've watched your show many times. It's a fun-filled riot of laughs.'

'Yeah,' Bunny Hentman murmured, glancing dourly at Chuck.

Chuck said, 'Dan is a new employee in my office; I'm meeting him for the first time.' He added, 'I'll be working with him from now on.'

'Naw,' Hentman said vigorously, 'You'll be working for me – don't you get it? I got the contract with me; I had my lawyers draw it up.' He groped in his coat pocket, scowling.

'Did I interrupt?' Mageboom said, drawing back circumspectly. 'I can come back later, Mr. Rittersdorf. Chuck, if I may call you that.'

Hentman eyed him. Then, shrugging, began to unfold the contract. 'See here. Look at what you're getting paid,' he jabbed at it with his cigar. 'Can this I-spy outfit pay you anything like that? I mean, making America laugh is patriotic; it helps the morale and defeats the Commies. In fact it's more patriotic than what you're doing; these simulacra, they all are cold fladballs – they give me the creeps.'

'I agree,' Dan Mageboom said. 'But, Mr. Hentman, there's another side to the argument, if I can take a moment of your time to explain. Mr. Rittersdorf, Chuck, here, does a job that no one else can do. Programming simulacra is an art; without expert programming they're nothing but hulks and anyone, even a child, can distinguish them from actual persons. But, properly programmed—' He smiled. 'You've never seen one of Chuck's simulacra in action. It's incredible.' He added, 'Mr. Petri does a good job, too. In fact in some ways better.'

Obviously it was Petri who had programmed this simulacrum. And was getting in a plug for himself. Chuck could not suppress a grin.

'Maybe I ought to hire this guy Petri,' Bunny Hentman said gloomily. 'If he's that good.'

'For your purposes,' Mageboom said, 'Petri might be better. I know the element in Chuck's scripts that appeals to you, but the problem is this: it's erratic. I doubt if he could sustain it as a full-time commodity, as he would have to, for your purposes. However as one ingredient among many it—'

'Butt out,' Hentman said crossly to Mageboom. To Chuck he said. 'I don't like three-way conversations; can't we go somewhere else?' He was visibly annoyed by Dan Mageboom ... he appeared to sense something amiss.

In Chuck's mind the slime mould's thoughts again formed. 'That splendid lovely girl, although as you noted lacking a nipple-dilation job, is entering the building, Mr. Rittersdorf, looking for you; I have already told her to come on up.'

Bunny Hentman obviously also receiving the thoughts of the slime mould, groaned in despair. 'Isn't there any way we can talk? Now who the hell is *this*?' He turned to face the door, glaring at it.

'Miss Trieste won't interfere with your conversation, Mr. Hentman,' Dan Mageboom said, and Chuck glanced at the simulacrum, surprised that it had an opinion about Joan. But it was on remote; he realized that all at once. Obviously this was not a programming; Petri was operating it from the CIA building in San Francisco.

The door opened and, hesitantly, Joan Trieste, wearing a

grey sweater and dirndl, no stockings but thin high heels, stood there. 'Am I bothering you, Chuck?' she asked. 'Mr. Hentman,' she said, and flushed scarlet. 'I've watched you hundreds of times I think you're the greatest comedian alive. You're as great as Sid Ceasar and all the great old-timers.' Her eyes bright, she came up to Bunny Hentman, stood close to him but carefully avoided touching him. 'Are *you* a friend of Bunny Hentman?' she asked Chuck. 'I wish you had told me.'

'We're trying,' Hentman groaned, 'to conduct a business deal. So I mean, how do we do it?' Perspiring freely he began to pace about the small living-room. 'I give up,' he announced. 'I can't sign you; it's out of the question. You know too many people. Writers are supposed to be recluse types, living lonely type lives.'

Joan Trieste had not shut the conapt door and now, through the entrance, the slime mould slowly undulated. 'Mr. Rittersdorf,' its thoughts came to Chuck, 'I have an urgent matter to take up with you alone, in private. Could you cross the hall to my apt for a moment, please?'

Hentman turned his back, squealed in frustration, walked to the window and stood looking out.

Puzzled, Chuck accompanied the slime mould across the hall to its own conapt.

'Shut the door and come closer to me,' the slime mould said. 'I don't want the others to pick up my thoughts.'

Chuck did so.

'That person, Mr. Dan Mageboom,' the slime mould thought at low volume. 'He is not a human being; he is a construct. There is no personality within him; an individual at some distance operates him. I thought I should warn you, since after all you are a neighbour of mine.'

'Thanks,' Chuck said, 'but I already knew that.' But now he felt uneasy; it would not do to have the slime mould prying into his thoughts, in view of the direction they had taken recently. 'Listen,' he began, but the slime mould anticpated him.

'I have already scanned that material in your mind,' it informed him. 'Your hostility toward your wife, your murderous impulses. Everyone at some time or another has such impulses, and in any case it would be improper for me to discuss them with anyone else. Like a priest or a doctor, a telepath must—'

'Let's not discuss it,' Chuck said. The slime mould's knowledge of his intentions put a new light on them; perhaps he would be unwise to continue. If the prosecutor could bring Lord Running Clam into court—

'On Ganymede,' the slime mould declared, 'vengeance is sanctified. If you do not believe me, have your attorney Mr. Nat Wilder look it up. In no way do I deplore the direction of your preoccupations; they're infinitely preferable to the previous suicidal impulse, which is contrary to nature.'

Chuck started back out of the slime mould's apt.

'Wait,' the slime mould said. 'One item more; in exchange for my silence ... I would like a favour.'

So there had been a catch to it. He was not surprised; after all, Lord Running Clam was a business-creature.

The slime mould said, 'I insist, Mr. Rittersdorf, that you take the job which Mr. Hentman is offering at this very moment.'

'What about my job with the CIA?' Chuck demanded.

'You need not give that up; you can hold both jobs.' The slime mould's thoughts were confident. 'By um, moonlighting it.'

' "Moonlighting." Where did you get hold of that term?'

'I am an expert on Terran society,' the slime mould informed him. 'As I envision it, you will hold the job with CIA by day, the job with Bunny Hentman by night. To accomplish this you will need drugs, thalamic stimulants of the hexo-amphetamine class, which are illegal on Terra. However I will provide them; I have contacts off this planet and can procure the drugs easily. You will need no sleep at all, once your brain metabolism has been stimulated by—'

'A sixteen-hour workday! I'd be better off letting you go to the police.'

'No,' the slime mould disagreed. 'Because here is the upshot; you will refrain from the murder, knowing that your intentions are clear to the authorities in advance. So you will not eradicate this evil woman; you will abandon your scheme and permit her to live.'

Chuck said, 'How do you know Mary's an "evil woman"?' In fact, he thought, what do you know about Terran women at all?

'From your thoughts I have learned the host of minor sadisms which Mrs. Rittersdorf has practised on you over the years; it is no doubt diabolical, by any culture's standard. Because of it you are ill and can't perceive reality correctly; for example, observe how you resist the exceedingly desirable job which Mr. Hentman is offering you.'

There was a knock on the conapt door; the door opened and Bunny Hentman looked in, glowering. 'I have to go. What's your answer, Rittersdorf? Yes or no? And if you join me you're not to bring any of these gelatinous non-Terran organisms with you; you come alone.'

The slime mould throught-radiated, 'Mr. Rittersdorf will accept your kind job-offer, Mr. Hentman.'

'What are you,' Bunny Hentman demanded, 'his agent?'

'I am Mr. Rittersdorf's colleague,' the slime mould declared.

'Okay,' Hentman said, handing the contract to Chuck. 'This calls for an eight-week assignment on your part, one full-hour script a week, and a once-a-week participation in conference with the other writers. Your salary is two thousand TERPLAN skins a week; okay?'

It was more than okay; it was twice what he had expected. Accepting the contract he signed, as the slime mould looked on.

'I'll witness your signature,' Joan Trieste said; she too had come into the apt and was standing nearby. She signed as witness on the three copies, which were then returned to Bunny Hentman; he stuffed them back into his coat pocket, then remembered that one went to Chuck – bringing it out he handed it back.

'Cheers,' the slime mould said. 'This calls for a celebration.'

'None for me,' Bunny Hentman said. 'I got to go. So long, Rittersdorf. I'll be in touch with you; get a vidphone installed in this rotten, nothing type pad you're living in. Or move to a better apt.' The door of Lord Running Clam's conapt closed after him.

'The three of us,' the slime mould said, 'can celebrate. I know of a bar willing to serve non-Ts. It is on me; the check, I mean.'

'Fine,' Chuck said. He did not want to be alone anyhow, and if he stayed in his conapt it was simply one further opportunity for Mary to find him.

When they opened the door they found, to their collective surprise, a familiar chubby-faced young man waiting in the hall. It was Dan Mageboom.

'Sorry,' Chuck apologized. 'I forgot about you.'

'We go to celebrate,' the slime mould explained to Mageboom as it oozed from its conapt. 'You are invited, despite the fact that you have no mind and are simply an empty husk.'

Joan Trieste glanced with curiosity at first Mageboom, then Chuck.

By way of explanation Chuck said to her, 'Mageboom here is a CIA robot, being operated from our S.F. office.' To Mageboom he said, 'Who is it? Petri?'

Smiling, Mageboom said, 'I'm on autonomous self-circuit right now, Mr. Rittersdorf; Mr. Petri cut himself off when you left the conapt. Don't you agree I'm doing a good job? See, you thought I was on remote and I'm not.' The simulacrum seemed marvellously pleased with itself. 'In fact,' it stated, 'I can pull off this entire evening on self-circuit; I can go out to a bar with you, drink and celebrate, comport myself exactly as a non-simulacrum would, perhaps in some ways better.'

So this, Chuck thought to himself as they walked to the down-ramp, is the instrument through which I'm to obtain redress against my wife.

Picking up his thoughts the slime mould cautioned. 'Remember, Mr. Rittersdorf, Miss Trieste is a member of the Ross Police Department.'

Joan Trieste said, 'So I am.' She had obtained the slime mould's thoughts but not Chuck's. 'Why did you think that to Mr. Rittersdorf?' she asked the slime mould.

'I felt,' the slime mould said to her, 'that because of that fact you would not countenance amorous activity on his part.'

The explanation seemed to satisfy her. 'I think,' she said to the slime mould, 'that you ought to mind your own business more. Being a telepath has made you Ganymedeans terrible busybodies.' She sounded cross.

'I am sorry,' the slime mould said, 'if I misjudged your desires, Miss Trieste; forgive me.' To Chuck it thought, 'Apparently Miss Trieste *will* entertain amorous activity on your part toward her.'

'Chrissake,' Joan Trieste complained. 'Mind your own business, please! Leave the whole topic alone, okay?' She had turned pale.

'It is difficult,' the slime mould thought morosely, to no one in particular, 'to please Terran girls.' For the rest of the trip to the bar it carefully did not think anything at all.

Later, as they sat in a booth – the slime mould in a great yellow heap on the imitation-leather-covered seat – Joan Trieste said, 'I think it's wonderful, Chuck, that you're going to work for Bunny Hentman; what a thrill it must be.'

The slime mould thought, 'Mr. Rittersdorf, it occurs to me that you should refrain, if at all possible, from acquainting your wife with the fact that you now have two jobs. If she knew she would ask for a much larger settlement and alimony.'

'True,' Chuck agreed. It was sound advice.

'Since she will learn that you are working for Mr. Hentman,' the slime mould continued, 'you had better concede that fact, while concealing the retention of your job at CIA. Ask your co-workers at CIA, in particular your immediate superior, Mr. Elwood, to cover for you.'

Chuck nodded.

'The results of this,' the slime mould pointed out, 'this singular situation of your holding two jobs simultaneously, will mean that despite the settlement and alimony payments you will have enough to live comfortably on. Had you thought of that?'

To be honest he had not looked that far ahead. The slime mould was much more provident than he, and it made him feel chagrined.

'You can see,' the slime mould said, 'how clearly I am looking out for your interests. My insistence that you accept Mr. Hentman's job-offer —'

Joan Trieste broke in, 'I think it's terrible the way you Ganymedeans play god with Terran lives.' She glared at the slime mould.

'But consider,' the slime mould said urbanely, 'that I brought you and Mr. Rittersdorf together. And I foresee – although admittedly I am not a precog – great and successful activity on your parts in the sphere of sexuality.'

'Shut up,' Joan said fiercely.

After their celebration at the bar Chuck left the slime mould off, got rid of Dan Mageboom, hailed a jet cab and accompanied Joan Trieste back to her own conapt.

As the two of them rode together in the rear of the cab Joan said, 'I'm glad to get out of Lord Running Clam's vicinity; it's a pain in the neck, having him read your mind all the time. But it is true that he brought us —' She broke off, cocking her head and listening intently. 'There's been an accident.' At once she gave new instructions to the cab. 'I'm needed. There's been a fatality.'

When they reached the scene they found a jet hopper upended; during its landing, its rotor had somehow failed and it had crashed against the side of a building, spilling out its passengers. Under a hastily-improvised blanket composed of coats and sweaters, an elderly man lay pale and silent; the police in charge waved everyone away and Chuck realized that this was the fatality.

At once Joan hurried over to him; Chuck accompanied her, finding himself permitted past by the police. Already an ambulance was on the scene; it whirred impatiently, eager to begin the trip to Ross Hospital.

Bending, Joan studied the dead man. 'Three minutes ago,' she said, half to herself, half to Chuck. 'All right,' she said. 'Just wait a minute; I'll put him back to five minutes ago.' She examined the billfold of the dead man; one of the police had handed it to her. 'Mr. Earl B. Ackers,' she murmured, and then she shut her eyes. 'This will only affect Mr. Ackers,' she said to Chuck. 'At least it's only supposed to. But you can never be sure with this...' Her face became squeezed, puffed out as she concentrated. 'You'd better move away,' she said to Chuck. 'So you're not affected.'

Rising, he walked off, strolled about in the cold night air, smoking a cigarette and listening to the din from the police cars' radios; a crowd had gathered and traffic moved sluggishly, waved on by the police.

What a strange girl to get mixed up with, he thought. A member of a police department and a Psi as well ... I wonder what she'd do if she knew what I have in mind for the Daniel Mageboom simulacrum. Probably Lord Running Clam is right; it would be catastrophic to let her know.

Waving to him Joan said, 'Come here.'

He walked hurriedly over.

Under the improvised blankets the elderly man was breathing; his chest rose and fell slightly and at his lips faint bubbles of saliva had formed.

'He's back in time four minutes,' Joan said. 'Alive again, but after the accident. It was the best I could do.' She nodded to the hospital simulacra; at once they approached, bent over the again-living injured man. Using what appeared to be a X-ray scanning device the senior simulacrum studied the anatomy of the injured man, seeking the source of the worst damage. Then it turned to its companion; the simulacra exchanged thoughts and all at once the junior member of the team opened its metal side, brought out a cardboard carton which it quickly tore open.

The carton contained an artificial spleen; Chuck saw, in the headlights of the police cars, the stamped information on the discarded pasteboard box. And now the simulacra, here in the spot, were beginning to operate; one administered a local anaesthetic while the other, utilizing a complex surgical hand, began to cut into the dermal wall of the injured man's abdominal cavity.

'We can go,' Joan said to Chuck, rousing him from his

fixed scrutiny of the simulacra at work. 'My job's done.' Hands in the pockets of her coat, small and slender, she walked back to their jet cab, entered and seated herself to wait for him. She looked tired.

As they drove away from the accident Chuck said, 'That's the first time I've seen medical simulacra in action.' It had been impressive; it made him even more aware of the enormous capabilities built into the artificial pseudo-men that General Dynamics had developed and constructed. Of course he had seen the CIA's simulacra countless times, but there had been nothing like this; in a vital, basic sense this was different. Here, the enemy was not merely another group of human beings with a differing political persuasion; the enemy here was death.

And, with the simulacrum Daniel Mageboom, it would be the diametric opposite; death, instead of being fought, would be encouraged.

Obviously, after what he had just witnessed, he could never tell Joan Trieste what he planned. And in that case didn't practicality dictate his not seeing her any further? It seemed almost self-destructive to engineer a murder while at the same time keeping company with an employee of a police agency – did he *want* to be caught? Was this a vitiated suicidal impulse?

'One half skin for you thoughts,' Joan said.

'Pardon?' He blinked.

'I'm not like Lord Running Clam; I can't read your mind. You seem so serious; I guess it's your marital problems. I wish there was some way I could cheer you up.' She pondered. 'When we get to my conapt you come on in and—' All at once she flushed, obviously remembering what the slime mould had said. 'Just a drink,' she said firmly.

'I'd like that,' he said, also remembering what Lord Running Clam had predicted.

'Listen,' Joan said. 'Just because that Ganymedean busybody stuck his pseudopodium or whatever they have into our lives that doesn't mean—' She broke off in exasperation her eyes shining with animation. 'Damn him. You know, he potentially could be very dangerous. Ganymedeans are so ambitious ... remember the terms under which they entered the Terra-Alpha War? And they're all like him – a million irons in the fire, always scenting out possibilities.' Her forehead wrinkled. 'Maybe you should move out of that building, Chuck. Get away from him.'

It's a little late for that, he realized soberly.

They reached Joan's building; it was, he saw, a modern pleasing structure, extremely simple in design and, like all new buildings, for the most part subsurface. Instead of rising it penetrated down.

'I'm on floor sixteen,' Joan said, as they descended. 'It's a bit like living in a mine ... too bad if you have claustrophobia.' A moment later, at her door, as she got out her key and inserted it in the lock she added philosophically, 'However this is affluent safety-wise in case the Alphanes attack again; we've got fifteen levels between us and an H-bomb.' She opened the door. The apt's lights came on, a soft, hazy illumination.

A bright streak of light seared into being, vanished; Chuck, blinded, peered and then saw, standing in the centre of the room with a camera in his hands, a man he recognized. Recognized and disliked.

'Hello, Chuck,' Bob Alfson said.

'Who is this?' Joan demanded. 'And why'd he take a picture of us?'

Alfson said, 'Keep calm, Miss Trieste. I'm your paramour's wife's attorney; we need evidence for the litigation which, by the way—' He glanced at Chuck. 'Is on the court calendar for next Monday at ten a.m. in Judge Brizzolara's courtroom.' He smiled. 'We had it moved up; your wife wants it accomplished as soon as possible.'

'Get out of this apt,' Chuck said.

Moving toward the door Alfson said, 'Glad to. This film I'm using— I'm sure you've run across it at CIA; it's expensive but helpful.' He explained to both Chuck and Joan, 'I've just taken an Agfom potent-shot. Does that strike a chord? What I have in this camera is not a record of what you did just now but what will go on here during the next half hour. I think Judge Brizzolara will be more interested in that.'

'Nothing is going to go on here during the next half hour,' Chuck said, 'because I'm leaving.' He pushed past the attorney and out into the corridor; he had to get away as soon as possible.

'I think you're wrong,' Alfson said. 'I think there'll be something of value on the film. Anyhow, what do you care? It's merely a technical device by which Mary can obtain the decree; there has to be the formal presentation of evidence. And I fail to see how you'll be hurt.'

Baffled, Chuck turned. 'This invasion of privacy—'

'You know there hasn't been any privacy for anybody for the last fifty years,' Alfson said. 'You work for an intelligence agency; don't kid me, Rittersdorf.' He strolled out into the hall, passed by Chuck and made his way unhurriedly to the elevator. 'If you want a print of the film—'

'No,' Chuck said. He stood watching the attorney until he was gone from sight.

Joan said, 'You might as well come on in. He's got it on the film anyhow.' She held the conapt door open for him and at last, reluctantly, he entered. 'What he did is illegal, of course. But I guess it goes on all the time in court cases.' Going into the kitchen she began fixing drinks; he heard the clink of glasses. 'How about Mercury Slumps? I've got a full bottle of—'

'Anything,' Chuck said, roughly.

Joan brought him his drink he accepted it reflexively.

I'll get back at her for this, he said to himself. Now it's decided; *I'm fighting for my life.*

'You look so grim,' Joan said. 'That really upset you, didn't it, that man here waiting for us with a potent-camera. Prying into our lives. First Lord Running Clam and now just when—'

'It's still possible,' Chuck said, 'to perform an act in secret. That no one else knows about.'

'Like what?'

He said nothing; he sipped his drink.

SIX

From head-high shelves, cats hopped down, three old orange toms and a mottled Manx, then several part-Siamese kittens with fuzzy, whiskery faces, a supple black young tom, and, with great difficulty, a heavy-with-young calico female; the cats, joined by a small dog, clustered around Ignatz Ledebur's feet, impeding his progress as he attempted to leave the shack.

Ahead lay parts of a dead rat; the dog, a ratting terrier, had caught it and the cats had eaten what they wished. Ignatz had heard them, at dawn, growling. He felt sorry for the rat, which had probably been after the garbage heaped on both sides of the shack's single door. After all, the rat had a right to life, too, as much so as any human. But, of course, the dog did not grasp that; to kill was an instinct implanted in the dog's weak flesh. So no moral blame was involved, and anyhow the rats frightened him; unlike their counterparts back on Terra these had agile hands, could – and did – fashion crude weapons. They were smart.

Ahead of Ignatz stood the rusting remains of an autonomic tractor, long out of service; it had been deposited here several years ago with the vague idea that it might be repaired. In the meantime Ignatz's fifteen (or was it sixteen?) children played on it, inducing what remained of its commune-circuit to converse with them.

He did not see what he was searching for: an empty plastic milk carton by which to start his morning fire. So instead he would have to break up a board. Among the great mound of discarded lumber next to his shack, he began to pick about, seeking a board frail enough for him to break by jumping on it, as it lay propped against the shack's porch.

The morning air was cold and he shivered, wishing that he had not lost his wool jacket; on one of his long walks he had lain down to rest, placing the jacket under his head as a pillow ... when he had awakened he had forgotten it and left it there. So much for the jacket. He could not, of course, remember where that had been; he knew only vaguely that it lay toward Adolfville, perhaps ten days' walk.

A woman from a nearby shack – she had been his, briefly, but he had got tired of her after fathering two children by her – appeared and yelled in a frenzy at a big white goat who had got into the vegetable garden. The goat continued to eat, almost until the woman had reached him, and then he bucked, kicked with his hind legs, and leaped away, out of reach, beet leaves still dangling from his maw. A flock of ducks, startled by his activity, honked in various stages of panic as they all scattered, and Ignatz laughed. Ducks took things so seriously.

After he had broken the board for his fire, he returned to the shack, the cats still trailing, he shut the door in their faces – not before one kitten managed to squeeze past and inside – and then he squatted by the cast iron trash burner and began building the fire.

On the kitchen table his current wife, Elsie, lay sleeping under a pile of blankets; she would not get up until he had started the fire and fixed coffee. He did not blame her. On these cold mornings no one liked to get up; it was late in the morning before Gandhitown stirred, except of course for those Heebs who had wandered all night.

From the sole bedroom of the shack a small child appeared, naked, stood with thumb in mouth, watching him silently as he lit the fire.

Behind the child blared the noise of the TV set; the sound worked but not the picture. The children could not watch, could only listen. I ought to fix that, Ignatz said to himself, but he felt no urgency; before the moon's TV transmitter at Da Vinci Heights had gone into operation, life had been simpler.

When he started to make coffee he found that part of the pot was missing. So, rather than spend time searching, he made boiled coffee; he heated a pan of water over the propane burner, then, just as it boiled, dropped in a large, unmeasured handful of ground beans. The warm, rich smell filled the shack; he inhaled with gratitude.

He was standing there at the stove, God knew how long, smelling the coffee, hearing the crackling of the fire as it warmed the shack, when by degrees he discovered that he was having a vision.

Transfixed, he remained there; meanwhile the kitten which had squeezed in managed to climb to the sink, where it found a mass of discarded food left over from last night – it ate greedily, and the sound and sight of it mixed with the other sounds and sights. And the vision grew stronger.

'I want cornmeal mush for breakfast,' the naked child at the bedroom door announced.

Ignatz Ledebur did not answer; the vision held him, now, in another land. Or rather in a land so real that it had no place; it obliterated the spacial dimension, was neither there nor here. And in terms of time —

It seemed always to have been, but as to this aspect he possessed no certitude. Perhaps what he saw did not exist in time at all, had no start and, no matter what he did, would never terminate, because it was too large. It had burst loose from time entirely perhaps.

'Hey,' Elsie murmured sleepily. 'Where's my coffee?'

'Wait,' he said.

'Wait? I can smell it, goddam it; where is it?' She struggled to a sitting position, throwing the covers aside, her body bare, breasts hanging. 'I feel awful. I feel like throwing up. I suppose those kids of yours are in the bathroom.' She slid from the table, walked unsteadily from the room. 'Why are you standing there like that?' she demanded, pausing at the entrance of the bathroom, suspiciously.

Ignatz said, 'Leave me alone.'

' "Leave me alone" my ass – it was your idea I live here. I never wanted to leave Frank.' Entering the bathroom she slammed the door; it swung back open and she pushed it, held it shut, with her foot.

The vision, now, had ended; Ignatz, disappointed, turned

away, went with the pan of coffee to the table, shoved the blankets to the floor, laid out two mugs – left over from last night's meal – and filled them with hot coffee from the pan; swollen grounds floated at the surface of each mug.

From the bathroom Elsie said, 'What was that, another of your so-called trances? You saw something, like God?' Her disgust was enormous. 'I not only have to live with a Heeb – I have to live with one who has visions, like a Skitz. Are you a Heeb or a Skitz? You *smell* like a Heeb. Make up your mind.' She flushed the toilet, came out of the bathroom. 'And you're as irritable as a Mans. That's what I hate about you the most, your perpetual irritability.' She found her coffee, drank. 'It's got grounds in it!' she yelled at him in fury. 'You lost the pot again!'

Now that the vision had departed he found it difficult to remember what it had been like. That was one trouble with visions. *How did they relate to the everyday world?* He always asked that of them.

'I saw a monster,' he said. 'It stepped on Gandhitown and crushed it underfoot. Gandhitown was gone; only a hole remained.' He felt sad; he liked Gandhitown, much more than any other spot on the moon. And then he felt afraid, much more than he ever had before in his life. And yet there was nothing he could do. No way to stop the monster; it would come and get them all, even the powerful Manses with all their clever ideas, their ceaseless activity. Even the Pares who tried to defend themselves against everything real and unreal alike.

But there had been more to the vision than that.

Behind the monster had been a wicked soul.

He had beheld it as it crept out on to the world like a shiny jello of rot; it had decayed everything it touched, even the bare soil, the skinny plants and trees. A cupful of it would corrupt an entire universe, and it belonged to a person of deeds. A creature who *wanted*.

So there were two evil things coming, the monster who crushed Gandhitown, and beyond that, the wicked soul; they were separable, and each would ultimately go its separate way. The monster was female, the wicked soul mate.

And – he shut his eyes. This was the portion of the vision that terrified him. The two would fight a dreadful battle. And it was not a battle between good and evil; it was a sightless, vacant struggle in the mire between two thoroughly contaminated entities, each as vicious as the other.

The battle, fought perhaps even to the death of one of the entities, would take place on this world. They were coming here now, to use this as a battleground deliberately, to fight out their timeless war.

'Fix some eggs,' Elsie said.

Reluctantly, Ignatz looked about in the litter by the sink for a carton of eggs.

'You'll have to wash the frying pan from last night,' Elsie said. 'I left it in the sink.'

'Okay.' He began to run cold water; with a rolled-up mass of newspaper he scrubbed at the encrusted surface of the frying pan.

I wonder, he thought. Can I influence the outcome of this struggle? Would the presence of good in the midst of this have any effect?

He could summon all his spiritual faculties and try. Not only for the benefit of the moon, for the clans, but for the two dismal entities themselves. Perhaps to ease their burden.

It was a thought-provoking idea, and as he scoured the frying pan he continued to entertain it, silently. No use telling Elsie; she would merely tell him to go to hell. She did not know his powers inasmuch as he had never revealed them to her. When in the right mood, he could walk through walls, read people's minds, cure illness, cause evil people to become ill, affect the weather, blight crops – he could do almost anything, given the right mood. It derived from his saintliness.

Even the suspicious Pares recognized him as a saint. Everyone on the moon did, including the busy, insulting Manses – when they took time out from their activity to glance up and notice him.

If anyone can save this moon from the two dingy organisms approaching, Ignatz realized, it is I. This is my destiny.

'It's not a world; it's just a moon,' Elsie said, with bleak contempt; she stood before the trash burner, dressing herself in the clothes she had taken off the night before. She had worn them for a week now, and Ignatz observed – not without a trace of relish – that she was well on her way to becoming a Heeb; it would not require much more.

And it was a good thing to be a Heeb. Because the Heeb had found the Pure Way, had dispensed with the unnecessary.

Opening the door of the shack he stepped out once more into the morning cold.

'Where are you going?' Elsie shrieked after him.

Ignatz said, 'To confer.' He shut the door behind him and then, with the cats trailing, set off on foot to find Omar Diamond, his colleague among the Skitzes.

By means of his Psionic, unnatural powers he teleported here and there about the moon until at last, sure enough, there was Omar, seated in council at Adolfville with a representative of each clan. Ignatz levitated to the sixth floor of the great stone building, bobbed against the window and rapped until those within noticed him and came to open the window for him.

'God, Ledebur,' Howard Straw, the Mans rep, declared. 'You smell like a goat. Two Heebs in the room at once – foul.' He turned his back on everyone, walked off and stood staring into space, fighting to hold back his Mans anger.

The Pare rep, Gabriel Baines, said to Ignatz, 'What's the purpose of this intrusion? We're in conference.'

Ignatz Ledebur communed silently with Omar Diamond, telling him the urgency of their need. Diamond heard him, agreed, and at once, by combining their skills, the two of them left the council chamber; he and Diamond walked together across a grassy field in which mushrooms grew. Neither spoke for a time. They amused themselves by kicking over mushrooms.

At last Diamond said, 'We were already discussing the invasion.'

'It's going to land in Gandhitown,' Ignatz said. 'I experienced a vision; those who are coming will —'

'Yes, yes,' Diamond said irritably. 'We know they're chthonic powers; I acquainted the delegates with that fact. No good can come from chthonic powers because they're heavy; like the corporeal animae they are they will sink down into the earth, become mired in the body of the planet.'

'Moon,' Ignatz said, and giggled.

'Moon, then.' Diamond shut his eyes, walked without missing a step even though he could no longer see where he journeyed; he had retreated, Ignatz realized, into a momentary, voluntary catatonia. All the Skitzes were prone to this, and he said nothing; he waited. Halting, Omar Diamond mumbled something which Ignatz could not catch.

Ignatz sighed, seated himself on the ground; beside him Omar Diamond, stood in his trance and there was no sound except the faint rustling of far distant trees beyond the limits of the meadow.

All at once Diamond said, 'Pool your powers with mine and we will envision the invasion so clearly that —' Again his words became arcane mumbling. Ignatz – even a saint could be annoyed – sighed again. 'Get hold of Sarah Apostoles,' Diamond said. 'The three of us will evoke a view of our enemy so real that it will actualize; we will control our enemy and his arrival here.'

Sending out a thought-wave, Ignatz contacted Sarah Apostles, asleep in her shack in Gandhitown. He felt her awaken, stir, mumble and groan as she rose from her cot to stagger to her feet.

He and Omar Diamond waited and presently Sarah appeared; she wore a man's coat and man's trousers, tennis shoes. 'Last night,' she said, 'I had a dream. Certain creatures are hovering near here, preparing to manifest themselves.' Her round face was twisted with worry and a nagging, corroding fear. This gave her an ugly contracted look, and Ignatz felt sorry for her. Sarah had never been able, in times of stress, to purge the destructive emotions from her being; she was bonded to the soma and its ails.

'Sit down,' Ignatz requested.

'We shall make them appear *now,*' Diamond said. 'And here at this spot. Begin.' He ducked his head; the two Heebs also ducked their heads, and together the three of them applied their mutually-reinforcing visionary powers. They struggled in unison, and time passed – none of them knew how much – while that which they contemplated bloomed in the vicinity like an evil bud.

'Here it is,' Ignatz said, and opened his eyes. Sarah and Diamond did also; they looked up into the sky – and saw, lowering itself tail first, a foreign ship. They had been successful.

Blowing vapours from its rear the ship settled to the ground a hundred yards to their right. It was a large ship, Ignatz perceived. The largest he had ever seen. He, too, felt fright, but as always he managed to control it; many years had passed since phobia had been a factor for him to deal with. Sarah, however, looked palpably terror-stricken as she watched the ship tremble to a halt, saw the hatch slide open as the occupants prepared to excrete themselves from the great tubular organism of metal and base plastic.

'Have them approach us,' Omar Diamond said, his eyes once again squeezed shut. 'Have them recognize our existence. We will force them to take note of us and honour us.' Ignatz joined him instantly, and after a pause so did frightened Sarah Apostoles, to the extent possible for her.

A ramp descended from the hatch of the ship. Two figures appeared, then lowered themselves step by step to the ground.

Ignatz said hopefully to Diamond, 'Shall we produce miracles?'

Eyeing him, Diamond said with doubt. 'Such as? I – do not customarily work magic.'

Sarah said, 'Together Ignatz and I can accomplish this.' To Ignatz she said, 'Why don't we transfigure them with the spectre of the world-spider as it spins its web of determination for all life?'

'Agreed,' Ignatz said, and turned his attention to the chore of summoning the world-spider ... or, as Elsie would say, the *moon*-spider.

Before the two figures from the ship, blocking their way, appeared a glistening manifold of web-strands, a hastily erected structure by the never-ceasing toils of the spider. The figures froze.

One of them said something unutterable.

Sarah laughed.

'If you let them amuse you,' Omar Diamond said severely, 'we will lose the power which we hold over them.'

'I'm sorry,' Sarah said, still laughing. But it was already too late; the heap of shimmering web-fragments dissolved. And, Ignatz saw to his dismay, so did Omar Diamond and Sarah; he found himself seated alone. Their triumvirate had been extinguished by one instant of weakness. Nor did he still sit on the field of grass; he sat instead on a heap of junk in his own front yard in the centre of Gandhitown.

The invading macro-organisms had regained control of their actions. Had managed to revert to their own plans.

Rising, Ignatz walked toward the two figures from the ship, who now stood uncertainly looking around them. Beneath Ignatz's feet his cats romped and raced; he tripped, almost sprawled; cursing to himself he pushed the cats aside, trying to retain a measure of gravity, of dignified countenance before these invaders. However this was impossible. Because behind him the door of the shack had opened and Elsie had come out; she had spoiled even this last-ditch stand on his part.

'Who are they?' she yelled.

Irritably Ignatz said, 'I don't know. I'm going to find out.'

'Tell them to get the hell out of here,' Elsie said, her hands on her hips. She had been a Mans for several years and she still retained the arrogant hostility learned at Da Vinci Heights. Without knowing what she was up against she was prepared to do battle ... perhaps, he thought, with a can opener and a skillet. That amused him and he began to laugh; once he started he could not stop, and it was in this condition that he came up face to face with the two invaders.

'What's so funny?' one of them, a female inquired.

Ignatz, wiping his eyes, said, 'Do you remember landing twice? Do you remember the world-spiders? You don't.' It was too funny; the invaders did not even recall the efforts of the triadic unnaturally-gifted saints. For them it had not even happened; it had not even been a delusion, and yet into it had gone all the efforts possible on the part of Ignatz Ledebur, Sarah Apostoles and the Skitz, Omar Diamond. He laughed on and on, and meanwhile the two invaders were joined by a third and then a fourth.

One of them, a male, sighed as he looked around. 'Lord, what a rundown dump this place is. You think it's all this way?'

'But you can help us,' Ignatz said. He managed to gain control of himself; pointing to the rusting hulk of the autonomic tractor on which the children played, he said, 'Could you put yourself out to the extent of lending a hand to repair my farming equipment? If I had a little help —'

'Sure, sure,' one of the men said. 'We'll help clean up this place.' He wrinkled his nose in disgust; evidently he had smelled or seen something that offended him.

'Come inside,' Ignatz said. 'And have coffee.' He turned toward the shack; after a pause the three men and the woman reluctantly followed. 'I have to apologize for the smallness of the place,' Ignatz said, 'and the condition it's in —' He pushed open the door and this time most of the cats managed to squirm into the shack; bending, he picked up one after another, tossed them back outdoors. The four invaders uncertainly entered, stood about looking acutely unhappy.

'Sit down,' Elsie said, summoning a modicum of politeness; she put the tea-kettle on the stove, lit the burner. 'Just clear off that bench,' she directed. 'Push the stuff anywhere; on the floor if you want.'

The four invaders reluctantly – with tangible aversion – pushed the mass of children's soiled clothing on to the floor, seated themselves. Each had a vague, stunned expression and Ignatz wondered why.

The woman, haltingly, said, 'Couldn't you – clean up your home here? I mean, how do you live in such—' She gestured, unable to continue.

Ignatz felt apologetic. But after all ... there were so many more important matters and so little time. Neither he nor Elsie could seem to find the opportunity to straighten things up; it was wrong, of course, to let the shack get like this, but – he shrugged. Sometime soon, perhaps. And the invaders could possibly help here, too; they might have a work-sim that could pitch in. The Manses had them, but they charged too much. Possibly the invaders would loan him a work-sim *free.*

A rat, from its hole behind the icebox, scuttled across the floor. The woman invader, seeing the clumsy little weapon which it carried, shut her eyes and moaned.

Ignatz, as he fixed the coffee, giggled. Well, no one had asked them to come here; if they didn't like Gandhitown they could leave.

From the bedroom several of the children appeared, gaped in silence at the four invaders. The invaders sat rigidly, saying nothing, waiting in pain for their coffee, ignoring the blank, staring eyes of the children.

In the large council room at Adolfville the Heeb rep, Jacob Simion, spoke up suddenly. 'They've landed. At Gandhitown. They're with Ignatz Ledebur.'

Furious, Howard Straw said, 'While we sit here talking. Enough of this time-wasting gabble; let's wipe them out. They have no business on our world – don't you agree?' He poked Gabriel Baines.

'I agree,' Baines said, and moved a trifle further away from the Mans delegate. 'How did you know?' he asked Jacob Simion.

The Heeb snickered. 'Didn't you see them here in the room? The astral bodies? It was Ignatz who came here – you don't remember that; he came and took Omar Diamond with him, but you've forgotten that because it never happened; the invaders made it unhappen by dividing the three into one and two.'

Staring hopelessly at the floor the Dep said, 'So already it's too late; they've landed.'

Howard Straw barked a sharp, cold laugh. 'But only in Gandhitown. Who cares about that? It *ought* to be mopped up; personally I'd be glad if they pulverized it out of existence – it's a cesspool and everybody living in it stinks.'

Shrinking back as if struck, Jacob Simion murmured, 'At least we Heebs, we're not cruel.' He blinked back helpless tears; at that, Howard Straw grinned with relish and nudged Gabriel Baines.

'Don't you have spectacular weapons at Da Vinci Heights?' Gabriel Baines asked him. He had a deep intuition, then, that the Mans' write-off of Gandhitown was indicative; the Manses probably intended to make no stand until their own settlement was endangered. They would not lend the inventiveness of their hyperactive minds for the general defence.

Gabriel Baines' long-time suspicions of Straw were now being justified.

Frowning with worry Annette Golding said, 'We can't let Gandhitown go down the drain.'

'"Down the drain,"' Straw echoed. 'Appropriate! Yes we certainly can. Listen; *we have the weapons*. They've never been put to use – they can wipe out any invading armada. We'll trot them out – when we feel like it.' He glanced around the table at the other delegates, enjoying the power of his position, his mastery; they were all dependent on him.

'I knew you'd behave like this as soon as a crisis arose,' Gabriel Baines said bitterly. God, how he hated the Manses. How unreliable morally they were, so egocentric and superior; they simply could not work for the common good. Thinking this he made himself a promise right on the spot. It his opportunity to get back at Straw ever came he would take it. Fully. In fact, he realized, if the opportunity came to pay back the whole bunch of them, the entire Mans settlement – it was a hope worth living for. The Manses held the advantage now, but it wouldn't last.

In fact, Gabriel Baines thought, it would almost be worth going to the invaders and making a pact with them on behalf of Adolfville; the invaders and ourselves against Da Vinci Heights.

The more he thought of it the more the idea appealed to him.

Annette Golding, eyeing him, said, 'Do you have something to offer us, Gabe? You look as if you've thought of something valuable.' Like all Polys she had acute perceptions; she had correctly read the changing expressions on his face.

Gabe chose to lie. Obviously he had to. 'I think,' he said aloud, 'we can sacrifice Gandhitown. We're going to have to give it to them, let them colonize in that area, set up a base or whatever they want to do; we may not like it but —' He shrugged. What else could they do?

Miserably, Jacob Simion stammered, 'Y-you people don't care about us just because we're – not so cleanly as you all. I'm going back to Gandhitown and join my clan; if they're going to perish I'll perish with them.' He rose to his feet, pushing his chair over with a discordant crash. 'Betrayers,' he added as he shambled, Heeb-wise, toward the door. The other delegates watched him go, displaying various shades of indifference; even Annette Golding, who generally cared about everything and everyone, did not seem perturbed.

And yet – fleetingly – Gabriel Baines felt grief. Because for the whole lot of them, here went their potential fate; every now and then a full Pare or Poly or Skitz or even Mans drifted by insidious, imperceptible degrees into Heebhood. So it could still come about. Any time.

And now, Baines realized, if that happens to any of us *there will be no place to go.* What became of a Heeb without Gandhitown? A good question; if frightened him.

Aloud he said, 'Wait.'

At the door the shambling, unshaven, sloppy figure of Jacob Simion paused; in the sunken Heeb eyes a flicker of hope manifested itself.

Gabriel Baines said, 'Come back.' Addressing himself to

the others, especially arrogant Howard Straw, he said, 'We have to act in concert. Today it's Gandhitown; tomorrow it'll be Hamlet Hamlet or ourselves or the Skitzes – the invaders will nab us bit by bit. Until only Da Vinci Heights remains.' His antagonism toward Straw made his voice grate with envenomed harshness; in his own ears it was scarcely recognizable. 'I vote formally that we employ all our resources in an effort to reconquer Gandhitown. We should make our stand there.' Right in the middle of the heaps of garbage, animal manure and rusting machinery, he said to himself, and winced.

After a pause Annette said, 'I – second the motion.'

The vote was taken. Only Howard Straw voted against it. So the motion carried.

'Straw,' Annette said briskly, 'you're instructed to produce these miracle weapons you've been bragging about. Since you Manses are so militant we'll let you lead the attack to retake Gandhitown.' To Gabriel Baines she said, 'And you Pares can organize it.' She seemed quite calm, now that it had all been decided.

Softly, Ingred Hibbler said to Straw, 'I might point out that if the war is fought near and in Gandhitown, damage will not occur to the other settlements. Had you thought of that?'

'Imagine fighting in Gandhitown,' Straw muttered. 'Wading around waist-deep in —' He broke off. To Jacob Simion and Omar Diamond he said, 'We'll need all the Skitz and Heeb saints, visionaries, miracle-workers and just plain Psis we can get; will your settlements produce them and let us employ them?'

'I think so,' Diamond said. Simion nodded.

'Between the miracle weapons from Da Vinci Heights and the talents of the Heeb and Skitz saints,' Annette said, 'we should be able to offer more than token resistance.'

Miss Hibbler said, 'If we could get the full names of the invaders we could cast numerological charts of them, discover their weak points. Or if we had their exact birthdates —'

'I think,' Annette interrupted, 'that the weapons of the

Manses, plus the oganizing powers of the Pares, in conjunction with the Heeb and Skitz unnaturals, will be somewhat more useful.'

'Thank you,' Jacob Simion said, 'for not sacrificing Gandhitown.' He gazed in mute appreciation at Gabriel Baines.

For the first time in months, perhaps even years, Baines felt his defences melt; he enjoyed – briefly – a sense of relaxation, of near-euphoria. Someone liked him. And even if it was only a Heeb it meant a lot.

It reminded him of his childhood. Before he had found the Pare solution.

SEVEN

Walking along the muddy, rubbish-heaped central street of Gandhitown, Dr. Mary Rittersdorf said, 'I've never seen anything like this in my life. Clinically it's mad. These people must all be hebephrenics. Terribly, terribly deteriorated.' Inside her something cried at her to *get out*, to leave this place and never return. To get back to Terra and her profession as marriage counsellor and forget she had ever seen this.

And the idea of attempting psychotherapy with these people —

She shuddered. Even drug-therapy and electroshock would be of little use, here. This was the tail-end of mental illness, the point of no return.

Beside her the young CIA agent, Dan Mageboom, said, 'Your diagnosis, then, is hebephrenia? I can report that back officially?' Taking her by the arm he assisted her over the remains of some major animal carcass; in the mid-day sun the ribs stuck up like tines of a great curved fork.

Mary said, 'Yes, it's obvious. Did you see the pieces of dead rat lying strewn around the door of that shack? I'm sick; I'm actually sick to my stomach. No one lives that way now. Not even in India and China. It's like going back four thousand years; that's the way Sinanthropus and Neanderthal must have lived. Only without the rusted machinery.'

'At the ship,' Mageboom said, 'we can have a drink.'

'No drink is going to help me,' Mary said. 'You know what this awful place reminds me of? The horrible shoddy old conapt my husband moved into when we separated.'

Beside her Mageboom started, blinked.

'You knew I was married,' Mary said. 'I told you.' She

wondered why her remark had surprised him so; on the trip she had freely discussed her marital problems with him, finding him a good listener.

'I can't believe your comparison is accurate,' Mageboom said. 'The conditions here are symptoms of a group psychosis; your husband never lived like that – he had no mental disorder.' He glared at her.

Mary halting, said, 'How do you know? You never met him. Chuck was – still is – sick. What I said is so; he has a latent streak of hebephrenia in him ... he always shrank from socio-sexual responsibility; I told you about all my attempts to get him to seek employment that guaranteed a reasonable return.' But of couse Mageboom himself was an employee of the CIA; she could hardly expect to obtain sympathy from him on that issue. Better, perhaps, to drop the whole topic. Things were depressing enough without having to rehash her life with Chuck.

On both sides of her Heebs – that was what they called themselves, a corruption of the obviously accurate diagnostic category hebephrenic – gazed with vacuous silliness, grinning without comprehension, even without real curiosity. A white goat wandered by ahead of her; she and Dan Mageboom stopped warily, neither of them familiar with goats. It passed on.

At least, she thought, these people are harmless. Hebephrenics at all their stages of deterioration, lacked the capacity to act out aggression; there were other far more ominous derangement-syndromes to be on the lookout for. It was inevitable that, very shortly, they would begin to turn up. She was thinking in particular of the manic-depressives, who, in their manic phase, could be highly destructive.

But there was an even more sinister category which she was steeling herself against. The destructiveness of the manics would be limited to impulse; at the worst it would have a tantrum-like aspect, temporary orgies of breaking and hitting which ultimately would subside. However, with the acute paranoid a systemized and permanent hostility could be anticipated; it would not abate in time but on the contrary would become more elaborate. The paranoid possessed an analytical, calculating quality; he had a good reason for his actions, and each move fitted in as part of the scheme. His hostility might be less conspicuously violent ... but in the long run its durability posed deeper implications as far as therapy went. Because with these people, the advanced paranoids, cure or even temporary insight was virtually impossible. Like the hebephrenic, the paranoid had found a stable and permanent maladaptation.

And, unlike the manic-depressive and the hebephrenic, or the simple catatonic schizophrenic, the paranoid *seemed* rational. The formal pattern of logical reasoning appeared undisturbed. Underneath, however, the paranoid suffered from the greatest mental disfigurement possible for a human being. He was incapable of empathy, unable to imagine himself in another person's role. Hence for him others did not actually exist – except as objects in motion that did or did not affect his well-being. For decades it had been fashionable to say that paranoids were incapable of loving. This was not so. The paranoid experienced love fully, both as something given to him by others and as a feeling on his part toward them. But there was a slight catch to this.

The paranoid experienced it as a variety of hate.

To Dan Mageboom she said, 'According to my theory the several sub-types of mental illness should be functioning on this world as classes somewhat like those of ancient India. These people here, the hebephrenics, would be equivalent to the untouchables. The manics would be the warrior class, without fear; one of the highest.'

'Samurai,' Mageboom said. 'As in Japan.'

'Yes.' She nodded. 'The paranoids – actually paranoiac schizophrenics – would function as the statesman class; they'd be in charge of developing political ideaology and social programmes – they'd have the overall world view. The simple schizophrenics...' She pondered. 'They'd correspond to the poet class, although some of them would be religious visionaries – as would be some of the Heebs. The Heebs, however, would be inclined to produce ascetic saints, whereas the schizophrenics would produce dogmatists. Those with polymorphic schizophrenia simplex would be the creative members of the society, producing the new ideas.' She tried to remember what other categories might exist. 'There could be some with over-valent ideas, psychotic disorders that were advanced forms of milder obsessive-compulsive neurosis, the so-called diencephalic disturbances. Those people would be the clerks and office holders of the society, the ritualistic functionaries, with no original ideas. Their conservatism would balance the radical quality of the polymorphic schizophrenics and give the society stability.'

Mageboom said, 'So one would think the whole affair would work.' He gestured. 'How would it differ from our own society on Terra?'

For a time she considered the question; it was a good one.

'No answer?' Mageboom said.

'I have an answer. Leadership in this society here would naturally fall to the paranoids, they'd be superior individuals in terms of initiative, intelligence and just plain innate ability. Of course they'd have trouble keeping the manics from staging a coup ... there'd always be tension between the two classes. But you see, with paranoids establishing the ideology, the dominant emotional theme would be hate. Actually hate going in two directions; the leadership would hate everyone outside its enclave and also would take for granted that everyone hated it in return. Therefore their entire so-called foreign policy would be to establish mechanisms by which this supposed hatred directed at them could be fought. And this would involve the entire society in an illusory struggle, a battle against foes that didn't exist for a victory over nothing.'

'Why is that so bad?'

'Because,' she said, 'no matter how it came out, the results would be the same. Total isolation for these people. That would be the ultimate effect of their entire group activity: to progressively cut themselves off from all other living entities.'

'Is that so bad? To be self-sufficient —'

'No,' Mary said. 'It wouldn't be self-sufficiency; it would be something entirely different, something you and I really can't imagine. Remember the old experiments made with people in absolute isolation? Back in the mid-twentieth century, when they anticipated space travel, the possibility of a man being entirely alone for days, weeks on end, with fewer and fewer stimuli ... remember the results they obtained when they placed a man in a chamber from which no stimuli at all reached him?'

'Of course,' Mageboom said. 'It's what now is called *the buggies*. The result of stimulus-deprivation is acute hallucinosis.'

She nodded. 'Auditory, visual, tactile and olfactory hallucinosis, replacing the missing stimuli. And, in intensity, hallucinosis can exceed the force of reality; in its vividness, its impact, the effect aroused by it ... for example, states of terror. Drug-induced hallucinations can bring on states of terror which no experience with the real world can produce.'

'Why?'

'Because they have an absolute quality. They're generated within the sense-receptor system and constitute a feedback emanating not from a distant point but from within a person's own nervous system. He can't obtain detachment from it. And he knows it. There's no retreat possible.'

Mageboom said, 'And how's that going to act here? You don't seem able to say.'

'I can say, but it's not simple. First, I don't know yet how far this society is advanced along the lines of isolating itself and the individuals who make it up. We'll know soon by their attitude toward us. The Heebs we're seeing here—' She indicated the hovels on both sides of the muddy road. 'Their attitude is no index. However, when we run into our first paranoids or manics – let's say this: undoubtedly some measure of hallucination, of psychological projection, exists as a component of their world view. In other words, we have to assume they're already partly hallucinating. But they still retain some sense of objective reality as such. Our presence here will accelerate the hallucinating tendency; we have to face that and be prepared. And the hallucination will take the form of seeing us as elements of dire menace; we, our ship, will literally be viewed – I don't mean interpreted, I mean actually perceived – as threatening. What they undoubtedly will see in us is an invading spearhead that intends to overthrow their society, make it a satellite of our own.'

'But that's true. We intend to take the leadership out of their hands, place them back where they were twenty-five years ago. Patients in enforced hospitalization circumstances – in other words, captivity.'

It was a good point. But not quite good enough. She said, 'There is a distinction you're not making; it's a slender one, but vital. We will be attempting therapy of these people, trying to put them actually in the position which, by accident, they now improperly hold. If our programme is successful they *will* govern themselves, as legitimate settlers on this moon, eventually. First a few, then more and more of them. This is not a form of captivity – *even if they imagine it is.* The moment any person on this moon is free of psychosis, is capable of viewing reality without the distortion of projection —'

'Do you think it'll be possible to persuade these people voluntarily to resume their hospitalized status?'

'No,' Mary said. 'We'll have to bring force to bear on them; with the possible exception of a few Heebs we're going to have to take out commitment papers for an entire planet.' She corrected herself, 'Or rather moon.'

'Just think,' Mageboom said. 'If you hadn't changed that to "moon" I'd have grounds for committing you.'

Startled, she glanced at him. He did not appear to be joking; his youthful face was grim.

'It was just a slip,' she said.

'A slip,' he agreed, 'but a revealing one. A symptom.' He smiled, and it was a cold smile. It made her shiver in bewilderment and unease; what did Mageboom have against her? Or was she becoming just a little bit paranoid? Perhaps so . . . but she felt enormous hostility directed her way from the man, and she barely knew him.

And she had felt this hostility throughout the trip. And strangely, from the very beginning; it had started the moment they met.

Putting the Daniel Mageboom simulacrum on homeostasis, Chuck Rittersdorf switched himself out of the circuit, rose stiffly from the seat before the control panel and lit a cigarette. It was nine p.m. local time.

On Alpha III M2 the sim would go about its business, functioning in an adequate manner; if any crisis came up Petri could take over. In the meantime he himself had other problems. It was time for him to produce his first script for the TV comic Bunny Hentman, his other employer.

He had, now, a supply of stimulants; the slime mould from Ganymede had presented them to him as he had started from his conapt that morning. So evidently he could count on working all night.

But first there was a little matter of dinner.

For what it was worth he paused at the public vidphone booth in the lobby of the CIA building and put in a call to Joan Trieste's conapt.

'Hi,' she said when she saw who it was. 'Listen, Mr. Hentman called here, trying to get hold of you. So you better get in touch with him. He said he tried to reach you at the CIA building in S.F. but they said they never heard of you.'

'Policy,' Chuck said. 'Okay. I'll call him.' He asked her, then, about dinner.

'I don't believe you'll be able to have dinner, with or without me,' Joan answered. 'From what Mr. Hentman told me. He's got some idea he wants you to listen to; he says when he springs it on you you'll drop.'

Chuck said, 'That wouldn't come as a surprise.' He felt resigned; obviously this was how the entire relationship with Hentman would function.

Temporarily forgetting any further efforts in Joan's direction he called the vidphone number which the Hentman organization had provided him.

'Rittersdorf!' Hentman exclaimed, as soon as the contact

was established. 'Where are you? Get right over here; I'm in my Florida apt – take an express rocket; I'll pay the fare. Listen, Rittersdorf; your test is showing up right now – this'll tell if you're any good or not.'

It was a long leap from the vacuous dump-like settlement of the Heebs on Alpha III M2 to Bunny Hentman's energetic schemes. The transition was going to be hard; perhaps it could be accomplished on the flight back East. He could eat, too, on the ship, but that let out Joan Trieste; already his job was undermining his personal life.

'Tell me the idea now. So I can mull it over on the flight.'

Hentman's eyes glowed with cunning. 'Are you kidding? Suppose someone overhears? Listen, Rittersdorf. I'll give you a *hint*. I had this in the back of my mind when I hired you but—' His grin increased. 'I didn't want to scare you off, you know what I mean? Now I got you hooked.' He laughed loudly. 'So now – wow! Anything goes, right?'

'Just tell me the idea,' Chuck said, patiently.

Lowering his voice to a whisper Hentman leaned close to the vidscanner. His nose, magnified, filled the screen, a nose and one winking, delighted eye. 'It's a new characterization I'm going to add to my repertoire. George Flibe; that's his name. As soon as I tell you what he is, you'll see why I hired you. Listen: Flibe is a CIA agent. And he's posing as a female marriage counsellor, in order to get information on suspects.' Hentman waited, expectantly. 'Well? What you say?'

After a long time Chuck said, 'It's the worst thing I've heard in twenty years.' It completely depressed him.

'You're out of your mind. I know and you don't. This could be the biggest character in TV comedy since Red Skelton's Freddy the Freeloader. And you're the one to write the script because you've had the experience. So get here to my apt as soon as possible and we'll get started on the first George Flibe episode. All right! If that's not such a hot idea what have got to offer?'

Chuck said, 'What about a female marriage counsellor who poses as a CIA agent in order to get information that'll cure her patients?'

'Are you pulling my leg?'

'In fact,' Chuck said, 'how about this? A CIA simulacrum —'

'You're putting me on.' Hentman's face became red; at least, on the vidscreen it darkened appreciably.

'I was never more serious in my life.'

'All right, what about the simulacrum?'

'This CIA simulacrum, see,' Chuck said, 'poses as a female marriage counsellor, see, but every now and then the simulacrum breaks down.'

'Do the CIA sims really do that? Break down?'

'All the time.'

'Go on,' Hentman said, scowling.

Chuck said, 'See, the whole point is, what the hell does a simulacrum know about human marital problems? And see, here it is advising people. It keeps giving out this advice; once it gets started it can't stop. It's even giving marital advice to the General Dynamics repairmen who're always fixing it. See?'

Rubbing his chin Hentman nodded slowly. 'Hmm.'

'There'd have to be a particular reason why this one sim acts this way. So we'd go into his origin. The episode, see, would start with the General Dynamics engineers who —'

'I've got it!' Hentman interrupted. 'This one engineer, call him Frank Fupp, is having trouble in his marriage; he's seeing a marriage counsellor. And she's given him this document, it's an analysis of his problem, and he's brought it to work, to G.D.'s labs, with him. And there's this new sim standing there, waiting to be programmed.'

'Sure!' Chuck said.

'And – and Fupp reads the document aloud to this other engineer. Call him Phil Grook. The simulacrum gets accidentally programmed; it thinks it's a marriage counsellor. But actually it's been contracted for by the CIA; it's shipped to the CIA and it shows up —' Hentman paused, pondering. 'Where would it show up, Rittersdorf?'

'Behind the Iron Curtain. Say in Red Canada.'

'Right! In Red Canada, in Ontario. It's supposed to pose as a – synthetic wabble-hide salesman; isn't that right? Isn't that what they do?'

'More or less; right.'

'But instead,' Hentman went on excitedly, 'it sets itself up in a little office, hangs out a sh-shingle. George Flibe, Psychologist, Ph.D. Marital Counselling. And these high Commie party officials with marital problems keep coming to it—' Hentman puffed with agitation. 'Rittersdorf, you've got the best frigging idea I've heard in as long as I can remember. And – and always these two General Dynamics engineers, they're showing up trying to tinker with it and get it working right. Listen; get on the express rocket for Florida right now; and sketch this out during the trip, maybe have some dialogue when you get here. I think we're really on to something; you know, your brain and mine really synchronize – right?'

'I think so,' Chuck said. 'I'll be right there.' He obtained the address and then rang off. Wearily, he left the vidphone booth; he felt drained. And he could not for the life of him tell if had come up with a good idea or not. Anyhow Hentman believed he had, and evidently that was what counted.

By jet cab he reached the San Francisco space port; there he boarded an express rocket which would carry him to Florida.

The conapt building of Bunny Hentman was luxury incarnate; all its levels were below the surface and it had its own uniformed police force patrolling the entrances and halls. Chuck gave his name to the first cop who approached him and a moment later he was descending to Bunny's floor.

Within the huge apt Bunny Hentman lounged in a hand-dyed Martian spider-silk dressing gown, smoking a green, enormous, Tampa, Florida cigar; he jerked his head in impatient greeting to Chuck and then indicated the other men in the living-room.

'Rittersdorf, there are two of your colleagues, my writers. This tall one—' He pointed with his cigar. 'That's Calv Dark.' Dark approached Chuck slowly and shook hands. 'And the short fat one with no hair on his head; that's my senior writer, Thursday Jones.' Also coming forward Jones, an alert, sharp-featured Negro, shook hands with Chuck. Both the writers seemed friendly; he had no sense of hostility on their parts. Evidently they did not resent him.

Dark said, 'Sit down, Rittersdorf. It's been a long trip for you. A drink?'

'No,' Chuck said. He wanted his mind clear for the session ahead.

'You had dinner on the rocket?' Hentman asked.

'Yes.'

'I've been telling my boys about your idea,' Hentman said. 'Both of them like it.'

'Fine,' Chuck said.

'However,' Hentman continued, 'they've batted it back and forth and a little while ago they came up with an evolution of their own ... you know what I mean?'

Chuck said, 'I'd be only too happy to hear their idea based on my idea.'

Clearing his throat Thursday Jones said, 'Mr. Rittersdorf, could a simulacrum commit a murder?'

After staring at him a moment Chuck said, 'I don't know.' He felt cold. 'You mean on its own, working by autonomic —'

'I mean could the person operating it from remote use it as an instrument for murder?'

To Bunny Hentman, Chuck said, 'I don't see any humour in an idea like that. And my wit's supposed to be moribund.'

'Wait,' Bunny cautioned. 'You forget the famous old funny thrillers, combinations of terror and humour. Like the *Cat and the Canary*, that movie with Paulette Goddard and Bob Hope. And the famous *Arsenic and Old Lace* – not to mention classic British comedies in which someone was murdered ... there were dozens of them in the past.'

'Like the marvellous *Kind Hearts and Coronets*,' Thursday Jones said.

'I see,' Chuck said, and that was all he said; he kept his mouth shut, while inside he seethed with disbelief and shock. Was this just some malign coincidence, this idea running parallel to his own life? Or – and this seemed more probable – the slime mould had said something to Bunny. But if so, why was the Hentman organization doing this? What interest did they have in the life and death of Mary Rittersdorf?

Hentman said, 'I think the boys have a good idea here. The scary with the ... well, you see, Chuck, you work for CIA so you don't realize this, but the average person is scared of the CIA; you got it? He regards it as a secret interplanetary police and spy organization which—'

'I know,' Chuck said.

'Well, you don't have to bite my head off,' Bunny Hentman said, with a glance at Dark and Jones.

Speaking up, Dark said, 'Chuck – if I can call you that already – we know our business. When the average Joe thinks of a CIA sim he's scared right off the bat. When you gave Bunny your idea you weren't thinking of that. Now here's this CIA operator; let's call him—' He turned to Jones. 'What's our working-name?'

'Siegfried Trots.'

'Here's Ziggy Trots, a secret agent ... trenchcoat made of Uranian molecricket fur, hat of Venusian wubfuzz pulled down over his forehead – all that. Standing in the rain on some dismal moon, maybe one of Jupiter's. A familiar sight.'

'And then, Chuck,' Jones said, picking up the narrative, 'once the pic is established in the viewer's mind, the stereotype – you see? Then the viewer discovers something about Ziggy Trots he didn't know, that the stereotype of the sinister CIA agent doesn't ordinarily contain.'

Dark said, 'See, Ziggy Trots is an idiot. A nurt who can never pull off anything right. And here's what he's trying to pull off.' He walked over, seated himself on the couch beside Chuck. 'He's going to try to commit a murder. Got it?'

'Yes,' Chuck said tightly, saying as little as possible, becoming merely a listening entity. He shrank within himself, more and more bewildered by – and suspicious of – what was going on around him.

Dark continued, 'Now, who's he trying to kill?' He

glanced at Jones and Bunny Hentman. 'We've been arguing about this part.'

Bunny said, 'A blackmailer. An international jewel magnate who operates from another planet entirely. Maybe a non-T.'

Shutting his eyes, Chuck rocked back and forth.

'What's wrong, Chuck?' Dark asked.

'He's thinking,' Bunny said. 'Trying the idea on. Right, Chuck?'

'That's – right,' Chuck managed to say. He was sure, now, that Lord Running Clam had gone to Hentman. And something vast and dismal was unfolding around him, catching him up; he was a midge in the midst of this, whatever it was. And there was no way for him to get out.

'I disagree,' Dark said. 'International jewel magnate who's maybe a Martian or a Venusian – that's not bad ... but—' He gestured. 'It's been done to death; we started with one stereotype; let's not revert to another. I think he should be trying to do away with – well, his wife.' Dark looked around at each of them. 'Tell me; what's wrong with that? He's got a nagging, shrew of a wife – get the picture? This hard, tough, CIA secret police spy type agent, who the average person is scared to death of ... we see how tough he is, pushing people around – and then he goes home and he's got this wife who pushes *him* around!' He laughed.

'It's not bad,' Bunny admitted. 'But it's not enough. And I wonder how many times I could do the characterization; I want something I can add permanently to the show. Not just a skit for one week.'

'I think the henpecked CIA man could go on forever,' Dark said. 'Anyhow—' He turned back to Chuck. 'So this Ziggy Trots is next seen on the job, at CIA headquarters, and there's all these police gadgets and electronic devices. *And all of a sudden it comes to him.*' Dark jumped to his feet and began striding about the room. 'He can use them against his wife! And then to top it off – in steps this new sim.' Dark's voice became metallic and crabbed as he mimicked a simulacrum. 'Yes, master, what may I do for you? I am waiting.'

Bunny, grinning, said, 'What you say, Chuck?'

With difficulty Chuck said, 'Is – his only motive for murdering his wife the fact that she's a shrew? That she browbeats him?'

'No!' Jones shouted, leaping up. 'You're right; we need a stronger motivation and I think I've got it. There's this girl. Ziggy's got a mistress in the side. An interplan female spy, beautiful and sexy – you get it? And his wife won't give him a divorce.'

Dark said. 'Or maybe his wife has discovered this girl friend and has —'

'Wait,' Bunny said. 'What are we getting here, a psychological drama or a comedy skit? It's getting too messy.'

'Right,' Jones said, nodding. 'We stick to just showing what a monster the wife is. Anyhow Ziggy sees this simulacrum —' He broke off. Because someone had entered the room.

It was an Alphane. One of the race of chitinous creatures who, a few years ago, had been locked in combat with Terra. Its multi-jointed arms and legs clicking it scuttled toward Bunny, feeling with its antennae – the Alphanes were blind – and then, touching him, delicately stroking Bunny's face, the Alphane turned and moved back, satisfied that it was where it wished to be ... its eyeless head swivelled and now it sniffed, picked up the presence of other humans.

'Am I interrupting?' it asked in its twangy, harp-like voice, its Alphane sing-song. 'I heard your discussion and it interested me.'

Bunny said to Chuck, 'Rittersdorf, this is one of my oldest and dearest friends. I never trusted nobody the way I trust my buddy here, RBX 303.' He explained, 'Maybe you don't know it but Alphanes have licence-plate type names, sort of mechanical codes. That's all there is, just RBX 303. Sounds sort of impersonal, but Alphs are real warmhearted. RBX 303 here has a heart of gold.' He sniggered 'Two of them, in fact; one on each side.'

'I'm glad to meet you,' Chuck said, reflexively.

The Alphane scrabbled up to him, stroked at his features

with its twin antennae; it was, Chuck decided, like having two houseflies run here and there across his face – a distinctly unpleasant impression. 'Mr. Rittersdorf,' the Alphane twanged. 'Delighted.' It withdrew, then. 'And who else is in this room, Bunny? I smell others.'

'Just Dark and Jones,' Bunny said, 'my writers.' Again turning to Chuck he explained, 'RBX 303's a tycoon, a big wheeler and dealer in interplan commercial enterprises of every sort. See, Chuck, here's the situation. RBX 303 here owns controlling stock in Pubtrans Incorporated. Does that mean anything to you?'

For a moment it meant nothing and then it came to Chuck. Pubtrans Incorporated was the company which sponsored Bunny Hentman's TV show. 'You mean,' Chuck said, 'it's owned by —' He broke off. He had started to say, 'Owned by one of our former enemies?' However, he did not say it; for one thing it obviously was so, and for another – they were, after all, the former, not the present, enemy. Terra and the Alphanes were at peace and the enmity was supposed to be over.

'You never met an Alph' close up before?' Bunny said acutely. 'You should; they're a great people. Sensitive, with a terrific sense of humour ... Pubtrans sponsors me partly because RBX 303 here personally believes in me and my talent – he did a lot to get me from being nothing but a comic doing the nightclub circuit with occasional guests on TV shows to having my own show, a show that's gone over partly because Pubtrans has done a hell of a good job publicizing it.'

'I see,' Chuck said. He felt ill. But he did not know quite why. Perhaps it was the whole situation; he could not understand it. 'Are Alphanes telepathic?' he asked, knowing they weren't and yet – there seemed to be an uncanny awareness about this Alphane. Chuck had the intuition that it knew everything; there were no secrets which the Alphane could not seek out.

'They're not telepaths,' Bunny said, 'but they depend on hearing a lot; that makes them different from us, because we have eyes.' He glanced at Chuck. 'What's with you and telepaths? I mean, you must have known the answer; during the war we were briefed up to our eyeballs about the enemy. And you're not too young to remember that; you must have grown up with it.'

Dark spoke up suddenly. 'I'll tell you what's bothering Rittersdorf; I used to feel the same way. Rittersdorf was hired for his ideas. And he doesn't want to see his brain picked clean. His ideas belong to him up until the moment he chooses to reveal them. If you brought in, say, a Ganymedean slime mould, hell, that would be an unfair invasion of all of our personal rights; it would turn us into machines that you mechanically pumped for ideas.' To Chuck he said, 'Don't worry about RBX 303; he can't read your thoughts; all he can do is very carefully listen to subtle, tiny nuances in what you say ... but it's surprising how much he can detect that way. Alphanes make good psychologists.'

'Seated in the next room,' the Alphane said, 'reading *Life* magazine, I listened to your conversation, about your new humourous character Siegfried Trots. Interested, I decided to come in; I put the audio tape down and arose. Is this satisfactory with all of you?'

'Nobody minds your presence,' Bunny assured the Alphane.

'Nothing,' the Alphane said, 'amuses and entertains – and fascinates – me as does a creative session by you gifted writers. Mr. Rittersdorf, I have never seen you in operation before, but already I can tell that you have a great deal to add. However, I sense your aversion – a very deeply-held aversion – to the line which the conversation has taken. May I ask what precisely you find so objectionable to Siegfried Trots and his desire to do away with his unpleasant wife? Are you married, Mr. Rittersdorf?'

'Yes,' Chuck said.

'Perhaps this plot-idea rouses guilt-feelings within you,' the Alphane said thoughtfully. 'Perhaps you have unacknowledged hostile impulses toward your wife.'

Bunny said, 'You're way off, RBX; Chuck and his wife are splitting up – she's already gone into court. Anyway Chuck's private life is his own business; we're not here to dissect his psyche. Let's get back to the material.'

'I still say,' the Alphane declared, 'that there is something very unusual and atypical in Mr. Rittersdorf's reaction; I would like to find out why.' It turned its knob-like blind head toward Chuck. 'Perhaps, if you and I see more of each other, I will find out why. And I have the feeling that knowing this would be of benefit to you, too.'

Scratching his nose thoughtfully Bunny Hentman said, 'Maybe he does know, RBX. Maybe he just doesn't want to say.' He eyed Chuck and said, 'I still say *it's his own business*, in either case.'

Chuck said, 'It simply doesn't sound like a comedy idea to me. That's the extent of my —' He had almost said *aversion*. 'Of my doubts.'

'Well, I don't have any doubts,' Bunny decided. 'I'll have our prop department put together a hollow simulacrum-type figure that somebody can get into; that'll be a lot cheaper and more reliable than buying a genuine one. And we'll need some girl to play the role of Ziggy's wife. *My* wife, because I'll be Ziggy.'

'How about the girlfriend?' Jones said. 'Is that in or not?'

Dark said, 'It would have one advantage; we could have her breast-heavy. You know, fracked. That would please a lot of viewers; otherwise we're stuck with one shrewish type woman who decidedly would *not* be breast-heavy. That kind never gets that operation performed.'

'You got someone particular in mind who could play that part?' Bunny asked him, pad of paper and pen in hand.

'You know that new fray your agent's handling,' Dark said. 'That fresh little one ... Patty something. Patty Weaver. She's *really* breast-heavy. The medics must have grafted in fifty pounds if it's an ounce.'

'I'll sign up Patty tonight,' Bunny Hentman said, nodding. 'I know her and she's good; she's exactly right for it. And then we need some bellicose old hag to play the shrewish wife. Maybe I'll let Chuck do the casting-select for that.' He laughed owlishly.

EIGHT

When, late that night, Chuck Rittersdorf wearily returned to his rundown conapt in Marin County, California, he was stopped in the hall by the yellow Ganymedean slime mould. This, at three a.m. It was too much.

'There are a pair of individuals in your apt,' Lord Running Clam informed him. 'It seemed to me you should be tipped off in advance.'

'Thanks,' Chuck said, and wondered what he had to cope with now.

'One of them is your superior at CIA,' the slime mould said. 'Jack Elwood. The second is Mr. Elwood's superior, a Mr. Roger London. They are here to interrogate you as to your other job.'

'I never concealed it from them,' Chuck said. 'In fact Mageboom operated by Pete Petri was right here on the spot when Hentman hired me.' Uneasily he wondered why they considered it their affair.

'True,' the slime mould agreed, 'but you see they had a tap on the vidline over which you talked this evening first to Joan Trieste and then to Mr. Hentman in Florida. So not only do they know that you're working for Mr. Hentman but they also know the script-idea which you —'

That explained it. He passed on by the slime mould, to the door of his apt. It was unlocked; he opened it, faced the two CIA men. 'This late in the night?' he said. 'It's that important?' Going to the closet – it was the ancient-style manual variety – he hung up his coat. The apt was comfortably warm; the CIA officials had turned on the non-thermostatically controlled radiant heat.

'Is this the man?' London said. He was a tall, stooped, greying man in his late fifties; Chuck had run into him a few times and had found him difficult. 'This is Rittersdorf?'

'Yes,' Elwood said. 'Chuck, listen carefully. There are facts about Bunny Hentman you don't know. Security facts. Now, we're aware of the reason why you accepted this job; we know you didn't want to but were forced to.'

'Oh?' Chuck said warily. They couldn't possibly know what pressure the telepathic slime mould across the hall had put on him.

Elwood said, 'We fully recognize your difficult situation regarding your ex-wife Mary, the enormous settlement and alimony payments which she was able to obtain; we know you need the money in order to meet those payments. However —' He glanced at London. London nodded, and Elwood bent to unzip his briefcase. 'I have Hentman's dossier here. His real name is Sam Little. During the war he was convicted on a charge of violating the trade-rules governing commerce with neutral states; in other words Hentman supplied needed commodities to the enemy by way of an intermediate source. He spent only one year in prison, however; he had a very good choir of attorneys. You want to hear more?'

'Yes,' Chuck said. 'Because I can hardly quit my job on the grounds that fifteen years ago —'

'All right,' Elwood said, after a further exchange of glances with his superior, London. 'After the war Sam Little – or Benny Hentman, as he now is known – lived in the Alpha system. What he did there no one knows; our data-gathering sources were of no use to us in Alpha-held territory. Anyhow about six years ago he returned to Terra and with plenty of interplan skins. He began doing a comedy routine in nightclubs and then Pubtrans Incorporated sponsored him —'

'I know,' Chuck interrupted, 'that an Alphane owns Pubtrans. I met him. RBX 303.'

'You MET him?' Both Elwood and London stared at him. 'Do you know anything about RBX 303?' Elwood demanded. 'His family, during the war, controlled the largest wargoods combine in the Alpha system. His brother is in the Alphane cabinet right now, directly responsible to the Alphane Doge. In other words when you're dealing with RBX 303 you're dealing with the Alphane government.' He tossed the dossier to Chuck. 'Read the rest.'

Chuck glanced through the neatly-typed pages. It was easy to make out the summary at the end; the CIA agents who had compiled the dossier believed that RBX 303 was acting as an untitled rep of a foreign power and that Hentman was aware of this. Therefore their activities were being watched by the CIA.

'His reason for giving you the job,' Elwood said, 'is not what you think. Hentman doesn't need another writer; he's got five already. I'll tell you our opinion. We think it has to do with your wife.'

Chuck said nothing; he continued, vacantly, to pore over the sheets which made up the dossier.

'The Alphanes,' Elwood said, 'would like to reacquire Alpha III M2. And the only way they can do it *legally* is to induce the Terrans inhabiting it to leave. Otherwise according to interplan law the Protocols of 2040 come into effect; the moon becomes the property of its settlers and since those settlers are Terran it's indirectly the property of Terra. The Alphanes can't *make* the settlers leave, but they've kept an eye on them; they're perfectly aware that it's a society made up of former mental patients of the Harry Stack Sullivan Neuropsychiatric Hospital which we established there before the war. The only agency that could get those settlers off Alpha III M2 would be Terran, either TERPLAN or the US Interplan Health and Welfare Service; we could conceivably evacuate the moon, and that would leave it up for grabs.'

'But no one,' Chuck said, 'is going to recommend that the settlers be evacuated.' It seemed to him entirely out of the question. One of two things would occur: either Terra would leave the settlers strictly alone or a new hospital would be built and the settlers would be coerced into entering it.

Elwood said, 'You may be right. But do the Alphanes know that?'

'And remember,' London said in his hoarse, low voice,

'the Alphanes are great gamblers; the entire war was one great longshot for them – and they lost. They don't know any other way to operate.'

That was true; Chuck nodded. And yet it still made no sense. What influence did he have over Mary's decisions? Hentman knew that he and Mary were legally separated; Mary was on Alpha III M2 and he was here on Terra. And even if they were both on the Alphane moon Mary would never listen to him. Her decision would be her own.

Yet, if the Alphanes knew that he had control of the Daniel Mageboom simulacrum—

He simply couldn't believe that they knew this; it was impossible.

'We have a theory,' Elwood said, retrieving the dossier and returning it to his briefcase. 'We believe that the Alphanes know—'

'Don't tell me,' Chuck said, 'that they know about Mageboom; that would mean they'd penetrated the CIA.'

'I – wasn't going to say quite that,' Elwood said uncomfortably. 'I was going to say that they know, just as we do, that your separation from Mary is purely legal, that you're still as emotionally involved with her as ever. As reconstructed by us, their view comes out like this: contact between you and Mary will shortly be resumed. Whether either of you anticipates it or not.'

'And what good will that do them?' Chuck said.

'Here their concept of the situation becomes positively lurid,' Elwood said. 'Now, this we've picked up strictly from peripheral indications, from snatches gathered here and there; we may be wrong, but it appears that the Alphanes are going to try to induce you to make an attempt to kill your wife.'

Chuck said nothing; he kept his features immobile. Time passed; no one spoke. Elwood and Roger London regarded him curiously, tangibly wondering why he did not respond.

'To be honest with you,' London growled finally, 'we have an informant in Hentman's immediate staff; never mind who. This informant tells us that the script-idea which Hentman and his writers presented you on your arrival in Florida had to do with a CIA simulacrum killing a woman. A man's wife. The man is a CIA agent. Is that correct?'

Chuck nodded slowly, his eyes fixed on a spot on the wall to the right of Elwood and London.

'This plot situation,' London continued, 'is supposed to give you the idea of trying to kill Mrs. Rittersdorf with a CIA sim. What Hentman and his Alphane buddies don't know, of course, is that a CIA sim is already on Alpha III M2 and that you're operating it; if they did know this they would—' He broke off, then said slowly, half to himself, 'Then they'd see there's no need to build an elaborate script up to give you the idea.' He studied Chuck. 'Because very possibly you already have thought of it.'

After a pause Elwood said, 'That's an interesting speculation. I hadn't come on to it, myself, but eventually I would.' To Chuck he said, 'Would you like to give up your operation of the Mageboom simulacrum? To prove beyond a doubt that you had no such action in mind?'

Chuck said, picking his words with care, 'Of course I won't give it up.' It was obvious that if he did he would be admitting that they were right, that they had uncovered something about him and his intentions. And, in addition, he did not care to relinquish the Mageboom task – for a very good reason. He wanted to continue his plan for killing Mary.

'If anything should happen to Mrs. Rittersdorf,' London said, 'in view of this, great suspicion would fall on you.'

'I realize that,' Chuck said woodenly.

'So while you're operating that Mageboom sim,' London said, 'you better see to it that it protects Mrs. Rittersdorf.'

Chuck said, 'You want my frank opinion?'

'Certainly,' London said, and Elwood nodded.

'This whole thing is an absurdity, a concoction based on isolated data by some imaginative agent in the field, someone who evidently has hung around TV personalities too long. *How is my killing Mary going to alter her decision regarding Alpha III M2 and its psychotic settlers?* If she's dead she'd simply be replaced and someone else would make the determination.'

'I think,' Elwood said, speaking to his superior, 'that what we're going to find ourselves dealing with here is not a murder but an attempted murder. Murder as a threat, held over Dr. Rittersdorf's head, to make her comply.' He added, speaking to Chuck, 'That of course is assuming that Hentman's campaign bears fruit. That you're influenced by the logic put forth by the TV script.'

'But you seem to think I would be,' Chuck said.

'I think,' Elwood said, 'that it's an interesting coincidence that you *are* operating a CIA simulacrum in Mary's vicinity, exactly as Hentman's script proposes. What are the chances —'

Chuck said, 'A more plausible explanation is that somehow Hentman has found out I'm operating the Mageboom simulacrum, that he developed his idea from the situation. And you know what that means.' The implication was obvious. Despite their denials the CIA *had* been penetrated. Or —

There existed one other possibility. Lord Running Clam had picked up the facts from Chuck's mind and had conveyed them to Bunny Hentman. First the slime mould had blackmailed him into taking the job with Hentman and now all of them were acting together to blackmail him into fulfilling their plan for Alpha III M2. The TV script was not designed to put the idea of killing Mary into his mind; by means of the slime mould the Hentman organization knew the idea was already there.

The TV script was to tell him, indirectly but clearly, *that they knew*. And unless he did as they directed it would be telecast, manifestly, to the entire Sol system. Seven billion people would know about his plans for killing his wife.

It was, he had to admit, a compelling reason for his stringing along with the Hentman organization, to do what they wanted; they rather had him. Look what they had accomplished already: they had made high officials in the West Coast branch of the CIA suspicious. And, as London had said, if anything happened to Mary —

And yet he still intended to go through with it. Or rather

to try to go through with it. And not just as a threat, as the Hentman organization wanted, to coerce Mary into advocating a certain policy regarding the psychotic settlers. It was his intention to go all the way, as he had originally planned. Why, he did not know; after all, he did not have to see her any more, live with her ... why did her death seem so vital to him?

Oddly, Mary might be the only person who could poke into his mind, if she were given the chance, and discover his motives; it was her job.

The irony pleased him. And, despite the proximity of the two astute CIA officials – not to mention the ever-present yellow slime mould eavesdropping on the far side of the hall – he did not feel badly at all. He was, wit-wise, confronting two distinct factions, both of them experienced; the CIA and the Hentman organization consisted of old-time pros and yet he felt, intuitively, that ultimately he would obtain what *he* wanted, not what they wanted.

The slime mould of course would be overhearing his thought. He hoped that it would carry it back to Hentman; he wanted Hentman to know.

As soon as the two CIA officials had left, the slime mould flowed under the locked door to his apt, materialized in the centre of the old-fashioned wall-to-wall carpeting. It spoke accusingly, with a ring of righteous indignation. 'Mr. Rittersdorf, I assure you; I had no contact with Mr. Hentman; I never saw him before that night recently when he came here to obtain your signature on a job contract.'

'You rascals,' Chuck said as he fixed himself coffee in the kitchen. The time was now past four o'clock; however thanks to the illegal stimulants which Lord Running Clam had provided him he felt no fatigue. 'Always listening in,' he said. 'Don't you have a life of your own?'

The slime mould said, 'I agree with you on one point; Mr. Hentman, in preparing that script, *must* have known your intentions toward your wife – otherwise the coincidence is just too great to be acceptable. Perhaps someone, Mr. Rittersdorf, is a telepath, someone in addition to me.'

Chuck glanced at him.

'It could be a fellow employee at CIA,' the slime mould said. 'Or it could be taking place while you are in the Mageboom simulacrum on Alpha III M2; one of the psychotic settlers there might be a telepath. I conceive it to be my job from now on to assist you to every extent possible, in order to palpably demonstrate my good faith; I am desperately anxious to clear my good name in your eyes. I'll do all I can to find this telepath who has gone to Hentman, thus —'

'Could it be Joan Trieste?' Chuck interrupted suddenly.

'No. I'm familiar with her mind; it has no such powers. She is a Psi, as you know, but her talent deals with time.' The slime mould pondered. 'Unless – you know, Mr. Rittersdorf, there is another way by which your intentions could be known. That would be the Psionic power of precognition ... assuming that one day, eventually, your scheme becomes public. A precog, looking ahead, might see this, possess this knowledge now. That is an idea we must not overlook. At least it proves that the telepathic factor is not the sole item which would account for Hentman's knowledge of what you intend to do vis-a-vis your wife.'

He had to admit that there was merit in the slime mould's logic.

'In fact,' the slime mould said, pulsing visibly with agitation, 'it could be the involuntary functioning of a precog talent – by someone close to you who does not even know he possesses it. Someone, for example, in the Hentman organization. Even Mr. Hentman himself.'

'Hmm,' Chuck said absently, as he filled his cup with hot coffee.

'Your future life-track,' the slime mould said, 'is filled with the spectacular violence of your murder of the woman you fear and hate. This enormous spectacle may have activated the latent precog talent of Mr. Hentman and without knowing what he was drawing from he had the "inspiration" for this script idea ... often, Psionic talent's function in this very way. The more I think of it the more I am convinced that this is precisely what occurred. Hence, I would say that your CIA people's theory is valueless; Hentman and his Alphane colleague do not mean to confront you with any so-called "evidence" of your intentions ... they are simply doing as they say: attempting to concoct a workable TV script.'

'What about the CIA's contention that the Alphanes are interested in acquiring Alpha III M2?' Chuck said.

'Possibly that portion is so,' the slime mould conceded. 'It would be typical of the Alphanes not to give up, to keep hoping ... after all, the moon is in their system. But frankly – may I so speak? – your CIA people's theory strikes me as a miserable bundle of random suspicions, a few separate facts strung together by an intricate structure of ad hoc theorizing, in which everyone is credited with enormous powers for intrigue. A much simpler view can be entertained with more common sense, and as a CIA employee you must be aware that, like all intelligence agencies, it lacks the faculty of common sense.'

Chuck shrugged.

'In fact,' the slime mould said, 'if I may say so, your colourful desire for vengeance on your wife is in part derived from your years of hanging around intelligence-apparatus personnel.'

'You will admit one thing, though,' Chuck said. 'It's colossal bad luck for me that Hentman and his writers have hit upon that particular idea for their TV script.'

'Bad luck, but rather amusing in that you personally will soon be sitting down to do the dialogue for this script.' The slime mould chuckled. 'Perhaps you can infuse it with authenticity. Hentman will be delighted with your insight into Ziggy Trots' motivations.'

'How did you know the character is to be named Ziggy Trots?' At once he was again suspicious.

'It's in your mind.'

'Then it must also be in my mind that I'd like you to leave so I can be alone.' He did not feel sleepy, however; he felt like sitting down and starting on the TV script.

'By all means.' The slime mould flowed off and presently

Chuck was alone in the apt. The only sound arose from the meagre traffic in the street below. He stood at the window drinking his cup of coffee for a little while and then he seated himself at his typewriter and pressed the button which raised a sheet of blank paper into position.

Ziggy Trots, he thought with aversion. Christ, what a name. What kind of person does it suggest? An idiot, like one of the Three Stooges. Someone defective enough, he thought acidly, to dwell on the concept of murdering his wife....

He began, with professional canniness, to conjure up the initial scene. It, of course, would be Ziggy at home, trying peacefully to do some harmless task. Perhaps Ziggy was reading the evening homeopape. And, like some Harpy, his wife would be there, giving him the business. Yes, Chuck thought. I can supply verisimilitude to this scene; I can draw on years of experience. He began to type.

For several hours he wrote, marvelling at the efficiency of the illegal hexo-amphetamine stimulants; he felt no fatigue – in fact, he worked more swiftly than had been his custom in times past. At seven-thirty, with the street outside touched by the long, golden rays of the morning sun, he rose stiffly, walked into the kitchen and began to prepare himself breakfast. Now for my other job, he said to himself. At eight-thirty, off to the CIA building in San Francisco. And Daniel Mageboom.

Piece of toast in hand he stood by the typewriter, glancing over the pages which he had written. They looked good – and dialogue to be spoken had been his trade for years. Now to air-express them to Hentman in New York; they would be in the comic's hands within an hour.

At twenty minutes after eight, as he was shaving in the bathroom, he heard the vidphone ring. His first call since having it installed.

Going to it he switched it on. 'Hello.'

On the tiny screen a girl's face formed, stunningly beautiful Irish features; he blinked. 'Mr. Rittersdorf? I'm Patricia Weaver; I just learned that Bunny Hentman wants me for a script you're doing. I wondered if I could see a copy; I'm dying to look it over. For simply years I've prayed for a chance to be on Bunny's programme; I just admire it to hell and back.'

Naturally he had a Thermofax copying machine; he could run off any number of duplicates of the script. 'I'll send you what I have. But it's not done and Bunny hasn't seen it to okay it; I don't know how much he'll want to keep. Maybe none.'

'From the way Bunny talked about you,' Patricia Weaver said, 'I'm sure he'll use all of it. Could you do that? I'll give you my address. Actually I'm not far from you at all; you're up in Northern California and I'm down in L.A., in Santa Monica. We could get together; would you like that? And you could listen to me read my part of the script.'

Her part. Good grief, he realized; he hadn't written any dialogue that included her, the slinky, breast-heavy, nipple-dilated female intelligence agent – he had only done scenes between Ziggy Trots and his shrewish wife.

There was only one solution. To take a half-day leave of absence from his CIA job, sit here in the conapt and write more dialogue.

'I'll tell you what,' he said. 'I'll bring a copy down to you. Give me until this evening.' He found a pen and paper. 'Let's have your address.' The hell with the Mageboom simulacrum, in view of this; he had never witnessed such an attractive girl in his life. All at once everything else had become mediocre, hurled back into proper perspective.

He got the girl's address, shakily hung up the vidphone, then at once packaged up the pages of the script for Bunny Hentman. On his way to San Francisco he put the envelope in the rocket express mail and that was that. While he worked at his CIA job he probably could dream up dialogue for Miss Weaver; by dinner time he would be ready to get it down on paper and by eight o'clock he would have the actual pages to show her. Things, he decided, are not going so badly after all. Certainly this is a vast improvement over my nightmarish life with Mary.

He reached the CIA building on Sansome Street in San Francisco and started to enter by the wide, familiar gate.

'Rittersdorf,' a voice said. 'Please come into my office.' It was Roger London, large and grimly sullen, eyeing him with displeasure.

More talk? Chuck asked himself as he followed London to his office.

'Mr. Rittersdorf,' London said, as soon as the door had shut, 'we bugged your conapt last night; we know what you did after we left.'

'What did I do?' For the life of him he could not remember having done anything that would arouse the CIA ... unless in his conversation with the slime mould he had said too much. The Ganymedean's thoughts, of course, would be imperceptible to the monitoring device. All that he could remember having uttered himself was some remark that it was a colossal piece of bad luck that the TV script idea which Hentman wanted written had to do with a man murdering his wife by means of a CIA sim. And surely that —

London said, 'You were up the balance of the night. Working. That would be impossible unless you had access to drugs currently banned on Terra. Therefore you have non-T contacts which are supplying you with the drugs, and in view of this —' He studied Chuck. 'You're temporarily suspended from your job. As a security risk.'

Stunned, Chuck said, 'But to hold both my jobs —'

'Any CIA employee foolish enough to make use of illegal non-T stimulant drugs can't possibly be capable of fulfilling his task here,' London said. 'As of today the Mageboom simulacrum will be operated by a team consisting of Pete Petri and a man you don't know, Tom Schneider,' London's coarse features twisted into a mocking smile. 'You still have your other job ... *or do you*?'

'What do you mean, or do I? Of course he still had his job with Hentman; they had signed a contract.

London said, 'If CIA's theory is correct Hentman will have no use for you the moment he learns that you've been denied access to the Mageboom simulacrum. So I would say that in roughly twelve hours —' London examined his wrist-watch. 'That, say, by nine tonight you'll discover the unpleasant fact that you have no employment at all. And then, I think, you'll be a trifle more co-operative with us; you'll be glad to revert to your former status of holding one job here, period.' London opened his office door, ushering Chuck out. 'By the way,' he continued, 'would you care to name your source of supply of your drugs?'

'I deny taking any illegal drugs.' Chuck said, but even in his own ears it did not sound convincing; London had him and they both knew it.

'Why not simply co-operate with us?' London inquired. 'Give up your job with Hentman, name your supplier – you could have access to the Mageboom simulacrum in fifteen minutes; I can personally arrange it. What reason do you have for —'

'The money,' Chuck said. 'I need the money from both jobs.' And I'm being blackmailed, he said to himself. By Lord Running Clam. But he couldn't say that, not to London.

'Okay,' London said. 'You may go. Get in touch with us when you've seen your way clear to drop your job with Hentman; perhaps we can settle on just that one stipulation.' He held the office door open for Chuck.

Dazed, Chuck found himself on the wide front stairs of the CIA building. It seemed incredible and yet it had happened; he had lost his job of many years, and on what seemed to him a pretext. Now he had no way to reach Mary. The hell with the loss of salary; his income from the Hentman organization more than made that up. But without the use of the Mageboom simulacrum he could not expect to carry out his plan – which he had obviously delayed too long anyhow – and in the vacuum left by the disappearance of this anticipation he felt a powerful sinking emptiness inside him; his entire raison d'être had, all at once, evaporated.

He started numbly back up the stairs once more, toward the main gate of the CIA building. A uniformed guard at once materialized out of nowhere and blocked his way. 'Mr. Rittersdorf, I'm sorry; I regret. But I've been given order, you see, not to admit you.'

Chuck said, 'I want to see Mr. London again. For a minute.'

Using his portable intercom the guard put through a call. 'All right, Mr. Rittersdorf; you may proceed to Mr. London's office.' He then stepped aside and the turnstile flew automatically open for Chuck.

A moment later he once more faced London in the man's large wood-panelled office. 'You're reached a decision, have you?' London asked.

'I have a point to make. If Hentman doesn't fire me, wouldn't that be de facto proof that your suspicions of him were incorrect?' He waited while London scowled ... scowled but did not answer. 'If Hentman does *not* fire me,' Chuck said, 'I'm going to appeal your decision to bar me from my job; I'm going before the Civil Service Commission and show that —'

'You're barred from your job,' London said smoothly, 'because of your use of illegal drugs. To be blunt, we've already searched your conapt and found them. It's GB-40 that you're on, isn't it? You can maintain a twenty-four hour a day work schedule indefinitely on GB-40; congratulations. However, now that you no longer have your position here with us, being able to work around the clock hardly seems a benefit. So lots of luck.' He walked off, seated himself at his desk and picked up a document; the interview was at an end.

'But you'll know you were wrong,' Chuck said, 'when Hentman doesn't fire me. All I ask is that you rethink the situation, once that's occurred. Good-bye.' He left the office, closing the door noisily behind him. Good-bye for lord knows how long, he said to himself.

Once more, outdoors on the early-morning sidewalk, he stood uncertainly, buffeted by the hordes of people pushing by. Now what? he asked himself. His life, for the second time in a month, had been inverted: first the shock of the separation from Mary, now this. Too much, he said to himself, and wondered if there was anything left.

The Hentman job was left. And only the Hentman job.

By autonomic cab he returned to his conapt and quickly

– in fact, desperately – seated himself at his typewriter. Now, he said to himself, to do dialogue for Miss Weaver; he forgot everything else, narrowing his world to the dimensions of the typewriter with its sheet of paper. I'll give you a damn good part, he reflected. And – maybe I'll get something back in exchange.

He began to work. And, by three that afternoon, he had finished; he rose creakily, stretched and felt the weariness of his body. But his mind was lucid. So they bugged my apt, he said to himself. With both audio and video aids. Aloud, for the benefit of the tap, he said, 'Those bastards at the office – spying on me. Pathological. Frankly it's a relief to be out of that atmosphere of suspicion and —' He ceased; what was the use? He went into the kitchen and fixed lunch.

At four, dressed in his best Titanian rouzleweave blue and black suit, powdered, shaved and dabbed with such masculine scents as only the modern chemistry lab could produce, he set off on foot, seeking a jet cab, the manuscript under his arm; he was on his way to Santa Monica and Patty Weaver's conapt, to – heaven only knew. But he had great hopes.

If this fell through, then what?

A good question, and one he hoped he would not have to answer. He had lost too much already; the structure of his world had undergone an insidious process of truncation, by the loss of his wife and his traditional job, both in such a short period; he felt bewilderment within his percept-system. It expected to see Mary at night and the San Francisco CIA office by day; now it encountered neither. *Something* would have to occupy his void. His senses craved it.

He flagged down a jet cab and gave it the Santa Monica address of Patty Weaver; then, sitting back against the seat, he got out the pages of dialogue and began going over them for last-minute small alterations.

An hour later, slightly after five o'clock, the cab began to descend to the roof field of Patty Weaver's remarkably handsome, large and stylish new conapt building. This is the big time, Chuck said to himself. Hobnobbing with a breast-heavy TV starlet . . . what more could he ask?

The cab landed. A little unsteadily, Chuck got out the fare.

NINE

As if a benign harbinger, Patricia Weaver was at home; she opened the door of her conapt and said, 'Oh goodness, so you're the man with my script. How early you are; you said on the vidphone —'

'I got finished earlier than I had expected.' Chuck entered her apt, glancing at the excessively modern furniture; it was neo-pre-Columbian in style, based on recent archeological discoveries of the Incan culture in South America. All the furniture of course was hand wrought. And on the walls hung the new animated action-paintings that never ceased moving; they consisted of two-dimensional machines that clattered away softly, like the rush of a distant ocean. Or, he thought more practically, like a subsurface autofac. He was not certain he liked them.

'You've got it with you,' Miss Weaver said delightedly. She wore – and this seemed odd for so early in the evening – a high-fashion Paris dress, the like of which he had witnessed in magazines but never before in actual life. This was a long way from his desk at CIA. The dress was lavish and complex, like the petals of a non-T flower; it must have cost a thousand skins, Chuck decided. This was a dress in which to get a job; her right breast, firm and uptilted, was totally exposed; it was a very fashionable dress indeed. Had she been expecting someone else? Bunny Hentman, for example?

'I was going out,' Patty explained. 'For a cocktail. But I'll call and cancel it.' She walked to the vidphone, her sharp, high heels clacking against the synthetic – Inca-style – dirt floor.

'I hope you like the script,' he said, wandering about and feeling small-time. This was a bit over his head, the elaborate, expensive dress, the hand-wrought furnishings ... he stood facing a painting, watched as its non-objective surfaces slid and altered, forming entirely new – and never to be repeated – combinations.

Patty returned from the vidphone. 'I was able to catch him before he left MGB Studios.' She did not specify who and Chuck decided not to ask; it would probably deflate him even further. 'A drink?' She went to the sideboard, opened a pre-Columbian wood and gold cabinet, revealing bottle after bottle. 'What about an Ionian Wuzzball? It's the snig; you must try it. I bet it hasn't got up into Northern California – you're so —' She gestured. 'So gas-headed up there.' She began to mix drinks.

'Can I help?' He came over beside her, feeling serious and protective ... or at least wanting to be.

'No thanks,' Patty expertly handed him his glass. 'Let me ask you something,' she said, 'even before I look at the script. Is my part large?'

'Um,' he said. He had made it as large as he could, but the fact of the matter was this: her role was minor. The head of the fish got thrown to her, but the fillets had – of necessity – gone to Bunny.

'You mean it's small,' Patty said, walking to the bench-like couch and seating herself; the petals of her dress spread out on each side of her. 'Let me see it, please.' She had now an astute and entirely professional air about her; she was absolutely calm.

Seating himself across from her Chuck handed her the pages of the script. It included what he had sent to Bunny – and the more recent portion, her part in particular, which Bunny had not yet seen. Perhaps this was improper, showing Patty her script before Bunny saw it ... but he had decided to do it, mistake or not.

'This other woman,' Patty said, shortly; it did not take her long to leaf through the pages. 'The wife. The shrew that Ziggy decides to kill. She's got a much bigger part; she goes all the way through it and I'm really only in this one scene. At his office, where she comes in ... at the CIA headquarters ...' She pointed to the part.

What Patty said was true. He had done his best, but that was it; a fact was a fact, and Patty was too wise professionally to be deceived.

'I made it as big as I could,' he said honestly.

Patty said, 'It's almost one of those awful parts where a girl is just brought in to stand and look sexy, and not really *do* anything. I don't just want to come in wearing a tight open-bodice dress and be an ornament. I'm an actress; I want lines.' She handed him the script back. 'Please,' she said, 'Mr. Rittersdorf, for chrissakes, build up my part. Bunny hasn't seen this, has he? This is still just between you and me. So maybe between us we can think up something. How about a restaurant scene? Ziggy is meeting the girl – Sharon – at this fancy little out-of-the-way restaurant, and the wife shows up ... Ziggy has it out with her there, not at home in their conapt, and then Sharon, my part, she can be involved in that scene, too.'

'Hmm,' he said. He sipped his drink; it was an odd, sweet concoction, much like mead. It occurred to him to wonder what it had in it. Across from him Patty had already drunk hers; she now returned to the sideboard to fix herself another.

He also rose, walked over to stand beside her; against him her small shoulder brushed and he could smell the peculiar strange scent of the drink which she was making. One ingredient, he noticed, came from a distinctly non-T bottle; the printing on it seemed Alphane.

'It's from Alpha I,' Patty said. 'Bunny gave it to me; he got it from some Alphs he knows; Bunny knows every kind of creature in the inhabited universe. Did you know he lived for a while in the Alpha system?' She raised her glass, turned to face him and stood sipping meditatively. 'I wish I could visit another star system. It must make you feel almost – you know – superhuman.'

Setting his glass down Chuck put his hands on Patty Weaver's slight, rather hard shoulders; the dress crinkled. 'I can make your part somewhat larger,' he said.

'Okay,' Patty said. She leaned against him, sighed as she rested her head on his shoulder. 'It does mean a lot to me,' she said. Her hair, long and auburn, brushed his face, tickling his nose. Taking her glass from her he sipped, then set it down on the sideboard.

The next he knew, they were in the bedroom.

The drinks, he thought. Mixing with the illegal GB-40 thalamic stimulant that Lord whatever-his name-is gave me. The bedroom was nearly dark but he could see, outlined beyond his right arm, Patty Weaver sitting on the edge of the bed, unhooking some intricate part of her dress. The dress came off at last and Patty carried it carefully to the closet to hang it up; she returned, doing something strange with her breasts. He watched her for a moment and then he realized that she was massaging her ribcage; she had been bound up in the dress and now she could relax, move about unhindered. Both breasts, he saw, were of an ideal size, albeit for the most part synthetic. As she walked they did not wobble in the slightest; the left, as well as the previously-exposed right, was strikingly firm.

As Patty dropped like a well-oiled stone into the bed next to the spot where he himself lay the vidphone rang.

'—.' Patty said, startling him. She slid from the bed, stood, groped for her robe; finding it she started barefoot from the room, tying its sash. 'I'll be right back, dear,' she said matter-of-factly. 'You just stay there.'

He lay staring at the ceiling, feeling the softness, smelling the fragrance, of the bed. A long, long time seemed to pass. He felt very happy. This kind of waiting was a great peaceful pleasure.

And then, suddenly, there stood Patty Weaver in the bedroom doorway, in her robe, her hair down over her shoulders in a loose cloud. He waited but she did not approach the bed. All at once he realized that she was not going to; she was coming no farther in. Instantly he sat up; his mood of supine relaxation dwindled, vanished.

'Who was it?' he said.

'Bunny.'

'So?'

'The deal is off.' She came in now, but to the closet; from it she took a simple skirt and blouse. Picking up her underclothing she departed, obviously to dress somewhere else.

'Why is it off?' He hopped from the bed, began feverishly to dress. Patty had disappeared; somewhere in the apt a door closed. She did not answer. Evidently she had not heard him.

As he sat on the bed fully dressed, tying his shoelaces, Patty reappeared; she, too, was fully dressed. She stood brushing her hair, her face expressionless; she watched him fumble with his laces, making no comment. It was, he thought, as if she were a light year away; the bedroom was pervaded by her neutral coolness.

'Tell me,' he repeated, 'why the deal is off. Tell me exactly what Bunny Hentman said.'

'Oh, he said he's not going to use your script, and if I called you or if you called me —' Now, for the first time since the vidcall, her eyes focused on him, as if she were seeing him at last. 'I didn't say you were here. But he said if I talked to you I was to tell you that he's thought your idea over and it isn't any good.'

'*My* idea?'

'The whole script. He got the pages you expressed to him and he thought they were terrible.'

Chuck felt his ears burn and freeze at once; the pain spread to his face, like frost, numbing his lips and nose.

'So,' Patty said, 'he's having Dark and Jones, his regular writers, do something entirely different.'

After a long time Chuck said huskily, 'Am I supposed to get in touch with him?'

'He didn't say.' She had finished brushing her hair; now she left the bedroom, again disappearing. Rising, he followed after her, finding her in the living-room; she was at the vidphone, dialling.

'Who are you calling?' he demanded.

Patty said remotely, 'Someone I know. To take me out to dinner.'

In a voice that cracked with chagrin Chuck said, 'Let me take you out to dinner. I'd love to.'

The girl did not even bother to answer; she continued to dial.

Going over to the pre-Columbian bench he began to gather up the pages of his script; he returned them to the envelope. Meanwhile Patty had got her party; he heard, in the background, her low, muted voice.

'I'll see you,' Chuck said. He put on his coat, strode to the door of the apt.

She did not look up from the vidphone screen; she was absorbed.

With anguished wrath he slammed the door after him, hurried down the carpeted hall to the elevator. Twice he stumbled, and he thought, God, the drink is still afflicting me. Maybe the whole thing's a hallucination, brought on by the mixture of GB-40 and the – whatever she called it. The Ganymedean Wuzzfur or whatever. His brain felt dead, cold and dry of animation; his spirit had completely frozen over and all he could think of was getting out of the building, getting out of Santa Monica and back up to Northern California and his own conapt.

Had London been right? He couldn't tell; perhaps it was just what the girl had said: the pages he had sent to Bunny had been terrible and that was all there was to it. But on the other hand —

I've got to get in touch with Bunny, he realized. Right now. In fact, I should have called him back there from the apt.

On the ground-level floor of the conapt building he found a pay vidphone booth; inside it he began dialling the number of the Hentman organization. And then, all at once, he put the receiver back on its hook. Do I want to know? he asked himself. Can I stand knowing?

He left the vidphone booth, stood momentarily, and then passed out through the main doors of the building, on to the early-evening street. At least I should wait until my wits are clear, he thought. Until that drink has worn off, that non-T intoxicant she gave me.

Hands in his pockets he began to walk aimlessly down the sidewalk runnel. And, each minute, feeling more and more scared and desperate. Everything was falling apart around him. And he seemed helpless to halt the collapse;

he could only witness it, completely impotent, snatched up and gripped by processes too powerful for him to understand.

A voice in his ear, female and recorded, was repeating, 'That will be one quarter skin, sir. Please deposit in coins, no bills.'

Blinking, he looked around him, discovered that he was once again in a vidphone booth. But whom was he calling? Bunny Hentman? Rummaging in his pockets he found the quarter skin, dropped it in the slot of the pay vidphone. At once the image cleared.

It was not Bunny Hentman that he was calling. On the screen facing him was the miniature image of Joan Trieste.

'What's the matter?' Joan said, perceptively. 'You look awful, Chuck. Are you sick? Where are you phoning from?'

'I'm in Santa Monica,' he said. At least he assumed he still was; he had no memory of a ride back up to the Bay Area. And it did not feel much later ... or did it? He examined his wristwatch. Two hours had passed; it was now after eight o'clock. 'I can't believe it,' he said, 'but this morning I was suspended by the CIA as a security risk and now—'

'Good grief,' Joan said, listening intently.

He grated, 'Evidently I've been fired by Bunny Hentman but I can't be sure. Because frankly I'm afraid to get in touch with him.'

There was silence. And then Joan said calmly, 'You must call him, Chuck. Or I can do it for you; I'll tell him I'm your secretary or something – I can handle it, don't worry. Give me the number of the phone booth you're in. And don't give way to depression; I know you well enough already to know that you're going back to considering suicide, and it you try it in Santa Monica I can't help you; I couldn't get to you in time.'

'Thanks,' he said. 'It's nice to hear someone cares.'

'You've just had too much disruption in your life lately,' Joan said in her intelligent, commonsense way. 'The breakup of your marriage, now —'

'Call him,' Chuck interrupted. 'Here's the number.' He held the slip of paper to the vidscreen and Joan wrote it down.

After he had hung up he stood in the phone booth smoking and meditating. His brain was beginning to clear now, and he wondered what he had done between the hours of six and eight. His legs felt stiff, aching with fatigue; perhaps he had been walking. Up and down the streets of Santa Monica, with no destination, no plans.

Reaching into his coat pocket he got out the tin of GB-40 capsules which he had brought along; without benefit of water he managed to swallow one. That would – he presumed – take away the fatigue effects. But nothing short of a frontal-lobe retirement would take away the realization of the disaster which his situation had become.

The slime mould, he thought. Maybe it can help me.

From Marin County info he obtained Lord Running Clam's vidphone number; at once he placed the call, deposited the coins, waited as the phone rang and the screen remained blank.

'Hello.' Words, not auditory but visual, greeted him, manifesting themselves on the screen; the slime mould, unable to talk, could not make use of the audio circuit.

'This is Chuck Rittersdorf,' he said.

More words. 'You are in trouble. I can't read your mind over such a distance, of course, but I catch the nuance in your voice.'

'Do you have influence with Hentman?' Chuck asked.

'As I informed you earlier —' The words, a narrow band, passed in sequence by the video scanner. 'I do not even know the man.'

Chuck said, 'Evidently he's fired me. I'd like you to try to talk him into taking me back.' God, he thought, I have to have *some* kind of a job. 'It was you,' he said, 'who induced me to sign the contract with him; there's a lot of responsibility that can be laid to your door.'

'Your job with the CIA —'

'Suspended. Because of my association with Hentman.'

Brutally Chuck said, 'Hentman knows too many non-Terrans.'

'I see,' the words formed. 'Your highly-neurotic security agency. I should have expected it, but I did not. *You* should have, since you are an employee of several years.'

'Look,' Chuck said. 'I didn't call to engage in a dispute as to who's to blame; I just want a job, any job.' I've got to have it tonight, he said to himself; I can't wait.

'I must ponder this,' the slime mould informed him, via the moving strip of words. 'Give me —'

Chuck savagely hung up the phone.

Again he stood closed up within the booth, smoking and waiting, wondering what Joan would say when she called back. Maybe, he thought, she won't call back. Especially if the news is bad. What a mess. What a state I've single-handedly —

The phone rang.

Lifting the receiver he said, 'Joan?'

On the screen her small image formed. 'I called the number you gave me, Chuck. I got someone on his staff, a Mr. Feld. Everything was in a state of agitation. All Feld would say was for me to look at the evening homeopape.'

'Okay,' Chuck said, and felt even colder than before. 'Thanks. I'll get a L.A. 'pape down here and maybe I'll see you later.' He broke the connection, hurriedly left the booth, walked outdoors to the sidewalk and began searching for a peripatetic 'pape vendor.

It took him only moments to get his hands on the evening 'pape; in the light of a store window he stood reading. There it was on page one. Of course it would be; Hentman was the top TV clown.

BUNNY HENTMAN ARRESTED BY CIA AS
AGENT OF NON-TERRAN POWER, FLEES
CAPTORS IN RUNNING LASER-BATTLE

He had to read the article twice before he could believe it. What had happened was this. The CIA had, through its network of data-collecting mechanisms, learned during the course of the day that the Hentman organization was dropping Chuck Rittersdorf. This, to the CIA minds, had proved their thesis; Hentman was only interested in Chuck because of *Operation Fifty-minutes* on Alpha III M2. Hence, they reasoned, Hentman was, as they had long suspected, an agent of the Alphanes, and the CIA had acted at once – because Hentman's own informant in CIA would, if they had dallied, tipped him off and permitted him to escape. It was all very simple and very terrible; his hands shook as he held the 'pape up to the light.

And Hentmen *had* got away. Despite the CIA's swift action. Perhaps Hentman's own machinery had been efficient enough to warn him; he had been expecting the flying action-squad of CIA men that had tried to close in on him at, as the article said, the TV network studios in New York.

So now where was Bunny Hentman? Probably on his way to the Alpha system. *And where was Chuck Rittersdorf?* On his way to nothing; ahead of him lay only a bog-like emptiness, filled with no persons, no tasks, no reason for existence. Hentman might call Patty Weaver, the TV starlet, and tell her that the script was out, but he hadn't bothered to —

The vidphone call from Hentman had come in the evening. After the aborted arrest. Therefore Patty Weaver knew where Hentman was. Or at least might know. But that was something to go on.

By cab he quickly made his way back to Patty Weaver's magnificent conapt building; he paid the cab and hurried to the entrance, pressed the buzzer for her apt.

'Who is it?' Her voice still was cool, impersonal, even more so.

Chuck said, 'This is Rittersdorf. I left part of my script in your apt.'

'I don't see any pages.' She did not sound convinced.

'If you'll let me in I think I can lay my hands right on them. It shouldn't take more than a couple of minutes.'

'Okay.' The tall metal door clicked, swung open; upstairs in her apt Patty had released it.

He ascended by elevator. The door to her apt was open

and he walked on in. In the living-room Patty greeted him with chilly indifference, she stood with her arms folded, gazing stonily out the window at the view of night-time Los Angeles. 'There are no pages of your goddam script here,' she informed him. 'I don't know what—'

'That call from Bunny,' Chuck said. 'Where was he calling from?'

She eyed him, one eyebrow raised. 'I don't remember.'

'Have you seen tonight's homeopape?'

After a long pause she shrugged. 'Maybe.'

'Bunny called you after the CIA made their arrest attempt. You know it and I know it.'

'So?' She did not even bother to look at him; in all his life he had never been so glacially ignored. And yet, it seemed to him that underneath the hardness of her manner she was frightened. After all she was very young, hardly twenty. He decided to take the chance on that.

'Miss Weaver, I'm an agent of the CIA.' He still had his CIA identification; reaching into his coat he now got it out, held it toward her. 'You're under arrest.'

Her eyes flew wide open in a startled reaction; she spun, stifling an exclamation of dismay. And he could see how radically her breathing had altered; the heavy red pullover sweater rose and fell rapidly. 'You really are a CIA agent?' she asked in a strangled whisper. 'I thought you were a TV scriptwriter; that's what Bunny said.'

'We've penetrated the Hentman organization. I posed as a TV scriptwriter. Come on.' He took hold of Patricia Weaver by the arm.

'Where are we going?' She tugged away, horrified.

'To the L.A. CIA office. Where you'll be booked.'

'For *what*?'

'You know where Bunny Hentman is,' he said.

There was silence.

'I don't,' she said, and sagged. 'I really don't. When he called I didn't know he'd been arrested or whatever it was – he didn't say anything about that. It was only when I went out to dinner, after you left, that I saw the 'pape headlines.' She moved morosely toward the bedroom. 'I'll get my coat and purse. And I'd like to put on a little lipstick. But I'm telling you the truth; honest I am.'

He followed after her; in the bedroom she got her coat down from a hanger in the closet, then opened a dresser drawer for her purse.

'How long do you think they'll keep me?' she asked as she rooted in her purse.

'Oh,' he answered, 'not more than —' He broke off. Because Patty held a laser pistol pointed toward him. She had found it in her purse.

'I don't believe you're a CIA agent,' she said.

'But I am,' Chuck said.

'Get out of here. I don't understand what you're trying to do, but Bunny gave me this and told me to use it when and if I had to.' Her hand shook, but the laser pistol remained pointed at him. 'Please go on,' she said. 'Get out of my apt – if you don't go I'll kill you; honestly I will – I mean it.' She looked terribly, terribly frightened.

Turning, he walked out of the apt, into the hall, down the hall to the elevator. It was still there and he stepped inside it.

A moment later he was back downstairs, stepping out on to the dark sidewalk. Well, that was that. It had scarcely worked out as he intended. On the other hand, he reflected stoically, he had lost nothing ... except perhaps his dignity. And that, given time, would return.

There was nothing to do now but return to Northern California.

Fifteen minutes later he was in the air, heading home to his dreary conapt in Marin County. All in all, his experience in L.A. had failed to be sanguine.

When he arrived he found the apt's lights on and the heater on; seated in a chair, listening to an early Haydn symphony on the FM, was Joan Trieste. As soon as she saw him she hopped to her feet. 'Thank God,' she said, 'I was so worried about you.' Bending, she picked up the San Francisco *Chronicle*. 'You saw the 'pape by now. Where does this put you, Chuck? Does it mean the CIA is after you, too? As a Hentman employee?'

'I dunno,' he said, shutting the door of the apt. As far as he could make out the CIA was not after him, but it was something to ponder; Joan was right. Going into the kitchen he put on the teakettle for coffee, missing, at a time like this, the autonomic coffee-making circuit of the stove he had got Mary – got her, left with her, along with almost everything else.

At the doorway Joan appeared. 'Chuck, I think you ought to call into CIA; talk with someone you know there. Your former boss. Okay?'

He said, with bitterness, 'You're so law-abiding. Always comply with the authorities – correct?' He did not tell her that in the hour of crisis, when everything was falling apart around him right and left, *his* impulse had been to seek out Bunny Hentman, not the CIA.

'Please,' Joan said. 'And I've been conversing with Lord R.C. and he feels the same way. I was listening to news on the radio and they said something about other employees of the Hentman machine being arrested —'

'Just leave me alone.' He got down the jar of instant coffee; his hands shaking, he put a large teaspoonful in a mug.

'If you don't contact them,' Joan stated, 'then I can't do anything for you. So I think it would be best if I left.'

Chuck said, 'What could you do for me anyhow? What have you done for me in the past? I'll bet I'm the first person you ever met who lost two jobs in one day.'

'Then what are you going to do?'

'I think,' Chuck said, 'I'll emigrate to Alpha.' Specifically, he thought, to Alpha III M2. Had he been able to find Hentman —

'The CIA's right, then,' Joan said; her eyes smouldered. 'The Hentman machine is in the pay of a non-Terran power.'

'Lord,' Chuck said, with disgust. 'The war's been over for years! I'm sick of this cloak-mit-dagger rubbish; I've had enough to last me forever. If I want to emigrate then let me emigrate.'

'What I should do,' Joan said, without enthusiasm, 'is arrest you. I'm armed.' She displayed for his benefit, then, the incredibly tiny but undoubtedly genuine side arm which she carried. 'But I can't do it. I feel so sorry for you. How could you make such a mess of your life? And Lord R.C. tried so hard to —'

'Blame him,' Chuck said.

'He only wanted to help; he could see you weren't taking responsibility.' Her eyes flashed. 'No wonder Mary divorced you.'

He groaned.

'You just won't try,' Joan said. 'You've given up; you —' She ceased. And stared at him. He had heard it, too. The thoughts of the Ganymedean slime mould, from across the hall.

'Mr. Rittersdorf, a gentleman is passing along the hall in the direction of your apt; he is armed and he intends to force you to accompany him. I can't tell who he is or what he wants because he's got a grid of some sort installed as a brain-box lining to shield him from telepaths; therefore he's either a military person or a member of the security or intelligence police or part of a criminal or traitorous organization. In any case prepare yourself.'

To Joan, Chuck said, 'Give me that little laser pistol.'

'No.' She lifted it from its holster, turned it toward the door of the apt; her face was clear and fresh. Evidently she had herself completely under control.

'My God,' Chuck said, 'you're going to get killed.' He knew it, foresaw it as fully as if he were a precog; reaching out with lashing speed he grasped the laser tube and yanked it from her hand. The tube got away from him; both he and Joan surged toward it, groping – they collided and with a gasp Joan tumbled against the wall of the kitchen. Chuck's clutching fingers found the tube; he straightened up, holding it...

Something struck his hand and he experienced heat; he dropped the laser tube and it clattered away. At the same time a man's voice – unfamiliar to him – rang in his ears. 'Rittersdorf, I'll kill her if you try to pick that tube up again.' The man, now in the living-room, shut the apt door after him and came a few steps toward the kitchen, his own laser beam held in Joan's direction. He was middle-aged, wearing a cheap grey overcoat of domestic material and odd, archaic boots; the impression that flashed over Chuck was that the man hailed from some totally alien ecology, perhaps from another planet entirely.

'I think he's from Hentman,' Joan said as she slowly rose to her feet. 'So he probably would do it. But if you think you could get hold of the tube before —'

'No,' Chuck said at once. 'We'd both be dead.' He faced the man, then. 'I tried to reach Hentman earlier.'

'Okay,' the man said, and gestured toward the door. 'The lady may stay here; I only want you, Mr. Rittersdorf. Come along and let's not fnop any time; we have a long trip.'

'You can check with Patty Weaver,' Chuck said as he walked ahead of the middle-aged man out into the hall.

Behind him the man grunted. 'No more talking, Mr. Rittersdorf. There's been too much glucking talk already.'

'Such as what?' He halted, feeling ominous gradations of fear.

'Such as your entering the organization as a CIA spy. We realize now why you wanted that job as TV scriptwriter; it was to get evidence on Bun. So what evidence did you get? You saw an Alphane; is that a crime?'

'No,' Chuck said.

'They're going to pelt him to death for that,' the man with the gun said. 'Hell, they've known for years that Bun lived in the Alpha system. The war's over. Sure he's got economic connections with Alpha; who that's in business hasn't? But he's a big figure nationally; the public knows him. I'll tell you what got the CIA where they decided to crack down on him. It was Bun's idea for a script about a CIA sim killing someone; the CIA figured he was beginning to use his TV show to —'

Ahead in the hall the Ganymedean slime mould, in a huge yellow heap, manifested itself, blocking the way; it had flowed out of its conapt.

'Let us by,' the man with the gun said.

'I am sorry,' Lord Running Clam's thoughts came to Chuck, 'but I am a colleague of Mr. Rittersdorf's and it is impractical for me to allow him to be carted off.'

The laser beam clacked on; red and thin it travelled by Chuck and disappeared into the centre of the slime mould. With a crackling tearing noise the slime mould shrivelled up, dried into a black, encrusted blob which smoked and sputtered, charring the wooden floor of the hallway.

'Move,' the man with the gun said to Chuck.

'He's dead,' Chuck said. He couldn't believe it.

'There's some more of them,' the man with the gun said. 'On Ganymede.' His fleshy face showed no emotion, only alertness. 'When we get into the elevator press the up button; my ship's on the roof, and what a louzled-up little field it is.'

Numbly, Chuck entered the elevator. The man with the gun followed and an instant later they had reached the roof; they stepped out into the cold of a foggy night. 'Tell me your name,' Chuck said. 'Just your name.'

'Why?'

'So I can find you again. For killing Lord Running Clam.' Sometime sooner or later he would be set down in the same vector with this person.

'I'll be glad to tell you my name,' the man said as he herded Chuck into the parked hopper; its landing lights glowed and its turbine buzzed faintly. 'Alf Cherigan,' he said as he stationed himself at the controls.

Chuck nodded.

'You like my name? You find it pleasant?'

Saying nothing Chuck stared ahead.

'You've stopped talking,' Cherigan observed. 'Too bad, because you and I'll be cooped up together until we reach Luna and Brahe City.' He reached to snap on the auto course-finding pilot.

Beneath them the hopper bucked and leaped but did not ascend.

'Wait here,' Cherigan said, with a wave of his laser pistol in Chuck's direction. 'Don't touch any of the controls.' Opening the hatch of the hopper he irritably put his head out, peering to see in the darkness, what had stalled the lift-action. 'Holy critter,' he said, 'the outside conduit to the rear rubes—' His speech stopped; he rapidly yanked himself back into the hopper once again, then fired with his laser beam.

From the darkness of the roof an answering beam paralleled his own, found its way through the open hatch and to him; Cherigan dropped his weapon and flopped convulsively against the hull of the cabin, then twisted and sagged like a gored animal, his mouth hanging, his eyes corrupted and vague.

Bending, Chuck picked up the discarded laser beam, looked out to see who it was, there in the darkness. It was Joan; she had followed him and Cherigan up the hall, had taken the manual emergency lift to the roof field and arrived behind them. He got hesitantly from the hopper and greeted her. Cherigan had made a mistake; he had not been informed that Joan was an armed policewoman and accustomed to emergencies. It was even hard for Chuck to realize what she had done so quickly, first with one shot at the guidance system of the hopper, then the second shot which had killed Alf Cherigan.

'Are you getting out?' Joan asked. 'I didn't hit you, did I?'

'I'm untouched,' Chuck said.

'Listen.' She approached the hatch of the hopper, regarded the slumped, discarded shape that had just now been Alf Cherigan. 'I can bring him back. Remember? Do you want me to, Chuck?'

He considered a moment; he remembered Lord Running Clam. And because of that he shook his head no.

'It's up to you,' Joan said. 'I'll let him stay dead. I don't like to, but I understand.'

'How about Lord—'

'Chuck, I can't do anything for him; it's too late. More than five minutes has passed. I had the choice of staying there with him or following you and trying to assist you.'

'I think it would have been better if you—'

'No,' Joan said firmly. 'I did the right thing; you'll see

why. Do you have a magnifying glass?'

Startled, he said, 'No, of course not.'

'Look in the repair case of the hopper, in the storage region under the control panel. There're micro-tools for fixing the miniaturized portions of the ship's circuits ... you'll find a loupe there.'

He opened the cabinet, rummaged about, mindlessly obeying her. A moment later his hands found the jeweller's loupe; he stepped from the hopper, holding it.

'We'll go back below,' Joan said. 'To where he is.'

Presently the two of them bent over the reduced cinder which had previously been their compatriot, the Ganymedean slime mould. 'Stick the loupe in your eye,' Joan instructed, 'and search around. Very closely, especially down in the pile of the carpet.'

'What for?'

Joan said, 'His spores.'

Taken aback he said, 'Did he have a chance to —'

'Sporification for them is automatic, the moment they're attacked; it would have functioned instantaneously, I hope. They'll be microscopic, brown and round; you should be able to find them with the loupe. It's of course impossible to with the naked eye. While you're doing that I'll prepare a culture.' She disappeared into Chuck's apt; he hesitated and then got down on his hands and knees to search the hall carpet for the spores of Lord Running Clam.

When Joan returned he had, in the palm of his hand, seven tiny spheres; under the lens they were smooth and brown and shiny, definitely spores. And he had located them near the spot where the waste-remains of the slime mould lay.

'They need soil,' Joan said as she watched him sprinkle the spores into the measuring cup which she had found in his kitchen. 'And moisture. And time. Find at least twenty, because of course not all of them will survive.'

At last he managed to acquire, from the dirty, much-used carpet, twenty-five spores in all. These were transferred to the measuring cup and then he and Joan descended to the lowest floor of the building, made their way out into the backyard. In the darkness they clutched handfuls of dirt, deposited the loose black soil into the measuring cup. Joan located a hose; she sprinkled drops of water on to the soil and then sealed the cup off from the air with a polyfilm wrapper.

'On Ganymede,' she explained, 'the atmosphere is warm and dense; this is the best I can do to simulate proper conditions for the spores but I think it'll work. Lord R.C. told me once that in an emergency Ganymedeans have managed to sporify successfully in open-air conditions on Terra. So let's hope.' With Chuck she returned to the building, carrying the cup with great care.

'How long will it take?' he asked. 'Before we know.'

'I'm not sure. As soon as two days or – and this has happened in some cases – depending on the phase of the moon as long as a month.' She explained, 'It may sound like superstition but the moon will affect the activation of these spores. So resign yourself to that. The fuller the better; we can look it up in tonight's homeopape.' They ascended to the floor of his apt.

'How much memory will there be in the new —' He hesitated. 'In the next generation of slime mould? Will it or they remember us and what took place here?'

As she sat examining the homeopape Joan said, 'It depends entirely on how quickly he managed to act; if he got off spores from his —' She shut the 'pape. 'The spores should react in a matter of days.'

'What would happen,' Chuck asked, 'if I took them off Terra? Away from Luna's influence?'

'They'd still grow. But it might take longer. What's on your mind?'

'If the Hentman organization would send someone to find me,' Chuck said, 'and something happened to him —'

'Oh yes of course,' Joan agreed. 'They'll be sending another. Probably in a few hours, as soon as they realize we got the first one. And he may have had a dead-man's-signal installed on him somewhere, so they had the information as soon as his heart stopped. I think you're right; you should get off Terra as soon as possible. But how, Chuck? To really disappear you'd have to have resources, some money and support, and you don't; you have no source of income at all now. Do you have anything at all saved up?'

'Mary got the joint account,' he said, pondering; he seated himself, lit a cigarette. 'I have an idea,' he said at last, 'of what I'm going to try. I'd prefer you didn't hear. Do you understand? Or do I just sound neurotic and fearful?'

'You just sound anxious. And you ought to be.' She rose. 'I'll go out into the hall; I know you want to place a call. While you're doing that I'll contact the Ross Police Department and have them come here to dispose of that man in the hopper up above us.' At the door of the apt she lingered, however. 'Chuck, I'm glad I was able to keep them from taking you. I barely made it. Where was the hopper going?'

'I'd rather not tell you. For your own protection.'

She nodded. And the door shut after her. Now he was alone.

At once he placed a call to the San Francisco CIA office. It took some time, but at last he was able to trace down his former boss, Jack Elwood. At home with his family, Elwood answered the vidphone with irritation. Nor was he pleased to see who it was.

'I'll make a deal with you,' Chuck said.

'A deal! We believe you directly or indirectly tipped off Hentman so that he had the opportunity to escape. Isn't that what happened? We even know whom you worked through: that starlet in Santa Monica that's Hentman's current mistress.' Elwood scowled.

This was new to Chuck; he hadn't realized this about Patty Weaver. However, it hardly mattered now. 'The deal,' Chuck said, 'that I intend to make with you – with the CIA, officially – is this. *I know where Hentman is.*'

'That doesn't surprise me. What does surprise me is that you're willing to tell us. Why is that, Chuck? A falling-out within the Hentman happy family, with you on the outside?'

'The Hentman organization has already sent one nurt out,' Chuck said. 'We were able to stop him but there'll be another and then another until finally Hentman gets me.' He did not bother to try to explain his difficult situation to Elwood; his former boss wouldn't believe him and anyhow his wants would remain the same. 'I'll tell you where Hentman is hiding out in exchange for a CIA C-plus ship. An intersystem ship, one of those small military-style pursuit-class vessels. I know you've got a few of them; you can spare one, and you're getting back something of enormous value.' He added, 'And I'll return the ship – eventually. It's just the use of it that I want.'

'You actually do sound as if you're tying to get away,' Elwood said with acuity.

'I am.'

'Okay.' Elwood shrugged. 'I'll believe you; why not? And so what? Tell me where Hentman is; I'll have the ship for you within five hours.'

In other words, Chuck realized, they'll hold up delivery until they have had a chance to check my information. If Hentman isn't found, there will be no ship; I'll be waiting in vain. But it was hopeless to expect the pros of the CIA to operate in any other fashion; this was their business – life for them was one great card game.

Resignedly he said, 'Hentman is on Luna, at Brahe City.'

'Wait at your apt,' Elwood said instantly. 'The ship will be there by two this morning. *If*.' He eyed Chuck.

Breaking the connection Chuck went to pick up his burned down cigarette from the edge of the living-room coffee table. Well, if the ship did not show up then this was the end; he had no other plans, no alternative solution. Joan Trieste might save him again, might even bring him back after a nurt of Hentman's had actually killed him . . . but if he stayed on Terra eventually they would find and destroy him or at the very least capture him: detection devices were simply too good, now. Given sufficient time they always found the target if it were still somewhere on the planet. But Luna, unlike Terra, had uncharted areas; detection there posed a problem. And there existed remote moons and planets where detection, by anyone, was a near impossibility.

One of those areas was the Alpha system. For example Alpha III and its several moons, including M2; most especially M2. And with a CIA faster-than-light ship he could reach it in a matter of days. As had Mary and the gang with her.

Opening the door to the hall he said to Joan, 'Okay, I made my one puny call. That's that.'

'*Are* you leaving Terra?' Her eyes were enormous and dark.

'We'll see.' He seated himself, prepared to wait it out.

With great care Joan set the measuring cup of Lord Running Clam's spores on the arm of the couch by Chuck. 'I'll give these to you. I know you want them; it was you he gave his life for and you feel responsible. Better let me tell you what to do as soon as the spores become active.'

He got pen and paper in order to write down her instructions.

It was actually several hours later – the Ross Police Department had shown up and lugged off the dead man on the roof, and Joan Trieste had departed – that he realized what he had done. Now Bunny Hentman was right; he *had* betrayed Hentman to the CIA. But he had done it to save his life. That, however, would hardly justify it in Hentman's eyes; he, too, was trying to save *his* life.

In any case it was done. He continued to wait, alone in his apt, for the C-plus ship from CIA. A ship which very likely was never going to arrive. And what then? Then, he decided, I'll be sitting here and waiting for something else, for the next nurt from the Hentman organization. And my life can be measured out in teaspoonfuls.

It was one hell of a long wait.

TEN

Bowing slightly, Gabriel Baines said, 'We constitute the sine quo non council possessing overall authority on this world, an ultimate form of authority which can't be overruled by anyone.' He, with stark, cold politeness, drew back a chair for the Terran psychologist, Dr. Mary Rittersdorf; she accepted it with a brief smile. It seemed to him that she looked tired. The smile showed genuine gratitude.

The other members of the council introduced themselves to Dr. Rittersdorf in their several idiosyncratic fashions.

'Howard Straw. *Mans.*'

'J-Jacob Simion.' Simion could not suppress his moronic grin. 'From the Heebs, where your ship set down.'

'Annette Golding. Poly.' Her eyes were alert and she sat erectly, watchful of the female psychologist who had barged into their lives.

'Ingred Hibbler. One, two, three. Ob-Com.'

Dr. Rittersdorf said, 'And that would be—' She nodded. 'Oh yes, of course. Obsessive–compulsive.'

'Omar Diamond. I will let you guess what clan I am from.' Diamond glanced about remotely; he seemed withdrawn into his private world, much to Gabriel Baines' annoyance. This was scarcely a time for individual activity, even of a mystical order; this was the moment in which they had to function as a whole or not at all.

In a hollow, despairing voice the Dep spoke up. 'Dino Watters.' He struggled to say more, then gave up; the weight of pessimism, of sheer hopelessness, was too great for him. Once more he sat staring down, rubbing his forehead in a miserable tic-like motion.

'And you know who I am, Dr. Rittersdorf,' Baines said, and rattled the document which lay before him; it represented the joint efforts of the council members, their manifesto. 'Thank you for coming here!' he began, and cleared his throat; his voice had become husky with tension.

'Thank you for allowing me to,' Dr. Rittersdorf said in a formal but – to him – distinctly menacing tone. Her eyes were opaque.

Baines said, 'You have asked to be permitted to visit settlements other than Gandhitown. In particular you requested permission to examine Da Vinci Heights. We have discussed this. We decided to decline.'

Nodding, Dr. Rittersdorf said, 'I see.'

'Tell her why,' Howard Straw spoke up. His face was ugly; he had not for an instant taken his eyes from the lady psychologist from Terra: his hatred for her filled the room and tainted the atmosphere. Gabriel Baines felt as if he were choking in it.

Raising her hand Dr. Rittersdorf said, 'Wait. Before you read me your statement.' She looked at each of them in turn, a slow, steady and totally professional scrutiny. Howard Straw returned it with malignance. Jacob Simion ducked his head, smiled emptily, letting her attention simply pass. Annette Golding nervously scratched at the cuticle of her thumbnail, her face pale. The Dep never noticed that he was under observation; he never once raised his head. The Skitz, Omar Diamond, returned Mrs. Rittersdorf's stare with sweet sublimity, yet underneath it, Baines guessed, there was anxiety; Diamond looked as if at any moment he might bolt.

As for himself he found Dr. Mary Rittersdorf physically attractive. And he wondered – idly – if the fact that she had arrived without her husband signified anything. She was, in fact, sexy. As an inexplicable incongruity, considering the purpose of this meeting, Dr. Rittersdorf wore a distinctly feminine outfit: black sweater and skirt, no stockings, gilded slippers with turned-up elfish toes. The sweater, Baines observed, was just a fraction too tight. Did Mrs. Rittersdorf realize this? He could not tell, but in any case he found his attention drawn away from what she was saying to her well-articulated breasts. They were admittedly small but quite distinct as regard to angle. He liked them.

I wonder, he wondered, if this woman – she was, he surmised, in her early thirties, certainly in her physical, nubile prime – if she is looking for something more than professional success, here. He had a powerful affective insight that Dr. Rittersdorf was animated by a personal spirit as well as a task-oriented one; again, she perhaps was not conscious of this. The body, he reflected, possesses ways of its own, sometimes in contradistinction to the purposes of the mind. This morning, on arising, Dr. Rittersdorf might merely have thought that she would like to wear this black sweater, without thinking any more about it. But the body, the well-formed gynaecologic apparatus within, knew better.

And to this an analogous portion of himself responded. However in his case it was a conscious reaction. And, he thought, *perhaps this can be turned to our group's advantage.* This dimension of involvement might not be the liability for us that it surely is for our antagonists. Thinking this he felt himself slide into a posture of contrived defence; he had schemes, automatic and plentiful, by which to protect not only himself but also his colleagues.

'Dr. Rittersdorf,' he said smoothly, 'before we could permit you to enter our several settlements, a delegation representing our clans would have to inspect your ship to see what armaments – if any – you have along with you. Anything else is unworthy of even cursory consideration.'

'We're not armed,' Dr. Rittersdorf said.

'Nevertheless,' Gabriel Baines said, 'I propose to you that you allow me and perhaps one other individual here to accompany you to your base. I have a proclamation here –' He rattled the manifesto. '– which calls for your ship to vacate Gandhitown within forty-eight Terran hours. If you don't comply —' He glanced at Straw, who nodded. 'We will initiate military operations against you on the grounds that you are hostile, uninvited invaders.'

In a low, modulated voice Dr. Rittersdorf said, 'I understand your comprehension. You've lived here in isolation for quite a time. But —' She was speaking directly to him;

her fine, intelligent eyes confronted him purposefully. 'I am afraid I have to call attention to a fact which you all may find distasteful. *You are, individually and collectively, mentally ill.*'

There was a taut, prolonged silence.

'Hell,' Straw said to no one in particular, 'we blew that place sky high years ago. That so-called "hospital." Which was really a concentration camp.' His lips twisted. 'For purposes of slave labour.'

'I am sorry to say it,' Dr. Rittersdorf said, 'but you are wrong; it was a legitimate hospital, and you must include the realization of this as a factor in any plans you might make regarding us. I'm not lying to you; I'm speaking the plain, simple truth.'

' "Quid est veritas?" ' Baines murmured.

'Pardon?' Dr. Rittersdorf said.

Baines said, ' "What is truth?" Hasn't it occurred to you, Doctor, that in the last decade we here might have risen above our initial problems of group adaptation and become—' He gestured. 'Adjusted? Or whatever term you prefer ... in any case capable of possessing adequate interpersonal relationships, such as you're witnessing here in this chamber. Surely if we can work together *we are not sick*. There's no other test you can apply except that of group-workability.' He sat back, pleased with himself.

With care Dr. Rittersdorf said, 'You are, admittedly, unified against a common enemy ... against us. But – I'd be willing to place a bet that before we arrived, and again after we depart, you will fragment into isolated individuals, mistrustful and frightened of one another, unable to collaborate.' She smiled disarmingly, but it was far too wise a smile for him to accept; it too much underscored her very clever statement.

Because of course she was right; she had put her finger on it. They did not function together regularly. But – she was also wrong.

This was her error. She supposed, probably as a matter of self-justifying protection, that the origin of the fear and hostility lay with the council. But in fact it was Terra who displayed menacing tactics; the landing of their ship was de facto a hostile act ... *were it not, an attempt would have been made to secure permission.* These Terrans themselves had manifested initial distrust; they alone were responsible for the present pattern of mutual suspicion. Had they wanted to they could readily have avoided it.

'Dr. Rittersdorf,' he said bluntly, 'the Alphane traders contact us when they want permission to land. We notice that you did not. And we have no problems in our dealings with them; we trade back and forth on a regular, constant basis.'

Obviously his gauntlet had been thrown down to good effect; the woman hesitated, did not have an answer. While she pondered, everyone in the room rustled with amusement, contempt and, as in the case of Howard Straw, pitiless animosity.

'We assumed,' Dr. Rittersdorf said at last, 'that had we formally requested permission to land you would have refused us.'

Smiling, feeling calm, Baines said, 'But you didn't try. You "assumed." And now, of course, you'll never know, because —'

'Would you have granted us permission?' Her voice snapped at him, firm and authoritative, penetrating and shattering the continuity of his utterance; he blinked, involuntarily paused. 'No, you wouldn't have,' she continued. 'And all of you know it. Please try to be realistic.'

'If you show up at Da Vinci Heights,' Howard Straw said, 'we'll kill you. In fact if you don't leave we'll kill you. And the next ship that tries to land will never touch ground. This is our world and we plan to retain it as long as we survive. Mr. Baines here can recite the details of your original imprisonment of us; it's all contained in the manifesto which he and I – with the help of the others in this room – prepared. Read the manifesto, Mr. Baines.'

'"Twenty-five years ago,"' Gabriel Baines began, '"a colony was established on this planet —"'

Dr. Rittersdorf sighed. 'Our knowledge of the assorted patterns of your mental illnesses —'

'"Sordid"?' Howard Straw burst in. 'Did you say "sordid"?' His face was mottled with dire rage; he half-rose from his chair.

'I said *assorted*,' Dr. Rittersdorf said patiently. 'Our knowledge informs us that the focus of your militant activity will be found in the Mans settlement – in other words, the manic group's settlement. Four hours from now we will break camp and leave the hebephrenic settlement of Gandhitown; we will set down in Da Vinci Heights and if you engage us in combat we'll bring in line-class Terran military forces.' She added, 'Which are standing by approximately half an hour from here.'

Again there was a taut and prolonged silence in the room.

Annette Golding at last spoke up, but barely audibly. 'Read our manifesto anyhow, Gabriel.'

Nodding, he resumed. But his voice shook.

Annette Golding began to cry, miserably, interrupting his reading. 'You can see what's in store for us; they're going to turn us back into hospital patients again. It's the end.'

Uncomfortably, Dr. Rittersdorf said. 'We're going to provide *therapy* for you. It'll cause you to feel more – well, relaxed with one another. More yourselves. Life will take on a more pleasant, natural significance; as it is you're all oppressed with such strain and fears ...'

'Yes,' Jacob Simion muttered. 'Fears that Terra will break in here and round us up like a lot of animals again.'

Four hours, Gabriel Baines thought. Not long. His voice trembling, he resumed the reading of their joint manifesto.

It seemed to him an empty gesture. Because there is just exactly nothing, he realized, that is going to save us.

After the meeting had ended – and Dr. Rittersdorf had departed – Gabriel Baines laid his plan before his colleagues.

'You're what?' Howard Straw demanded with contemptuous derision, his face made into a parody of itself by his grimace. 'You say you're going to seduce her? My God, maybe she's right; maybe we ought to be in a neuropsychiatric hospital!' He sat back and wheezed bleakly to himself. His disgust was too great; he could make no further motions of abuse – he left that to the others in the room.

'You must think a lot of yourself,' Annette Golding said, finally.

'What I need,' Gabriel said, 'is someone with enough telepathic ability to tell me if I'm right.' He turned to Jacob Simion. 'Doesn't that Heeb saint, that Ignatz Ledebur, have at least a little capacity for telepathy? He's sort of a jack-of-all-trades, Psi talent-wise.'

'None that I know of,' Simion said. 'But you might, you just might try Sarah Apostoles.' He winked at Gabriel, shaking his head in mirth.

'I'll phone Gandhitown,' Gabriel Baines said, picking up the phone.

Simion said, 'The phone-lines in Gandhitown are out again. For six days now. You'll have to go there.'

'You'd have to go there anyhow,' Dino Watters said, rousing himself at last from the slumber of his endless depression. He, alone, seemed somewhat taken by Baines' scheme. 'After all that's where he is, in Gandhitown, where anything goes, everyone has children by everyone. By now she may in the spirit of the thing.'

With a grunt of agreement Howard Straw said, 'It's luck for you, Gabe, that she's among the Heebs; she ought to be more receptive to you because of that.'

'If this is the only way we can comport ourselves,' Miss Hibbler said stiffly, 'I think we deserve to perish; I truly do.'

'The universe,' Omar Diamond pointed out, 'possesses an infinitude of ways by which it fulfills itself. Even this must not out-of-hand be despised.' He nodded gravely.

Without another word, without even saying good-bye to Annette, Gabriel Baines strode from the council chamber, down the wide stone stairs and out of the building, to the parking lot. There he boarded his turbine-driven auto and presently, at a meagre seventy-five miles an hour, was on his way to Gandhitown. He would arrive before the four-hour deadline, he calculated, assuming that nothing had fallen on to the road, blocking it. Dr. Rittersdorf had returned to Gandhitown by rocket-driven launch; she was already there. He cursed at the archaic mode of transportation which he had to rely on, but there it was; this was their world and the reality for which they were fighting. As a satellite of the Terran culture once more they would regain modern means of transportation ... but this in no way would make up for what they stood to lose. Better to travel at seventy-five miles an hour and be free. Ah, he thought. A slogan.

And yet it was a trifle annoying. Considering the vitalness of his mission ... council-sanctioned or not.

Four hours and twenty minutes later, physically wearied by his travel but mentally alert, even keyed-up, he reached the rubbish-strewn outskirts of Gandhitown; he smelled the odour of the settlement, the sweet smell of rot mixed with the acrid stench of countless small fires.

During the trip he had evolved a new idea. So at this last moment he turned – not toward Sarah Apostoles' shack – but toward that of the Heeb saint Ignatz Ledebur.

He found Ledebur tinkering with an ancient, rusty gasoline generator in his yard, surrounded by his children and cats.

'I have seen your plan,' Ledebur said, raising a hand to stop Gabriel from breaking into an explanation. 'It was traced in blood on the horizon just a short while ago.'

'Then you know specifically what I want from you.'

'Yes.' Ledebur nodded. 'And in the past, with a number of women, I have made successful use of it.' He put down the hammer which he held, strolled toward the shack; the cats but not the children followed. So did Gabriel Baines. 'However it is a microscopic idea that you possess,' Ledebur said reprovingly, and chuckled.

'Can you read the future? Can you tell me if I'll succeed?'

'I am no seer. Others may foretell but I remain silent. Wait a minute.' Within the one main room of the shack he paused, while the cats trotted and hopped and mewed on all sides. Then he reached above the sink, lifted down a quart jar with a dark substance inside; he unscrewed the lid of the jar, sniffed, shook his head, put the lid back on the jar and restored it to its place. 'Not that.' He wandered off, then finally opened the ice box, rummaged within, came out with a plastic carton which he inspected with a critical frown.

His present common-law wife – Gabriel Baines did not know her name – appeared from the bedroom, glanced dully at the two of them, then started on. She wore a sack-like dress, tennis shoes and no socks, her hair a mass of uncombed dirty material coating the top and back of her head. Gabriel Baines looked away in gloomy disgust.

'Say,' Ledebur said to the woman. 'Where's that jar of you-know-what? That mixture we use before we—' he gestured.

'In the bathroom.' The woman padded on by, going outdoors.

Disappearing into the bathroom Ledebur could be heard moving objects about, glasses and bottles; at last he returned carrying a tumbler filled with a liquid that slopped against the sides as he walked. 'This is it,' Ledebur said, with a grin that showed two missing teeth. 'But you have to induce her to take it. How are you going to manage that?'

At that moment Gabriel Baines did not know. 'We'll see,' he said, and held out his hand for the aphrodisiac.

After leaving Ledebur he drove to the single shopping centre in Gandhitown, parked before the dome-shaped wooden structure with its peeling paint, its stacks of dented cans, heaps of discarded cardboard cartons littering the entrance and parking area. Here the Alphane traders rid themselves – dumped, actually – great masses of seconds.

Within he bought a bottle of Alph' brandy; seated in his auto he opened it, poured out a portion of the contents, added the dingy, heavily-sedimented aphrodisiac which the Heeb saint had given him. The two liquids managed somehow to mix; satisfied, he recapped the bottle, started up the car and drove on.

This was, he reflected, no time for him to depend on his natural talents; as the council had pointed out he did not particularly excel in this direction. And excellence, if they wished to survive, was mandatory.

Visually, he managed without difficulty to locate the Terran ship; it loomed high and shiny and metallically-clean above the litter of Gandhitown, and as soon as he sighted it he turned his auto in that direction.

An armed Terran guard, wearing a grey-green uniform familiar from the late war, halted him a few hundred yards from the ship, and from a nearby doorway Baines saw the muzzle of a heavy weapon trained on him. 'Your ident papers, please,' the guard said, warily scrutinizing him.

Gabriel Baines said, 'Tell Dr. Rittersdorf that a plenipotentiary from the supreme council is here to make a final offer by which bloodshed on both sides can be avoided.' He sat tautly bolt-upright behind the tiller of his car, gazing straight ahead.

By intercom the arrangements were made. 'You may go ahead, sir.'

Another Terran, also in full military dress with side arms and decorations, conducted him on foot to the ramp that led up to the open hatch of the ship. They ascended and presently he was bumping his way morosely down a corridor, searching for Room 32-H. The confining walls made him uneasy; he longed to be back outdoors where he could breathe. But – too late now. He found the proper door, hesitated, then knocked. Under his arm the bottle gurgled slightly.

The door swung open and there stood Dr. Rittersdorf, still wearing the slightly-too-tight black sweater, the black skirt and elfish shoes. She regarded him uncertainly. 'Let's see, you're Mr. —'

'Baines.'

'Ah. The Pare.' Half to herself she added, 'Schizophrenic paranoia. Oh, I beg your pardon.' She flushed. 'No offence meant.'

'I'm here,' Gabriel Baines said, 'to drink a toast. Will you join me?' He walked past her, into her diminutive quarters.

'A toast to what?'

He shrugged. 'That ought to be obvious.' He allowed just the right shade of irritation to enter his voice.

'Are you giving in?' Her tone was sharp, penetrating; closing the door she came a step toward him.

'Two glasses,' he said, in a deliberately resigned, muted voice. 'Okay, Doctor?' He got the bottle of Alphane brandy – and its alien additive – from its paper bag, began to unscrew the cap.

'I think you're definitely doing the wise thing,' Dr. Rittersdorf said. She looked distinctly pretty as she scurried about searching for glasses; her eyes shone. 'This is a good sign, Mr. Baines. Really.'

Sombrely, still the incarnation of defeat, Gabriel Baines poured from the bottle until both glasses were full.

'We can land, then, at Da Vinci Heights?' Dr. Rittersdorf asked, as she lifted her glass and sipped.

'Oh sure,' he agreed listlessly; he, too, sipped. It tasted awful.

'I'll inform the security member of our mission,' she said. 'Mr. Mageboom. So no accidental—' She all at once became silent.

'What's wrong?'

'I just had the strangest—' Dr. Rittersdorf frowned. 'A sort of flutter. Deep inside me. If I didn't know better—' She looked embarrassed. 'Never mind, Mr. – is it Baines?' Rapidly she drank from her glass. 'I feel so tense all of a sudden. I guess I was worried; we didn't want to see...' Her voice trailed away. Walking to the corner of the compartment she seated herself on the chair, there. 'You put something in that drink.' Rising, she let the glass drop; she crossed as swiftly as possible toward a red button on the far wall.

As she passed him he caught her around the waist. The plenipotentiary from the inter-clan council of Alpha III M2 had made his move. For better or worse the plan was being enacted, their struggle to survive.

Dr. Rittersdorf bit him on the ear. Nearly severing the lobe.

'Hey,' he said feebly.

Then he said, 'What are you doing?'

After that he said, 'Ledebur's concoction really works.'

He added, 'But I mean, there's a limit to everything.'

Time passed and he said gaspingly, 'At least there should be.'

A knock sounded on the door.

Raising herself up slightly Dr. Rittersdorf called, 'Go away!'

'It's Mageboom,' a muffled male voice sounded from the corridor.

Springing to her feet, disentangling herself from him, Dr. Rittersdorf ran to the door and locked it. At once she spun and, with a ferocious expression, dived – it looked to him as if she were diving – directly at him. He shut his eyes and prepared for the impact.

But was this going to get them what they wanted? Politically.

Holding her down, keeping her to one spot on the floor, a little to the right of the heap of her tossed-away clothing, Baines grunted, 'Listen, Dr. Rittersdorf —'

'Mary.' And this time she bit him on the mouth; her teeth clinked against him with stunning force and he winced with pain, shut his eyes involuntarily. That turned out to be his cardinal mistake. Because in that moment he was tilted; the next he knew he was somehow on the bottom, pinned in place – her sharp knees dug into his loins and she grasped him just above the ears, gathering his hair between her fingers and tugging upward as if to pull his head from his shoulders. And at the same time —

He managed to call out weakly, 'Help!'

The person on the other side of the door, however, had evidently already departed; there was no response.

Baines made out the sight of the red button on the wall which Mary Rittersdorf had been about to press – had intended to but now, beyond any doubt whatsoever, would never in a million years press – and began to squirm inch by inch in its direction.

He never made it.

And the thing that gets me, he thought later on in despair, is that in addition this is getting the council nowhere politically.

'Dr. Rittersdorf,' he grated, wheezing for breath, 'let's be reasonable. For God's sake let's talk, okay? Please.'

This time she bit the top of his nose; he felt her sharp teeth meet. She laughed; it was a long, echoing laugh that chilled him.

I think that what's going to kill me, he decided finally after the passage of what seemed an unending amount of time in which neither of them managed to say any more, is the biting; I'm being bitten to death and there is nothing I can do. He felt as if he had stirred up and encountered the libido of the universe; it was a mere elemental but enormous power that had him pinned to the rug, here, with no possibility of escape. If only someone would break in, one of the armed guards for instance—

'Did you know,' Mary Rittersdorf whispered wetly against his cheek, 'that you're the prettiest man alive?' At that she backed off slightly, sitting on her haunches, adjusting herself – he saw his opportunity and rolled away; scrambling, he broke for the button, groped frantically to press it, to summon someone, anyone – Terran or not.

Panting, she seized him by the ankle, brought him crashing down; his head hit the side of a metal cabinet and he moaned as the darkness of defeat and annihilation – of a sort he had never been prepared for by anything previous in his life – seeped over him.

With a laugh, Mary Rittersdorf rolled him about and once more pounced on him; her bare knees again dug into him, her breasts dangled above his face as she clamped her hands over his wrists and bore him flat. It obviously did not matter to her whether he was conscious really, he discovered, as the darkness became complete. One last thought entered his mind, a final determination.

Somehow, some way, he would get the Heeb saint Ingatz Ledebur for this. If it was his last act in life.

'Oh, you're so lovely,' Mary Rittersdorf's voice, uttered within a quarter-inch of his left ear, rang, deafening him. 'I could just eat you up.' She quivered from head to foot, an undulation that was like a storm of mobility, a tossing of the surface of the earth itself.

He had, as he passed out, a terrible feeling that Dr. Rittersdorf had just begun. And Ledebur's concoction did not account for this because it had not affected *him* this way. Gabriel Baines and the Heeb saint's concoction had provided an opportunity for something already in Dr. Mary Rittersdorf to emerge. And he would be lucky if the combination did not turn out to be – as it seemingly was turning out to be – not a so-called love potion but a clear-cut potion of death.

At no time did he truly lose consciousness. Therefore he was aware that, much later, the activity in which he was caught began by degrees to abate. The artificially-induced whirlwind diminished and then at last there was a fitful peace. And then – by an agency which remained obscure to him – he was physically moved from his place on the floor, from Dr. Mary Rittersdorf's compartment, to some other place entirely.

I wish I was dead, he said to himself. Obviously the last of the grace-period had trickled away; the Terran ultimatum had expired and he had failed to halt events. And where was he? Cautiously Baines opened his eyes.

It was dark. He lay outdoors, under stars amd around him rose the junk-heap which was the Heeb settlement of Gandhitown. In no direction – he peered frantically – could he make out the spape of the Terran ship. So obviously it had taken off. To land at Da Vinci Heights.

Shivering, he sat weakly up. Where, in the name of all that was sacred to the species, were his clothes? Hadn't she cared enough to give them back? It seemed a gratuitous coda; he lay back and shut his eyes and cursed to himself in a sing-song voice ... and he, the Pare delegate to the supreme council. Too much, he thought bitterly.

A noise to his right attracted him; again he opened his eyes, this time peering shrewdly. An antique vehicle of some obsolete sort put-putted toward him. He made out, now, bushes; yes, he realized, he had been tossed in the bushes, too, fulfilling the ancient saw: Mary Rittersdorf had reduced him to the status of a participant in a folk-saying. He hated her for that – but his fear of her, much greater, did not budge. What was coming was nothing more than a typical Heeb internal combustion engine car; he could distinguish its yellow headlights.

Climbing to his feet he waved the car to a halt, standing in the centre of the nebulous Heeb-built cowpath, here on the outskirts of Gandhitown.

'What's the matter?' the Heeb driver in his drawly, jejune voice inquired; he was so deteriorated as to be devoid of caution.

Baines walked up to the door of the car and said, 'I was – attacked.'

'Oh? Too bad. Took your clothes, too? Get in.' The Heeb banged on the door behind him until it swung creakily open. 'I'll drive you to my place. Get you something to wear.'

Baines said grimly, 'I'd prefer it if you took me to Ignatz Ledebur's shack. I want to talk to him.' But, if it had all been there, buried inside the woman in the first place, how could he blame the Heeb saint? No one could have predicted it, and surely if it generally affected women this way Ledebur would have ceased to employ it.

'Who's that?' the Heeb driver inquired as he started up the car.

There was that little intercommunication in Gandhitown; it was a symptom, Baines realized, that rather bore out Mary Rittersdorf's statements about them all. However, he drew himself together and described as best he could the location of the Heeb saint's shack.

'Oh yeah,' the driver said, 'the guy who has all those cats. I ran over one the other day.' He chuckled. Baines shut his eyes, groaned.

Presently they had halted before the dimly-lit shack of the Heeb saint. The driver banged open the car door; Baines climbed stiffly out, aching in every joint and still suffering unbearably from the million and one bites which Mary Rittersdorf, in her passion, had inflicted. He made his way step by step across the littered yard, in the uneven yellow light of the car's headlights, found the shack's door, nudged an undetermined collection of cats from his way, and rapped on the door.

Seeing him, Ignatz Ledebur rocked with laughter. 'What a time it must have been – you're bleeding all over. I'll get you something to wear and Elsie'll probably have something for those bites or whatever they are ... it looks as if she worked you over with a pair of cuticle scissors.' Chuckling, he shuffled off somewhere in the rear of the shack. A horde of grimy children regarded Baines as he stood by the oil heater warming himself; he ignored them.

Later, as Ledebur's common-law wife dabbed ointment on the bites – which constellated around his nose, mouth and ears – and Ledebur laid out tattered but reasonably clean clothes, Gabriel Baines said, 'I've got her figured out. Obviously she's the oral sadistic type. That's where things went wrong.' Mary Rittersdorf, he realized soberly, was as sick as, or even more than, anyone on Alpha III M2. But it had been latent.

Ledebur said, 'The Terran ship took off.'

'I know.' He began now to dress.

'There has been a vision,' Ledebur said, 'that has reached me in the last hour. About the arrival of another Terran ship.'

'A warship,' Baines guessed. 'To take Da Vinci Heights.' He wondered if they'd go as far as to H-bomb the Manses' settlement – in the name of psychotherapy.

'This is a tiny, fast pursuit ship,' Ledebur said. 'According to my psychic presentation related by the primordial forces. Like a bee. It hurtled down, landed near the Poly settlement, Hamlet Hamlet.'

At once Baines thought of Annette Golding. He hoped to heaven that she was all right. 'Do you have any kind of vehicle? Anything I can ride back to Adolfville in? There was his own car, presumably parked at the spot the Terran ship had occupied. Hell, he could walk to it from here. And he would not drive to his own settlement, he decided; he would go to Hamlet Hamlet, make certain that Annette had not been raped, beaten up or lasered. If she were harmed in any way —

'I let them down,' he said to Ledebur. 'I claimed I had a plan – they depended on me, naturally, because I'm a Pare.' But he had not given up yet; his Pare mind was filled with schemes, active and alive. He would go to his grave this way, still planning how to defeat the enemy.

'You should eat something,' Ledebur's woman suggested. 'Before you go anywhere. There's some kidney stew left; I intended to give it to the cats but you're welcome to it.'

'Thanks,' he said, managing not to gag; Heeb cooking left something to be desired. But she was right. He needed to regain a certain amount of energy, otherwise he'd fall dead in his tracks. It was amazing he had not already, considering what had befallen him.

After he had eaten he borrowed a flashlight from Ledebur, thanked him for the clothes, ointment and meal, then set off on foot through the narrow, twisted, junk-filled streets of Gandhitown. Fortunately his car was still where he had left it; neither Heebs or Terrans had seen fit to cart if off, saw it up or pulverize it.

Getting in he drove from Gandhitown, took the road east toward Hamlet Hamlet. Once more at a pitiful seventy-five miles an hour he was on his way across the open, exposed landscape between settlements.

With him rode a dreadful sense of urgency, of a sort he had never before experienced. Da Vinci Heights had been invaded, perhaps already had fallen; what was left? How, without the fantastic energy of the Mans clan, could they survive? If perhaps this single small Terran ship meant something ... might not that be a hope? At least it was unexpected. And, within the realm of the expected, they had no chance, were doomed.

He was not a Skitz, or a Heeb. And yet in his own dim way he had his vision, too. It was a vision of the off-chance, the one possibility plucked from the many. His first plan had fallen through but there was still this; he believed in this. And he did not even know why.

ELEVEN

On her trip home from the council meeting at Adolfville, a meeting which had seen the Terran ultimatum expire and the enemy go into action against Da Vinci Heights, Annette Golding considered the possibility of suicide. What had happened to them, even to the Manses, was overpowering; how did one combat the arguments put forth by a planet which had recently defeated the whole Alphane empire?

Obviously it was hopeless. And, on a biological level, she recognized it ... and was willing to succumb to it. I'm like Dino Watters, she said to herself as she scrutinized the murky road ahead, the glow of her headlights against the plastic ribbon which connected Adolfville with Hamlet Hamlet. When the chips are down, I prefer not to fight; I prefer to give up. And no one's making me give up: *I just want to.*

Tears filled her eyes as she realized this about herself. I guess I must basically admire the Manses, she decided. I venerate what I'm not; I'm not harsh, aloof, unyielding. But theoretically, being a Poly, I could become that. In fact I could become anything. But instead —

She saw, then, to her right, a streak of retro-rocket exhausts tailed out along the night sky. A ship was descending, and very close to Hamlet Hamlet. In fact if she kept on this road she would encounter it. She experienced at once – typical of a Poly – two equal, opposite emotions. Fear made her cringe, and yet curiosity, a blend of eagerness and anticipation and excitement, caused her to speed her car up.

However, before she reached the ship her fear won out; she slowed, drove the car on to the soft dirt shoulder and cut the switch. The car glided in silence to a stop; she sat with headlights off, listening to the night sounds and wondering what to do.

From where she sat she could dimly perceive the ship, and occasionally from near it a light flashed; someone was doing something. Terran soldiers, perhaps, preparing to invest Hamlet Hamlet. And yet – she heard no voices. And the ship did not appear large.

She was of course armed. Every delegate to the council had to be, although the Heeb rep traditionally forgot his. Reaching into the glove compartment she fished out the old-fashioned lead-slug pistol; she had never used it and it seemed incredible to her that she might soon find herself using it now. But it seemed that she had no choice.

On foot, quietly, she sneaked past scrubby bushes, until all at once she had reached the ship; startled, she backed away, and then saw a flash of light, the activity near the base of the ship continuing.

One man, utterly absorbed, was busy with a shovel, digging a pit; he laboured away, perspiring his face wrinkled with concentration. And then suddenly he hurried back to the ship.

When he reappeared he carried a carton which he set down beside the pit. His light flashed into the carton and Annette Golding saw five grapefruit-like spheres, faintly moist and pulsing; they were alive and she recognized them. Newly-born initial constituents of Ganymedean slime moulds – she had viewed pics of them in edutext tapes. The man of course was burying them; in the soil they would grow at great speed. This portion of their life-cycle fulfilled itself immediately. And so the man hurried. The spheres might die.

She said, surprising even herself, 'You'll never get them all in the ground in time.' One sphere, in fact, had already darkened and become sunken; it was withering before their eyes. 'Listen.' She approached the man, who continued working, digging with the small shovel. 'I'll keep them moist; do you have any water?' She bent down beside him waiting. 'They really are going to perish.' Obviously he knew this, too.

Roughly the man said, 'In the ship. Get a big container.

You'll see the water tap; it's marked.' He snatched the withering sphere from its fellows, set it gently into the pit, began to cover it with loose soil which he broke with his fingers.

Annette entered the ship, found the water tap and then a bowl.

Back outside with the bowl of water she doused the swiftly-deteriorating spheres, reflecting philosophically that this was the way with fungi: everything happened fast with them, birth, growth, even death. Perhaps they were lucky. They had their tiny time to strut about.

'Thanks,' the man said as he took a second – now wet – sphere and began to bury it, too. 'I don't hope to save them all. The spores germinated on my trip – I had no place to put the plants, I just had a pot for the microscopic-size spores.' He glanced up at her briefly as he dug to enlarge the pit. 'Miss Golding,' he said.

Crouched by the carton of spheres Annette said, 'Why is it that you know me but I've never seen you before?'

'This is my second trip here,' the man said cryptically.

Already the first-buried sphere had begun to grow; in the light of the hand torch Annette saw the ground quiver and bulge, tremble as the diameter of the sphere radically increased. It was an odd, funny sight and she laughed. 'I'm sorry,' she apologized. 'But you scuttled about, popped it into the ground and now look at it. In a while it'll be as big as we are. And then it can move on.' Slime moulds, she knew, were the sole mobile fungus; they fascinated her for that reason.

'How come you know so much about them?' the man asked her.

'For years I had nothing to do but educate myself. From the – I guess you would call it hospital . . . anyhow from it, before it was razed, I got tapes on biology and zoology. It's true, is it, that when they're fully ripe a Ganymedean slime mould is intelligent enough so you can converse with it?'

'More than that intelligent.' The man swiftly planted another sphere; in his hands it quivered, jelly-like, soft.

'How wonderful,' she said. 'I find that terribly exciting.'

It would be worth staying here, to see this. 'Don't you love this?' she said, kneeling down on the far side of the carton to watch his work. 'The night smells, the air, the sounds of creatures – little ones, like hipfrogs and bell-crickets – stirring about, and then this, making these fungi grow instead of just letting them die? You're very humane; I can see that. Tell me your name.'

He glanced at her sideways. 'Why?'

'Because. So I can remember you.'

'I have someone's name,' the man said, 'so I could remember him.'

Now only one sphere remained to plant. And the first had burgeoned out, exposing itself; it had become, she discovered, a multitude of spheres, now, gummed together into a mass. 'But,' the man said, 'I wanted his name so that I could —' He did not finish, but she got the idea. 'My name is Chuck Rittersdorf,' he said.

'Are you related to Dr. Rittersdorf, the psychologist in that Terran ship? Yes, you must be her husband.' She was positive of it; the fact was totally obvious. Remembering Gabriel Baines' plan she put her hand over her mouth, giggling with mischievous excitement. 'Oh,' she said, 'if you only knew. But I can't tell you.' Another name you should remember, she thought, is Gabriel Baines. She wondered how Gabe's plan to reduce Dr. Rittersdorf by love-making had gone; she had a feeling that it had failed. But for Gabe it might well have been – even still be at this moment – a good deal of fun.

Of course all that was over, now, because Mr. Rittersdorf had arrived.

'What was your name,' she asked, 'when you were here before?'

Chuck Rittersdorf glanced at her. 'You think I change my —'

'You were someone else,' It had to be that; otherwise she would remember him. Have recognized him.

After a pause Rittersdorf said, 'Let's just say I came here and met you and returned to Terra and now I'm back.' He glared at her as if it was her fault. The last sphere having been planted he reflexively gathered up the empty carton and the small shovel, started toward the ship.

Following, Annette said, 'Will slime moulds take over our moon, now?' It occurred to her that perhaps this was part of Terra's plan for conquest. But the idea did not ring right; this man had all the appearance of someone working in stealth alone. It was too much a Pare-like idea for her.

'You could do a lot worse,' Rittersdorf said laconically. He disappeared into the ship; after hesitating she went in after him, blinking in the bright overhead light.

There on a counter lay her lead-slug pistol; she had put it down when she was involved in filling the container with water.

Picking up the pistol Rittersdorf inspected it, then turned to her with a peculiar expression, almost a grin, on his face. 'Yours?'

'Yep,' she said, humiliated. She held out her hand, hoping he would give it back. However he did not. 'Oh please,' she said. 'It's mine and I laid it down because I was trying to help; you know that.'

He studied her a long, long time. And then handed her the pistol.

'Thank you.' She felt gratitude. 'I'll remember you did that.'

'Were you going to save this moon by means of that?' Now Rittersdorf smiled. He was not bad-looking, she decided, except that he had a hectic, careworn expression and too many wrinkles. But his eyes were a clean nice blue. Perhaps, she guessed, he was in his mid-thirties. Not really old, but somewhat older than herself. His smile had a pained quality, not as if it were contrived but – she pondered. As if it were unnatural, as if for him being happy, even briefly, was difficult. He was, perhaps like Dino Watters, addicted to gloom. She felt very sorry for him if that were so. It was a terrible malady to have. Far worse than the several others.

She said, 'I don't think we can save this moon. I just wanted to protect myself personally. You know our situation here, don't you? We—'

A voice inside her mind croaked into abrupt, rudimentary life. 'Mr. Rittersdorf ...' It creaked, faded out, then returned, like the feeble sputter of a crystal set radio. '... wise thing. I see that Joan ...' The voice was gone now.

'What in God's name was that?' Annette said, appalled.

'The slime mould. One of them. I don't know which.' Chuck Rittersdorf seemed transfixed with relief. Loudly he said, 'It carries the continuity!' He shouted at her as if she were a mile away. 'He's back again! What do you say, Miss Golding? Say something!' He grabbed her all at once by the hands, whirled her in a dance-like circle of joyous, child-like celebration. '*Say* something, Miss Golding!'

'I'm glad,' Annette said dutifully, 'to see you so happy. You ought to be as joyous as often as possible. Of course I don't know what happened. Anyhow—' She disengaged her fingers from his. 'I know you deserve this, whatever it is.'

Behind her something stirred. She looked back and saw at the doorway of the ship a yellow lump which progressed sluggishly forward, undulating over the doorstep, entering. So this is how they look, she realized. In their final stage. It was breathtaking. She retreated, not in fear but in awe; it was certainly a miracle the way it had developed so rapidly. And now – as she recalled – it would stay this way indefinitely, until killed at last by too cold or too warm a climate, or by too much dryness. And, in its last extremity, it would sporify; the cycle would repeat.

As the slime mould entered the ship a second slime mould crept into sight behind it, following. And behind it a third.

Startled, Chuck Rittersdorf said, 'Which is you, Lord Running Clam?'

In Annette's mind a series of thoughts progressed. 'It is a custom for the first-born to take the formal identity of the parent. But there is no actual distinction. In a sense we are all Lord Running Clams; in another sense none of us is. I – the first – will assume the name, the others are instead inventing new names that gratify them. To me comes the feeling that we will function and thrive on this moon; the atmosphere, the humidity and the pull of gravity seem quite in order to us. You have helped diversify our location; you've carried us more than – allow me to compute – three lights years from our source. Thank you.' It – or rather they – added, 'Your ship and you yourself are about to be attacked, I'm afraid. Perhaps you should take off as soon as possible. That is why we came inside, those of us who had developed in time.'

'Attacked by whom?' Chuck Rittersdorf demanded, pressing a button at the control panel which slid the hatch of the ship shut. Seating himself he prepared the ship for departure.

'As we ferret it out,' the thoughts came to Annette from the three slime moulds, 'a group of natives is involved, those who refer to themselves in their own minds as Manses. Evidently they have succeeded in blowing up some other ship —'

'Good grief,' Chuck Rittersdorf grated. 'That would be Mary's.'

'Yes,' the slime mould agreed. 'The approaching Manses are quite consciously congratulating themselves in their typically prideful fashion on successfully fighting off Dr. Rittersdorf. However she is not dead. Those in the first ship were able to escape; they are at unknown loci on the moon at present, and the Manses are hunting them.'

'What about the nearby Terran warships?' Rittersdorf asked.

'What warships? The Manses have thrown some novel variety of protective screen about their settlement. So for the moment they are safe.' The slime mould, then, amplified with a conjecture of its own. 'But it will not last long and this they know. They are on the offensive only temporarily. But they still love it. They are extremely happy, while all the while the baffled Terran line-ships buzz about uselessly.'

The poor Manses, Annette thought to herself. Unable to look ahead, dwelling on the now, sallying forth to do battle as if they had a reasonable chance. And yet, was her own view much better? Was her willingness to accept failure an improvement?

No wonder all the clans of the moon depended on the Manses; it remained the only clan with courage. And the vitality which that courage gave.

The rest of us, Annette realized, lost long ago. Before the first Terran, Dr. Mary Rittersdorf, showed up.

Gabriel Baines, driving at a paltry seventy-five miles an hour toward Hamlet Hamlet, saw the small, brisk ship race up into the night sky and knew that he was too late, knew it without having any understanding directly of the situation. Annette, his near-Psionic talent informed him, was in the ship or else the ship – those aboard it – had destroyed her. In any case she was gone and so he slowed the car, feeling bitterness and despair.

There was virtually nothing he could do, now. Hence he might as well turn back toward Adolfville, to his own settlement and people. Be with them in these last, tragic days of their existence.

As he started to turn his car around, something rumbled and clanked past him, heading toward Hamlet Hamlet; it was a crawling monster if not a super-monster. Cast of high process iron as only the Manses knew how to bring off, sweeping the landscape ahead with its powerful lights, it advanced flying a red and black flag, the battle symbol of the Manses.

Evidently he was seeing the initial stages of a surface counter-attack. But against precisely what? The Manses were certainly in action, but surely not against Hamlet Hamlet. Perhaps they had been attempting to reach the small, swift ship before it took off. But for them, as for himself, it was too late.

He honked his horn. The turret of the Mans tank flopped open; the tank circled back toward him and a Mans, unfamiliar to him, stood up and waved in greeting to him. The Mans's face was inflamed with enthusiasm; obviously he was hotly enjoying this experience, his military duties in defence of the moon, for which they had prepared so long.

The situation, depressing as it was to Baines, had an opposite effect on the Mans: for him it permitted a flowery, bellicose puffing and posturing. Gabriel Baines was not surprised.

'Hi,' the Mans in the tank yelled, grinning broadly.

Baines called back with as little sourness as he could manage, 'I see the ship got away from your people.'

'We'll get it.' The Mans did not lose his cheerfulness; he pointed instead toward the sky. 'Watch, buddy. For the missile.'

A second later something flashed overhead; luminous fragments rained down and Gabriel Baines realized that the Terran ship had been hit. The Mans was correct. As usual ... it was a clan characteristic.

Horrified, because of his intuition that Annette Golding had been within the ship, he said, 'You barbaric, monstrous Manses —' The main debris was descending to his right; slamming his car door he started up the engine, left the road and bumped across the open countryside. The Mans tank, meanwhile, shut its turret and began to follow, filling the night with its screeching clankings.

Baines reached the remains of the ship first. Some kind of emergency parachute device, a huge globe of gas, had sprung from the rear of the ship, letting it down more or less gently; it now lay half-buried in the soil, its tail up, smoking as if – and this horrified Baines still further – it was about to disintegrate; the atomic furnace within had reached, he thought, near-critical mass, and once it went that would be that.

Getting out of his car he sprinted toward the hatch of the ship. As he reached it the hatch swung open; a Terran energed unsteadily, and after him came Annette Golding and then, with immense technical difficulty, a homogenous yellow blob that flowed to the lip of the hatch and dropped with a plop to the ground below.

Annette said, 'Gabe, don't let the Manses shoot this man; he's a good person. He's even kind to slime moulds.'

Now the Mans tank had clattered up; once again the turret of the tank popped aside and again the Mans within raised himself up. This time, however, he held a laser beam, which he aimed at the Terran and Annette, Grinning, the Mans said, 'We got you.' It was clear that as soon as he had fully savoured his enjoyment he would kill them; the ferocity of the Mans mind was unfathomable.

'Listen,' Baines said, waving to the Mans. 'Leave these people alone; this woman is from Hamlet Hamlet – she's one of us.'

'One of us?' the Mans echoed. 'If she's from Hamlet Hamlet she's not one of us.'

'Oh, *come on,*' Baines said. 'Are you Manses so hopped up that you don't recognize or remember the common brotherhood of the clans at a time of crisis? Put your gun down.' He walked slowly back to his parked car, not taking his eyes from the Mans. In the car, under the seat, he had his own weapon. If he could get his hands on it he would use it on the Mans to save Annette's life. 'I'll report you to Howard Straw,' he said, and opening the car door groped within. 'I'm a colleague of his – I'm the Pare rep to the council.' His fingers closed over the butt of the gun; he lifted it out, aimed it and at the same time clicked off the safety.

The click, audible in the still night air, caused the Mans in the tank instantly to swivel; the laser beam was now pointed at Gabriel Baines. Neither Baines nor the Mans said anything; they faced each other, not moving, not firing – the light was not adequate and neither could make out the other fully.

A thought, emanating from heaven knew where, entered Gabriel Baines' mind. 'Mr. Rittersdorf, your wife is in the vicinity; I'm picking up her cephalic activity. Therefore I advise you to drop to the ground.'

The Terran, and also Annette Golding, both fell at once on their faces; the Mans in the tank, startled, moved his gun away from Gabriel Baines, peered into the night uncertainly.

An almost perfectly-directed bolt from a laser weapon passed over the prone figure of the Terran, entering the hull of the ruined ship and vanishing in a sizzle of liquefied metal. The Mans in the tank leaped, sought to pinpoint the origin of the shot; he clutched his own weapon in a spasm of instinctive response but did not fire. Neither he nor Gabriel Baines could make out what was happening. Who was shooting at whom?

To Annette, Gabriel Baines shouted, '*Get in the car!*' He held the door open; Annette lifted her head, gazed at him, then turned to the Terran beside her. The two of them exchanged a glance and then both stumbled up and snaked their way swiftly to the car.

In the turret of the tank the Mans opened fire, but not at Annette and the Terran; he was firing into the darkness, in the direction from which the laser bolt had come. Then all at once he popped back down inside his tank; the turret slammed shut and the tank, with a shudder, started up and rumbled forward, in the direction toward which the Mans had fired. At the same time a missile departed from the forward tube of the tank; it went straight, parallel to the ground and then, all at once, detonated. Gabriel Baines, trying to turn his car around, the Terran and Annette in the front seat beside him, felt the ground leap and devour him; he shut his eyes but what was happening could not be closed out.

Beside him the Terran cursed. Annette Golding gave a moan.

Those — Manses, Baines thought savagely as he felt the car lift, picked up by the shock-waves of the exploding missile.

'You can't use a missile like that,' the Terran's voice came very faintly over the uproar, 'at such close range.'

Whipped, carried by the concussion of the blast, the car spun over and over; Gabriel Baines bounced against the safety-padding of the roof, then against the safety-padding of the dashboard; all the security devices that an intelligent Pare would install in his vehicle to protect himself against attack came on automatically, but they were not enough. On and on the car rolled, and in it Gabriel Baines said to himself, *I hate the Manses.* I'll never advocate co-operation with them again.

Someone, thrown against him, said, 'Oh God!' It was Annette Golding; he caught her, hung on to her. All the windows of the car had burst; bits of plastic rained, showering on him and he smelled the acrid stench of something buring, perhaps his own clothing – it would not have surprised him. Now the protective anti-thermal foam spouted in gobs from the nozzles on all sides of him, activated by the temperature; in a moment he was floundering in a grey, sea, unable to catch hold of anything ... he had lost Annette again. Goddamn, he thought, these protective devices that cost me so much time and skins are almost worse than the blast itself. Is there a moral there? he asked himself as he tumbled in the slimy foam. It was like being lathered up for some great orgy of body-hair cutting; he cringed and gagged, struggled to get free of the sticky stuff.

'Help,' he said.

No one and nothing answered.

I'm going to blow up that tank, Gabriel Baines thought to himself as he floundered. I swear it; I'll get back at them, at our enemy, the arrogant Manses ... I always knew they were against us.

'You are mistaken, Mr. Baines,' a thought appeared in his mind, calm and sensible. 'The soldier who fired the missile did not intend to hurt you. Before he fired he made a careful calculation – or so he believed. You must beware of seeing malice behind accidental injury. At this moment, he is attempting to reach you and drag you from your flaming car. And those with you as well.'

'If you can hear me,' Baines thought back, 'help me.'

'I can do nothing. I am a slime mould; I can't under any circumstances approach the flames, being too heat-sensitive, as recent events demonstrate clearly. Two of my brethren have in fact already perished trying. And I am not ready at this time to sporify again.' It added, gratuitously, 'Anyhow, if I were to try to save anyone it would be Mr. Rittersdorf. There with you in the car ... the man from Terra.'

A hand grabbed Gabriel Baines by the collar; he was lifted, dragged from the car, tossed off to one side. The

Mans, with typical abnormal physical strength, now reached into the burning car and tugged Annette Golding to safety.

'Next Mr. Rittersdorf,' the slime mould's anxious thoughts came, reaching Gabriel Baines where he lay.

Once more, with complete disregard for his own safety – also typical of the hyperactive temperament – the Mans disappeared into the car. This time when he returned he was pulling the Terran out.

'Thank you,' the slime mould thought, with relief and gratitude. 'In exchange for your deed allow me to give you information; your missile did *not* reach Dr Rittersdorf, and she and the CIA simulacrum, Mr. Mageboom, are still nearby out of sight in the darkness, seeking an opportunity to fire at you again. So you had better return as soon as possible to your tank.'

'Why me?' the Mans said angrily.

'Because your clan destroyed their ship,' the slime mould thought back. 'Hostilities between you and them are overt. Hurry!'

The Mans soldier sprinted for his tank.

But he did not reach it. Two-thirds of the way there he pitched forward on his face as a laser beam appeared from the darkness, touched him briefly and then winked out.

And now we're going to get it, Gabriel Baines realized wretchedly as he sat wiping the foam from himself. I wonder if she recognizes me, remembers me from our encounter earlier today ... and if so, would that cause her to want to spare me – or to kill me sooner?

Beside him the Terran, also named Rittersdorf by some peculiar freak of coincidence, struggled to a sitting position, said, 'You had a gun. What became of it?'

'Still in the car. I suppose.'

'Why would she kill us?' Annette Golding gasped.

Rittersdorf said, 'Because she knows why I'm here. I came to this moon to kill her.' He seemed calm. 'By the time tonight's over one of us will be dead. Either she or I.' Obviously he had made up his mind.

Overhead the roar of a retro-rocket sounded. It was another ship, a huge one, Gabriel Baines realized, and he felt hope; possibly they had a chance of escaping from Dr. Rittersdorf – who certainly, as he had suspected, was deranged – after all. Even if the ship contained Terrans. Because it was so clear that Dr. Rittersdorf was acting out a feral impulse of her own, without official sanction. At least he hoped so.

A flare burst above them; the night became white and everything, each small object down to the stones on the ground, stood out with august clarity. The wrecked ship of Mr. Rittersdorf, the abandoned tank of the dead Mans, the corpse of the Mans himself, sprawled not far off, Gabriel Baines's car, burning itself into a clinker, and there, a hundred yards away, a vast molten, seething pocket where the missile had exploded. And – among trees to the far right, two human figures. Mary Rittersdorf and whoever else the slime mould had said. Now, too, he saw the slime mould; it had taken refuge near the wrecked ship. In the light of the flare it was a macabre sight; he suppressed an impulse to heehaw.

'A Terran warship?' Annette Golding said.

'No,' Rittersdorf said. 'Look at the rabbit on its side.'

'A rabbit!' Her eyes widened. 'Is it a race of sentient rabbits? Is there such a thing?'

'No,' the slime mould's thoughts came to Gabriel Baines. With seeming regret the slime mould said, 'This apparition is Bunny Hentman, searching for you, Mr. Rittersdorf. It was, as you anticipated, pessimistically, a relatively easy guess on his part that you came here to Alpha III M2; he left Brahe City shortly after you departed from Terra.' It explained, 'I am just now obtaining these thoughts from his mind; of course up to now I have been ignorant of this, being in the spore stage only.'

I don't understand this, Gabriel Baines said to himself. Who in God's name is Bunny Hentman? A rabbit deity? And why is he looking for Rittersdorf? As a matter of fact he was not even certain who Rittersdorf was. Mary Rittersdorf's husband? Her brother? The whole situation was confused in his mind and he wished he were back at Adolfville, in the prepared security positions which his clan had elaborated over the years for just such abominations as this.

Evidently, he decided, *we are doomed*. They are all ganged up against us – the Manses, Dr. Rittersdorf, the fat ship overhead with its bunny totem painted on its side, and, somewhere nearby, the Terran military authorities waiting to move in ... what chance do we have? A massive clot of defeatism rose up within him – and well it might, he thought grimly.

Leaning toward Annette Golding, who sat weakly trying to shake the anti-thermal foam from her arms, he said, 'Good-bye.'

She looked at him with large, dark eyes. 'Where are you going, Gabe?'

'What the heck,' he said bitterly, 'does it matter?' They had no chance here, caught by the flare, in sight of Dr. Rittersdorf and her laser beam – the weapon which had already killed the Mans soldier. He rose unsteadily to his feet, slopping off foam, shaking himself like a wet dog. 'I'm leaving,' he informed Annette, and then he felt sad, because of her; not his own death but hers – that was what distressed him. 'I wish I could do something for you,' he said, on impulse. 'But that woman is insane; I know firsthand.'

'Oh,' Annette said, and nodded. 'It didn't go well, then. Your plan regarding her.' She glanced at Rittersdorf, then, covertly.

' "Well," did you say?' He laughed; it was really amusing. 'Remind me to describe it to you sometime.' Bending, he kissed her; Annette's face, slippery and damp from the foam, pressed against his muzzle and then he straightened up and walked away, seeing clearly by the light of the still-functioning flare.

As he walked he waited for the laser beam to touch him. So brilliant was the glare that, involuntarily, he half-shut his eyes; squinting, he made his way along step by step, in no particular direction ... why hadn't she shot? It would come, he knew; he wished it would hurry. Death at the hands of this woman – it was a good fate for a Pare; ironic and deserved.

A shape blocked his way. He opened his eyes. Three shapes, and all of them familiar to him; he faced Sarah Apostoles, Omar Diamond and Ignatz Ledebur, the three ultimate visionaries on the moon, or, put another way, he thought to himself, the three greatest nuts from among all the clans. What are they doing here? Levitated or teleported or whatever they do; anyhow got here by their neo-magic. He felt only irritation at seeing them. The situation was enough of a mess as it was.

'Evil confronts evil,' Ignatz Ledebur intoned sententiously. 'But out of this our friends must be preserved. Have faith in us, Gabriel. We will see that you are conducted very soon, psychopomp-wise, to safety.' He extended his hand, then, to Baines, his face transfigured.

'Not me,' Baines said. 'Annette Golding; help her.' It seemed to him, then, that all at once the weight of being a Pare, of defending himself against all harm, had been lifted from him. For the first time in his life he had acted, not to save himself, but to save someone else.

'She will be saved too,' Sarah Apostoles assured him. 'By the same agency.'

Above their heads the retro-rockets of the big bunny-inscribed ship continued to roar; the ship was descending slowly. Coming down to land.

TWELVE

Beside Mary, the CIA man Dan Mageboom said, 'You heard that slime mould's statement; that ship contains the TV comic Bunny Hentman, who's on our top-want list.' Agitated, Mageboom plucked at his throat, obviously groping for the intercom transmitter which linked him with the powerful CIA relay aboard the nearby Terran ships of the line.

'I also heard the slime mould declare,' Mary said, 'that you're not a person but a simulacrum.'

'Person, shmerson,' Mageboom said. 'Does it matter?' Now he had found the microphone of the 'com; he spoke into it, ignoring her, telling his superiors that Bunny Hentman had turned up at last. And this, Mary thought, on the basis of a verbal utterance by a Ganymedean fungus. The credulity of the CIA passed all understanding. However, it was probably true. No doubt Hentman was aboard the ship; it did have as its ident marking the rabbit symbol familiar to viewers of the TV show.

She recalled, then, the ugly episode when she had approached the Hentman organization in her efforts to obtain a job for Chuck as scriptwriter. They had neatly, adroitly propositioned her and she had never forgotten this; nor would she ever. A 'side-deal,' they had euphemistically called it. The lewd skunks, she thought as she watched the ship settle down like some enormous over-ripe football.

'My instructions,' Mageboom spoke up suddenly, 'are to approach the Hentman ship and attempt to arrest Mr. Hentman.' He scrambled to his feet; amazed, she watched him trot toward the parked ship. Should I let him go? she asked herself. Why not? she decided, and lowered her laser beam. She had nothing against Mageboom, human or simulacrum, whatever he was. In any case he was decidedly ineffectual, like all CIA personnel she had met, during her years with Chuck. Chuck! At once she turned her attention back to him, where he huddled with Annette Golding. You've come a long way, dear, she thought. Just to pay me back. Is it worth it? But, she thought, you've also found a new woman; I wonder how you're going to enjoy having a polymorphic schizophrenic for a mistress. Pointing the laser tube she fired.

The harsh white light of the flare abruptly winked out; darkness returned. For a moment she could not understand what had happened and then she realized that now, since the ship had landed, it had no further use for illumination; hence it had shot the flare down. It preferred darkness to light, like some photophobic insect scuttling behind a bookcase.

She could not tell if her shot had touched Chuck.

Damn it, she thought in angered dismay. And then she felt fear. After all, it was she who was in danger; Chuck had become an assassin, here to murder her – she was perfectly, rationally, wholly conscious of that: his presence on the moon verified what with professional acumen she had long suspected. It occurred to her now that during the trip and initial days on Alpha III M2 Chuck might easily have been the inhabitant of the Mageboom simulacrum. Why hadn't he done it then, instead of waiting? In any case that was not true now, since the simulacrum would be operated from Terra; that was CIA policy, as she well knew from remarks Chuck had made over the years.

I should get away, she said to herself. Before he does do it. Where can I go? The big warships can't come in because those lunatics and maniacs have that shield up; they're still trying to trace a path through it, I suppose – whatever the reason she had lost contact with Terran military. And now Mageboom had gone; she no longer could reach the lineships through him. I wish I was back on Earth, she said miserably to herself. This whole project has turned out terribly. It's insane, Chuck and I trying to slay each other; how did something ghastly and psychotic like this develop?

I thought we had managed to separate ... didn't the divorce accomplish that?

She thought, I never should have had my attorney Bob Alfson get those potent-pics of Chuck and that girl. That's probably what made him do this. However, it was too late; she had not only got the pics but had in addition used them in court. They were now a matter of public record; anyone with a little morbid curiosity who wanted to could search up the court record, animate the pics and enjoy the sequences of Chuck and the Trieste fray making love. In hoc signo vinces, my dear...

Chuck, she thought, I'd like to surrender; I'd like to get back out of this, if not for your sake then for mine. Can't we be – friends?

It was a squandered hope.

Now something peculiar squirmed at the horizon; she started at it, wondering at its magnitude. Surely it was too immense to be a human construct. The atmosphere was alive with something real; the stars had become dull, partially extinguished in that region and the thing, whatever it was, now began to assume a nearly-luminous shape.

The shape was that of a master lizard and she realized at once what she was witnessing; this was a schizophrenic projection, part of the primordial world experienced by the advanced psychotic, and evidently a familiar entity here on Alpha III M2 – except why was *she* seeing it?

Could a schizophrenic – or possibly several of them acting in concert – have co-ordinated their psychotic perceptions with a Psionic talent? Weird idea, she thought nervously, and hoped that this was not the explanation. Because such a combination would be lethal, if these people had stumbled on to it during their quarter-century of freedom.

She remembered the hebephrenic whom she had met at Gandhitown ... he whom perhaps rightly they had called a saint, Ignatz Ledebur. At the time she had felt, despite the squalor, something of that about him, the invigorating and yet terrifying scent of unnatural abilities directed lord only knew where. In any case she had been fascinated at last by him.

The lizard – seemingly quite real – stretched itself, writhed its elongated neck and opened its jaws. And from it a fireball-like apparition vomited out, igniting that portion of the sky; the fireball drifted upward as if carried by the atmosphere, and she breathed a sigh of relief: at least it was departing, rather than descending. Frankly she was apprehensive about it. She did not relish this sight one bit; it was too much like covert dream-sequences which she had experienced in her own sleep – experienced and not discussed or contemplated, not wanting even to scrutinize them in secrecy, much less discuss them with anyone else, any professional psychiatrist. God forbid.

The fireball ceased ascending. And began to break up into streamers of luminosity. The streamers drifted down, and, to her numbed surprise, quivered, as if shaped by hand, into enormous words.

The words comprised a sign. In the most literal sense. And – a sign, she realized with embarrassment and horror, directed at her. The words blazed out:

DR. RITTERSDORF, AVOID BLOODSHED
AND
YOU WILL BE PERMITTED TO LEAVE US.

And then in smaller blazing letters, as if by afterthought, this:

THE HOLY TRIUMVIRATE.

They're out of their minds, Mary Rittersdorf said to herself, and felt a hysterical laugh rise up in her throat. It's not *I* who am seeking bloodshed; it's Chuck! Why in God's name pick on me? If you're so holy you ought to be able to perceive something as obvious as that. But she realized, perhaps it was not so obvious. She had fired at Chuck, and before that – she had killed the Mans soldier as he fled back to his tank. So perhaps after all her conscience – her intentions – were not so unstained.

More words formed.

PLEASE REPLY.

'Good grief,' she protested. '*How?*' She could hardly be

expected to write her own answering letters of fire in the sky; she was scarcely a triumvirate of holy hebephrenic saint-psychotics. This is just terrible, she said to herself. Just grotesque to have to endure. And if I'm to listen to them, to believe them, I'm somehow to blame – somehow responsible for the malignance that exists between me and Chuck. And I'm not.

There all at once was a red glow of laser-beam activity from the vicinity of the Bunny Hentman ship. Dan Mageboom, CIA simulacrum and agent in the field, was evidently fighting it out; she wondered what success he or it was having. Probably very little, if you knew the CIA. Anyhow she wished him luck.

She wondered whether the Holy Triumvirate had any instructions for him, too. Mageboom could use help; alone, he busily engaged in his frontal attack on the Hentman ship, firing away with what she now perceived to be an unhuman dedication. He may be a simulacrum, obviously is in fact a simulacrum, she said to herself, but no one can say he's a coward. And the rest of us, she reflected, she herself, Chuck and the girl with him, the slime mould, even the Mans soldier who had loped futilely for the protection of his tank – every one of us are now pinned down by fright, motivated by nothing more than the animal instinct to save our individual hides. Out of all of them only Dan Mageboom, the simulacrum, had gone on to the offensive. And, or at least so it appeared to her, Mageboom's assault on the Hentman ship was destined for ludicrous failure.

New glowing, enormous words now appeared in the sky. And, thank heaven, these were not specifically directed at her; she was spared the humiliation, this time, of being singled out.

CEASE YOUR WARFARE AND LOVE ONE ANOTHER.

All right, Mary Rittersdorf thought agreeably. I'll begin; I'll love my ex-husband Chuck, who came here to kill me; how's that for a new start in the midst of all this?

The red glow of laser beams near and around the parked Hentman ship picked up in intensity; the simulacrum had failed to respond to the great warning words: it continued its futile – but highly gallant struggle.

For the first time in her life she fully admired someone.

From the instant that Bunny Hentman's ship appeared the slime mould had become apprehensive; its thoughts, reaching Chuck Rittersdorf, were saturated with concern, now.

'I am receiving ghastly malappraisals of the recent events,' the slime mould thought to Chuck. 'All emanating from the Hentman ship; he and his staff, and in particular the several Alphanes around him, have dreamed up a philosophy which places you, Mr. Rittersdorf, dead centre in the fictitious conspiracy against them.' The slime mould was silent for an interval and then it thought, 'They have dispatched a launch.'

'Why?' Chuck said, and felt his heart-rate change.

'Pics taken during the exposure of the flare revealed your presence here on the surface. The launch will land; you will be nabbed; it is inevitable.'

Scrambling to his feet Chuck said to Annette Golding, 'I'm going to try to get away. You stay here.' He started to run, away from the scene, in no direction in particular; he simply hobbled across the uneven ground as best he could. Meanwhile, the Hentman ship had landed. And, as he ran, he now made out an odd phenomenon; red trails of laser beams lit up in the form of dull streaks near the parked ship. Someone – or some group – had initiated an overt conflict with the Hentman ship as soon as it had opened its hatch.

Who? he wondered. Not Mary, surely. One of the clans here on the moon? Perhaps a spearhead of the Manses ... but didn't they already have their hands full, fighting off Terra, maintaining the dubious protective shield over Da Vinci Heights? And the Manses employed some other form of weapon rather than the old-fashioned laser beam; therefore this sounded more like the CIA.

Mageboom, he decided. The simulacrum had received instructions to engage the Hentman ship in battle. And being a machine it had accordingly done so.

The Manses, he thought, are fighting Terra; Mageboom, representing the CIA, is busy shooting it out with Hentman. My ex-wife is fighting me. And Hentman is my enemy. Logically, what does this add up to? It must be possible to draw up a rational equation, extracted from this baroque interchange; it surely can be simplified. If the Manses are fighting Terra, and Hentman is fighting Terra, then the Manses and Hentman are allies. Hentman is fighting me, so I am his enemy and hence the ally of Terra. Mary is fighting me and I am fighting Hentman, so Mary is the ally of Hentman, hence the enemy of Terra. However, Mary leads the Terran task-force of do-gooding psychologists who landed here; she came as a rep of Terra. So, logically, Mary is both the enemy and the ally of Terra.

The equation simply could not be worked out ... there were just too many participants in the struggle, doing too many illogical things, some, as in Mary's case, entirely on their own.

But wait; his efforts to make a rational sensible equation out of the situation had borne fruit after all; as he trotted through the darkness he had an insight into his own dilemma. He was fighting to save himself from Hentman, the compatriot of the Alphanes and the enemy of Terra; this meant that by rigorous, unassailable logic, he himself was an ally of Terra *whether he recognized it or not*. Forgetting Mary for a moment – her actions undoubtedly were not sanctioned by the Terran establishment – the situation could be viewed clearly for a moment: his personal hope lay in reaching a Terran warship, seeking sanctuary there. Aboard a Terran ship of the line he would be safe – safe there and only there.

But the clans of Alpha III M2 were fighting Terra, he remembered all at once; the equation was even more complex than he had first seen. If he were – logically – an ally of Terra, then he was an enemy of the clans, an enemy of Annette Golding, of everyone on the moon.

Ahead of him his shadow, feebly, was cast. Some light, originating from the sky, had materialized. Another flare? Turning, he briefly came to a halt.

And saw, in the sky, huge letters of fire, a message directed at of all people – his wife. *Avoid bloodshed*, the sign admonished. *And you will be permitted to leave us.* Evidently this was a manifestation of the demented, silly tactics of the psychotics living here, probably of the deteriorated ones, the hebephrenics of Gandhitown. Mary, of course, would pay no attention. However, the glowing sign made him realize one further factor: the clans of this moon recognized Mary as their enemy. Mary was his enemy, too; he had tried to kill her and she him. Hence, by logic, this made him an ally of the clans. But his relationship to Terra made him an enemy of the clans. So there was no way of ignoring the conclusion of the entire line of his logical reasoning, melancholy as it was. He was both an ally and an enemy of the clans of Alpha III M2; he was for and against them.

At that point he gave up. Forewent the use of logic. Turning, he once more began to run.

The old adage, derived from the meditations of the sophisticated warrior-kings of ancient India, that 'my enemy's enemy is my friend' had just not worked out in this situation. And that was that.

Something buzzed low over his head. And a voice, artificially magnified, howled at him, 'Rittersdorf! Stop, stand still! Or we'll kill you on the spot.' The voice boomed and echoed, bouncing back from the ground; it had been beamed at him, directed full-force from what he knew to be the Hentman launch overhead. They had, as predicted by the slime mould, located him.

Panting, he stopped.

The launch hovered in the air at the ten-foot level. A metal ladder flopped noisily down and once more the artificially-reinforced voice instructed him. 'Climb the ladder, Rittersdorf. Without messing around or any delay!' In the night gloom, illuminated only by the glowing sign in the sky, the magnesium ladder quivered insubstantially like some link with the supernatural.

Taking hold, Chuck Rittersdorf, with leaden, heart-clutched reluctance, began to climb. A moment later he stepped from the ladder and found himself in the control cab of the launch. Two wild-eyed Terrans, with laser pistols, faced him. Paid enemies of Bunny Hentman, he realized. One was Gerald Feld.

The ladder was drawn back up; the launch scooted for the parent ship at the greatest velocity possible.

'We saved your life,' Feld said. 'That woman, your ex-wife, would have ripped you apart if you had stayed out there.'

'So?' Chuck said.

'So we're returning good for evil. What more can you ask? You won't find Bunny upset or sore; he's too big a man not to take all this in his stride. After all, no matter how bad things go he can always migrate to the Alphane empire.' Feld managed to smile, as if the thought struck him as a happy one. From Hentman's point of view it meant things were not intolerable after all; a way out existed.

The launch reached its parent ship; an aperture tube opened, the launch fitted itself in place and then slid without use of power down the tube and to its berth, deep within the big ship.

When the launch had opened its hatch Chuck Rittersdorf found himself confronted by Bunny Hentman, who mopped his florid forehead worriedly and said, 'Some lunatic's attacking us. One of the psychotics, here, evidently, from the way he's acting.' The ship vibrated. 'See?' Hentman said, with anger. 'He's charging us with a hand weapon.' Waving Chuck toward him he said, 'Come along with me, Rittersdorf; I want to have a conference with you. There's been a hell of a misunderstanding between you and I but I think we can still work it out. Right?'

'Between you and me,' Chuck said, in automatic correction.

Hentman led the way down a narrow corridor; Chuck followed. No one appeared at this point to have a laser beam trained on him, but he obeyed anyhow; one probably existed potentially – he was still patently a prisoner of the organization.

A girl, naked to the waist, wearing only shorts, strolled across-corridor ahead of them, smoking a cigarette meditatively. There was some aspect about her that Chuck found familiar. And then, as she disappeared through a doorway, he realized who she was. Patty Weaver. In his flight from the Sol system Hentman had been provident enough to bring at least one of his mistresses with him.

'In here,' Hentman said, unlocking a door.

Within the small, barren cabin Hentman shut the two of them up, then began immediately to pace with a restless, frantic intensity. For the time being he said nothing; he remained preoccupied. Every now and then the ship again vibrated under the attack directed at it. Once the overhead light went so far as to dim, but soon returned. Hentman glared up, then resumed his pacing.

'Rittersdorf,' Hentman said, 'I've got no choice; I've had to go—' A knock sounded at the door. 'Jeez,' Hentman said, and went to open the door a crack. 'Oh, it's you.'

Outside, now with a cotton shirt on, the tails not tucked in, the buttons not buttoned, Patty Weaver said, 'I just wanted to apologize to Mr. Rittersdorf for—'

'Go away,' Hentman said, shutting the door. He turned back to face Chuck. 'I've had to go over to the Alphanes.' More perspiration, in huge wax-like drops, emerged on his forehead; he did not bother to wipe them away. 'Do you blame me? My TV career's ruined by that goddam CIA; I've got nothing left on Terra. If I can—'

'She has big breasts,' Chuck said.

'Who? Patty? Oh yes.' Hentman nodded. 'Well, it's that operation they give in Hollywood and New York. It's more the rage now than the dilation, and she's had that done, too. She would have looked great on the show. Like a lot of things, too bad it didn't work out. You know, I darn near didn't get out of Brahe City. They thought they had me, but of course I was tipped off. Just in time.' He glared at Chuck with nervous accusation. 'If I can deliver Alpha III M2 to the Alphanes then I'm in; I can live the rest of my life in peace. If I can't, if Terra manages to take over this moon, then I'm not in.' He looked tired and depressed, now; he seemed to have shrunk. Telling Chuck this had been too much for him. 'What's your comment?' Hentman murmured. 'Speak up?'

'Hmm,' Chuck said.
'That's a comment?'
Chuck said, 'If you imagine I still have any influence with my ex-wife and her report to TERPLAN on this —'
'No,' Hentman agreed, nodding curtly. 'I know you can't influence her decision as to this operation; we saw you all down there, taking potshots at each other. Like animals.' He glowered, his energy returning. 'You kill my brother-in-law, Cherigan; you're ready to – in fact eager to – kill your wife ... what kind of lives do you people lead? I never saw such a thing. And leaking my location to the CIA, on top of everything else.'
'The Paraclete has deserted us,' Chuck offered.
'The parakeet? What parakeet?' Hentman wrinkled up his nose.
'There's a war on, here. Let's say that. Maybe that explains some of it. If it doesn't —' He shrugged. It was the best he could do.
'That somewhat hefty girl you were lying with,' Hentman said. 'Out there where your ex was shooting at you. She's a local nut, isn't she? From one of the settlements here?' He eyed Chuck keenly.
'You could say that,' Chuck said, with reluctance; the choice of wording did not especially appeal to him.
'Can you reach their governing inter-settlement supreme type council through her?'
'I suppose.'
Hentman said, 'Here's the only workable solution. With or without your damn parakeet or whatever it is. Have their council meet and listen to you, to your proposal.' Drawing himself up, Hentman said with firmness. 'Tell them to ask for Alphane protection from Terra. Tell them they've got to ask the Alphanes to come in here and occupy this moon. So it'll legally become Alphane territory under those damn protocols, whatever they are; I don't quite understand them but the Alphs do and so does Terra. And in exchange —' He did not take his eyes from Chuck's face; tiny, unwinking, his eyes challenged everyone, all things. 'The Alphanes will guarantee the civil liberties of the clans. No

hospitalization. No therapy. You won't be treated as nuts: you'll be treated as bona fide colonists, owning land and engaging in manufacture and commerce, whatever it is you all do.'

'Don't say "you,"' Chuck said. 'I'm not a clan member, here.'

'You think they'd go for that, Rittersdorf?'

'I – don't honestly know.'

'Sure you do. You were here before, in that CIA simulacrum. Our agent, our informant at CIA, told us every move you made.'

So there was a Hentman person at CIA. He had been right; the CIA had been infiltrated. That was just about par for it, too.

'Don't look at me like that,' Hentman said. 'They've got some nurt of theirs in here; don't forget that. Unfortunately I could never make out who he is. Sometimes I think it's Jerry Feld; other days I think it's Dark. Anyhow it was through our man at CIA that we learned you had been suspended, and so naturally we let you go – what good were you to us if you couldn't reach your wife here on Alpha III M2? I mean, let's be reasonable.'

Chuck said, 'And through their agent in your organization —'

'Yeah, the CIA knew within minutes that I'd cancelled the script idea and dropped you so off they went, slamming – they thought – the door on me ... as you read in the 'papes. But of course through my agent with them I knew the blade was about to fall, so I got away. And their agent in my organization let them know I had left Terra, only he didn't know where exactly I had gone. Only Cherigan and Feld knew that.' Philosophically Hentman said, 'Maybe I'll never find out who the CIA has in here. It's not important, now. I kept most of my dealings with the Alphs top secret, even from members of my staff, because of course I knew we'd been infiltrated right from the start.' He shook his head. 'What a mess.'

Chuck said, 'Who's your agent at CIA?'

'Jack Elwood.' Hentman grinned lopsidedly, gleeful at

Chuck's reaction. 'How come do you suppose Elwood was willing to release that expensive pursuit ship to you? *I* told him to. I wanted you to get here. Why do you imagine Elwood urged you so strongly originally to take control of the Mageboom simulacrum? That was my strategy. From the start. Now, let's hear your info about these clans here and which way they'll jump.'

No wonder Hentman and his writers had been able to whip together the so-called 'TV script' which they had dropped in his lap; through Elwood they had manoeuvred at dead-centre, just as Hentman was now admitting.

But that was not entirely true. Elwood could inform the Hentman organization of the existence of the Mageboom simulacrum, who operated it and where it was bound. But that was all. Elwood did not know the rest.

'Admittedly I was here before,' Chuck said. 'And spent some time here, but at the Heeb settlement, which isn't representative; the Heebs are at the bottom of the scale. I have no knowledge of either the Pares or the Manses and they're the ones who run the affair, here.' He recalled Mary's brilliant analysis of the situation, her account of the intricate caste system in operation on Alpha III M2. It had proved correct.

Hentman, his eyes intense, said, 'Will you try it? I personally believe the whole bunch of them have something to gain; if I was them I'd take it. Their alternative is to go back into enforced hospitalization – and that's it. Take it or leave it ... put it that way to them. And I'll tell you what you'll get out of it.'

'By all means,' Chuck said. 'Dilate on that aspect.'

'If you do this we'll instruct Elwood to take you back into the CIA.'

Chuck remained silent.

'Kriminy,' Hentman said plaintively. 'You don't even bother to answer. Okay, you saw Patty here in the ship. We'll instruct her to be nice to you. Know what I mean?' He winked, a hasty, nervous twitch.

'No,' Chuck said emphatically. That had turned out too unpleasantly.

'All right, Rittersdorf.' Hentman sighed. 'We'll really up it. If you'll do this for us we'll toss you a big bone, something out of the class of what I've named.' He took a deep raucous breath. 'We'll guarantee to do the job of killing your wife for you. As painlessly and quickly as possible. And that's very painless ... and very quick.'

After what seemed like an endless time to both men Chuck said, 'I can't make out why you think I'd like Mary dead.' He was able to meet Hentman's shrewd gaze, but the effort required was great.

Hentman said, 'Like I said – I watched you two scrunched down taking potshots at each other like a couple of wild animals.'

'I was defending myself.'

'Sure,' Hentman said, nodding in a parody of compliance.

'Nothing you saw here on this moon involving me and Mary would have told you that. You must have come to Alpha III M2 with that knowledge. And you didn't get it from Elwood because he couldn't have known it either, so spare yourself the nuisance of telling me that Elwood —'

'Okay,' Hentman said brusquely. 'Elwood retailed to us the part about the simulacrum, you and Mageboom; that's how *that* got into the script. But I'm not telling you where I got the rest. And that's it.'

Chuck said, 'I won't go before the council. That's it, too.'

Glaring, Hentman said, 'What does it matter how I found out? I know; let it rest at that. I didn't ask for the info; we wrote it in as an afterthought because when she told me —' He stopped himself at once.

'Joan Trieste,' Chuck said. Working with the slime mould; it had to be that. So now it had emerged. However it hardly mattered at this point.

'Let's not get sidetracked. Do you want your wife killed or not? Make up your mind.' Hentman waited impatiently.

'No,' Chuck said. He shook his head. There was no doubt in his mind. The solution lay at hand and he rejected it. And with finality.

Wincing, Hentman said, 'You want to do it yourself.'

'No,' he said. That was not the case. 'Your offer made me remember the slime mould and Cherigan's killing it there in the hall of my conapt. I could see that happening again, only with Mary instead of Lord Running Clam.' And, he thought, that's not what I want at all. Evidently I've been wrong. That terrible event told me something – and I can't forget it. But what, then, *do* I want in regard to Mary? He did not know; it was obscure to him, and perhaps it would remain so forever.

Once more Hentman had got out his handkerchief to mop his forehead. 'What a foul-up. You and your domestic life; it's wrecking the plans of two inter-system empires, Terra's and Alpha's – did you ever think of it that way? I give up. Frankly I'm glad you said no, but we couldn't seem to find any other inducement we could offer you; we thought that was what you wanted out of all this.'

'I thought so, too,' Chuck said. It must be that I'm still in love with her, he realized. A woman who murdered that Mans soldier as he tried to get back to his tank. But – at least in her own eyes – she had been trying to protect herself, and who could blame her for that?

Again there was a knock at the door. 'Mr. Hentman?'

Bunny Hentman opened the door. Gerald Feld stepped rapidly aside.

'Mr. Hentman, we've picked up the telepathic thought-emanations of a Ganymedean slime mould. It's somewhere nearby outside the ship. It wants to be allowed in so—' He glanced at Chuck. 'So it can be with Rittersdorf, here; it says it wants to "share his fate."' Feld grimaced. 'It's very concerned about him, obviously.' He looked disgusted.

'Let the damn thing in,' Hentman instructed. As Feld departed Hentman said to Chuck. 'To be honest I don't know what's going to become of you, Rittersdorf; you seem to have managed to create a complete mess of your life in every direction. Your marriage, your job, taking your long trip here and then changing your mind ... what *do* you have?'

'I think perhaps the Paraclete is back,' Chuck said. It

would seem so, in view of the fact that he had declined, at the final moment; to take Hentman up on his offer regarding Mary.

'What's this thing you're talking about?'

'The Holy Spirit,' Chuck said. 'It's in every man. But hard to find.'

Hentman said, 'Why don't you fill the vacuum with something noble, like saving these nuts here on Alpha III M2 from mandatory hospitalization? At least you'd be getting back at the CIA. There are a couple of highly-priced Alphane military characters on the ship ... in a matter of hours they can bring in official craft to take formal, legal possession of this moon. Of course Terran warships are hanging around here, too, but this just shows how carefully it has to be handled. You're an ex-CIA man; you ought to be able to work something tricky like this out.'

'I wonder how it would feel,' Chuck said, 'to spend the rest of my life on a moon populated solely by psychotics.'

'How the hell do you think you've *been* living? I'd call your inter-personal relationship with your wife psychotic. You'll make out; you'll find some fray to bed down with to replace Mary. As a matter of fact when our flare went off we got a reasonably good look – via the pics – of the one you were huddled with. She's not so bad, is she?'

'Annette Golding,' Chuck said. 'Polymorphous schizophrenia.'

'Yeah, but even so, won't she do?'

After a pause Chuck said, 'Possibly.' He was not a clinician, but Annette had not seemed very ill to him. Much less so, in fact, than Mary. But of course he knew Mary better. Still —

Once more there came a rap at the door; it opened and Gerald Feld said, 'Mr. Hentman, we've discovered the identity of the individual attacking us. It's the CIA simulacrum, Daniel Mageboom.' He explained, 'The Ganymedean slime mould in gratitude for our letting it into the ship gave us that information. I have an idea.'

'The same idea,' Hentman said, 'occurs to me. Or if it isn't I don't want to hear it.' He turned to Chuck. 'We'll contact Jack Elwood at the San Francisco office of the CIA; we'll have him pull the operator off the simulacrum, whoever it is that's operating it, probably Petri.' Obviously Hentman was completely familiar with the working of the CIA's San Francisco office. 'Then, Rittersdorf, we'll have you take over operation of the simulacrum from here. As long as his radio contact is maintained you can do it, and we basically need only a handful of instructions for it; simply programme it out of action and off to the sidelines. Will you do that much?'

Chuck said, 'Why should I?'

Blinking, Hentman said, 'B-because it's going to get our power supply and blow us up, using that damn laser beam as it is; that's why.'

'You'll be killed, too,' Feld pointed out to Chuck, 'in that event. Both you and your Ganymedean slime mould.'

'If I go before the supreme council of this moon,' Chuck said to Hentman, 'and ask them to seek Alphane protection, and they do – it may set off another major war between Alpha and Terra.'

'Oh hell no,' Hentman said emphatically. 'Terra doesn't care that much about this moon; *Operation Fifty-minutes*, that's just a minor, minor afterthought, nothing of importance. Believe me, I've got lots of contacts; I know this. If Terra really cared that much they would have gone in here years ago. Right?'

'What he says is true,' Feld said. 'Our man at TERPLAN verified this some time ago.'

Chuck said, 'I think the idea is a good one.'

Both Hentman and Feld visibly sighed with relief.

'I'll take it to Adolfville,' Chuck said, 'and if I can get the clans to reconvene their supreme council I'll put the idea before them. But I intend to do it in my own way.'

'What does that mean?' Hentman inquired nervously.

'I'm not a public speaker or a politician,' Chuck said. 'My job has been programming material for simulacra. If I can get control of Mageboom I'll have him appear before the council – I can feed him better lines to speak, better arguments, than I could possibly give my own self.' And also – but he did not say this aloud – he would be a great deal safer here in Hentman's ship than in Adolfville. Because the Terran military could at any moment break the Manses' shield, and one of their first acts would be to round up the inter-clan council. Someone before the council right then, proposing a switch of loyalties to the Alphane empire, would be unlikely to emerge. The proposal, coming from a Terran citizen – as he himself was – would be identified, and correctly, as an act of treason.

What I'm doing, Chuck realized with shock, is nothing less than throwing my lot in with Hentman's.

The thoughts of the slime mould came to him, reassuringly. 'You have made a wise choice, Mr. Rittersdorf. First your decision to permit your wife to live, and now this. If worst comes to worst we will all wind up subjects of the Alphanes. But under their rule I'm certain we can survive.'

Hentman, also hearing the thoughts, grinned. 'Shall we shake on it?' he asked Chuck, holding out his hand.

They shook. The treasonable deal, for better or worse, had been made.

THIRTEEN

The bulky Mans tank, clanking and rattling, its headlights blazing, coasted up beside Gabriel Baines and Annette Golding and hiccoughed to a halt. The turret flew open and the Mans within stood up cautiously.

From the surrounding darkness there emerged no laser beam attack by Dr. Mary Rittersdorf. Perhaps, Gabriel Baines thought hopefully, Mrs. Rittersdorf had acceded to the request posted by the Holy Triumvirate, to the letters of fire in the sky. In any case this appeared to be his and Annette's opportunity, as promised by Ignatz Ledebur.

In one swift motion he leaped up, tugged Annette to her feet, and with her scrambled up the side of the Mans tank. The driver helped them inside, banged the hatch shut after them; together the three of them sprawled within the cramped cab of the tank, panting sweatily.

We got away, Gabriel Baines informed himself. But he felt no joy. It did not seem important; in the great scheme it was a very little matter which they had accomplished. Still, it was something. Reaching out he put his arm around Annette.

The Man said, 'You're Golding and Baines? The council members?'

'Yes,' Annette said.

'Howard Straw ordered me to round you both up,' the Mans explained; he got behind the controls of his tank and started it into motion once more. 'I'm supposed to take you to Adolfville; there's a further meeting of the inter-clan council about to take place and Straw insists you have to be there.'

And so, Gabriel Baines reflected, because Howard Straw needs us for a vote, we survive; Mary Rittersdorf doesn't get to pick us off in the first light of dawn. Ironic. But it demonstrated the importance of the bond linking the clans. The bonds were life-giving, and to all of them. Even to the lowly Heebs.

When they reached Adolfville the tank let them off at the large central stone building; Gabriel Baines and Annette made their way up the familiar stairs, neither of them speaking; weary and soiled from lying hour after hour out in the open at night they were in no mood to exchange trivialities.

What we need, Baines decided, is not a meeting but six hours' sleep. He wondered what the purpose of this meeting was; hadn't the moon already taken its course of action by fighting the Terran invaders the best it knew how? What more could be done?

At the antechamber of the council room Gabriel Baines paused. 'I believe I'll send my simulacrum in first,' he said to Annette. With his special key he unlocked the supply closet in which – by legal right – he kept his Mans-made simulacrum. 'You never know,' And it would be a shame to lose one's life at this point, after just now escaping from Mrs. Rittersdorf.

'You Pares,' Annette said with a trace of forlorn amusement.

The Gabriel Baines simulacrum wheezed into life as he activated its mechanism. 'Good day, sir.' It then nodded to Annette. 'Miss Golding. I shall go in now, sir.' Politely, it bowed its way past the two of them, started somewhat jerkily but briskly into the council room.

'Hasn't all this taught you anything?' Annette asked Gabriel Baines as they waited for the simulacrum's return and report.

'Like what?'

'That there is no perfect defence. *There is no protection.* Being alive means being exposed; it's the nature of life to be hazardous – it's the stuff of living.'

'Well,' Baines said astutely, 'you can do the best you can by way of shielding yourself.' It never hurt to try. That was part of life, too, and every living creature engaged itself perpetually in attempting it.

The Baines simulacrum now returned and made its formal report. 'No deadly gas, no electrical discharge of a dangerous degree, no poison in the water pitcher, no sign of peep-holes for laser rifles, no concealed infernal machines. I would offer the suggestion that you can safely enter.' It ceased, then, having completed its task ... but then, to Baines' surprise, it all at once clacked back on again. 'However,' it stated, 'I would call your attention to the unusual fact that there is *another* simulacrum within the council room, other than myself. And I don't like that one bit, not one bit.'

'Who?' Baines demanded, astounded. Only a Pare would be so concerned with his self-defence as to employ an expensive sim. And he was of course the sole Pare delegate.

'The person to address the council,' his Baines-simulacrum replied. 'On whom the delegates wait; it is a simulacrum.'

Opening the door Gabriel Baines peeped in, saw the other delegates already assembled, and, standing before them, the companion of Mary Rittersdorf, the CIA man Daniel Mageboom, who, according to the slime mould, had been with her in the laser-beam attack on her husband, on the Mans tankman, himself and Annette Golding. What was Mageboom doing here? A lot of good his Baines-simulacrum had been, after all.

Against his better judgment, flying in the face of every instinct, Gabriel Baines slowly entered the council room, took his seat.

The next thing, he thought, is for Dr. Rittersdorf to gun us all down collectively from some concealed spot.

'Let me explain,' the Mageboom simulacrum said at once, as soon as Baines and Annette Golding were seated. 'I am Chuck Rittersdorf, now operating this simulacrum from a nearby spot on Alpha III M2, from the inter-system ship of Bunny Hentman. You may have noticed it; it has a rabbit painted on its side.'

Howard Straw said keenly, 'So the fact is you're no

longer an extension of the Terran intelligence service, the CIA.'

'Correct,' the Mageboom simulacrum agreed. 'We have pre-empted, at least temporarily, the CIA control of this artifact. Here, as quickly as possible, is the proposal which we feel advances the best hope for Alpha III M2, for all the clans. You must formally, as the supreme governing body on the moon, at once request the Alphanes to come in and annex. They guarantee not to treat you as hospital patients but as legitimate settlers. This annexation can be accomplished through the agency of the Hentman ship, since two high-ranking Alphane officials at this moment are —'

The simulacrum bucked, convulsed, ceased speaking.

'Something's wrong with it,' Howard Straw said, standing up.

Abruptly the Mageboom simulacrum said, 'Wrzzzzzzzzimus. Kadrax an vigdum niddddd.' Its arms flapped, its head lolled and it declared, 'Ib srwn dngmmmmmm *kunk*!'

Howard Straw stared at it, pale and tense, then turned to Gabriel Baines and said, 'The CIA on Terra has cut into the hyper-space transmission from the Hentman ship here.' He slapped his thigh, found his side arm, lifted it up and closed one eye to aim precisely.

'What I have just said,' the Mageboom simulacrum stated, in a now somewhat altered, more agitated and higher-pitched voice, 'must be disregarded as a treasonable snare and an absurd delusion. It would be a suicidal act for Alpha III M2 to seek so-called protection from the Alphane empire because for one reason —'

With a single shot Howard Straw disabled the simulacrum; pierced through its vital cephalic unit the simulacrum dropped with a crash spread eagle to the floor. Now there was silence. The simulacrum did not stir.

After a time Howard Straw put his side arm away and shakily reseated himself at his place. 'The CIA in San Francisco succeeded in pre-empting Rittersdorf,' he said, unnecessarily in that every delegate, even the Heeb Jacob Simion, had followed the sequence of events firsthand. 'However, we have heard Rittersdorf's proposal, and that's what matters.' He glanced up and down the table. 'We'd better act swiftly. Let's have the vote.'

'I vote to accept the Rittersdorf Proposal,' Gabriel Baines said, thinking to himself that this had been a close call; without Straw's quick action the simulacrum, again under Terran control, might have blown itself up and got them all.

'I agree,' Annette Golding said, with great tension.

When the total vote had been verified everyone but Dino Watters, the miserable Dep, turned out to have declared in the affirmative.

'What was wrong with you?' Gabriel Baines asked the Dep curiously.

In his hollow, despairing voice the Dep answered, 'I think it's hopeless. The Terran warships are too close. The Manses' shield just can't last that long. Or else we won't be able to contact Hentman's ship. *Something* will go wrong and then the Terrans will decimate us.' He added, 'And in addition I've been having stomach pains ever since we originally convened; I think I've got cancer.'

Howard Straw signalled by pressing a buzzer and a council servant entered, carrying a portable radio transmitter. 'I will now make contact with the Hentman ship,' Straw stated, and clicked on the transmitter.

In contact with the remnants of his organization on Terra, Bunny Hentman lifted his head and with a haggard expression on his face said to Chuck Rittersdorf, 'What happened is this. That guy London, chief of the San Francisco branch of the CIA and Elwood's superior, caught on to what was happening; he was monitoring the sim's activities – must have already been suspicious, no doubt because I got away.'

'Is Elwood dead?' Chuck asked.

'No, just in the grang at the S.F. Presidio. And Petri took over once more.' Hentman rose to his feet, shut off the line to Terra temporarily. 'But they didn't regain control of Mageboom in time.'

'You're an optimist,' Chuck said.

'Listen,' Hentman said vigorously. 'Those people in Adolfville may be legally and clinically insane, but they're not stupid, especially in matters pertaining to their security. They heard the proposal and I bet right now they're voting in favour of it. We should get a call from them by radio any time.' He examined his watch. 'I say within fifteen minutes.' He turned to Feld. 'Get those two Alphanes in here, so they can relay the request immediately to their ships of the line.'

Feld hurried off. After a pause Hentman, sighing, reseated himself.

Lighting a fat, green, Terran cigar Bunny Hentman leaned back, hands behind his head, regarding Chuck.

Moments passed.

'Does the Alphane empire need TV comics?' Chuck asked.

Hentman grinned. 'As much as they need simulacrum-programmers.'

Ten minutes later the call came through from Adolfville.

'Okay,' Hentman said, nodding as he listened to Howard Straw. He glanced at Chuck. 'Where are those two Alphanes? Now's the time; now or just plain never.'

'I'm here, representing the Empire.' It was the Alphane RBX 303; it had hurried flappingly into the room with Feld and its companion Alphane. 'Assure them once again that they will not be treated as invalids but as settlers. We are absolutely anxious to make that point clear. Alphane policy has always been—'

'Don't make a speech,' Hentman said incisively. 'Ring up your warships and get them down to the surface.' He handed the transmitter's microphone to the Alphane, rose wearily and walked over to stand beside Chuck. 'Jeez,' he murmured. 'At a time like this it wants to recap on its foreign policy over the last sixty years.' He shook his head. His cigar had gone out; now with great deliberateness he relit it. 'Well, I guess we're going to learn the answers to our ultimate queries.'

'What queries?' Chuck said.

Hentman said briefly, 'Whether the Alphane empire can use TV comics and sim-programmers.' He walked away, stood listening to RBX 303 trying by means of the ship's transmitter to raise the Alphane battle fleet. Puffing cigar smoke, hands in his pockets, he silently waited. One would never know from his expression, Chuck reflected, that literally our lives depend on the successful establishment of this conduit of communication.

Twitching with nervous agitation, Gerald Feld came up to Chuck and said, 'Where's the Frau Doktor right now?'

'Probably wandering around somewhere below,' Chuck said. The Hentman ship, now in an orbit three hundred miles at apogee, no longer had contact, except by radio, with events occurring on the moon's surface.

'She can't do anything, can she?' Feld said. 'To fnug this up, I mean. Of course she'd like to.'

Chuck said, 'My wife, or ex-wife, is a scared woman. She's alone on a hostile moon, waiting for a Terran fleet which probably will never come, although of course she doesn't know that.' He did not hate Mary now; that was gone, like so many other things.

'You feel sorry for her?' Feld asked.

'I – just wish that destiny hadn't crossed her and me up quite so completely as it has. Her in relationship to me, I mean. I have the feeling that in some obscure way which I can't fathom Mary and I could somehow still have made it together. Maybe years from now—'

Hentman announced, 'He's got the line ships. We're in.' He beamed. 'Now we can get so goddamn completely absolutely bagged that – well, you name it. I've got the booze here on the ship. Nothing, you understand, nothing at all more is required from any of us; we've done it. We're now citizens of the Alphane empire; we'll pretty soon have licence-plate numbers instead of names, but that's okay with me.'

Finishing his statement to Feld, Chuck said, 'Maybe someday when it doesn't matter I can look back and see what I should have done that would have avoided this, Mary and me lying in the dirt shooting back and forth at each other.' Across the darkened landscape of an unfamiliar world, he thought to himself. Where neither of us is at home, and yet where I – at least – will probably have to live out the remainder of my life. Maybe Mary too, he thought sombrely.

To Hentman he said, 'Congratulations.'

'Thanks,' Hentman said. To Feld he said, 'Congratulations, Jerry.'

'Thank you,' Feld said. 'Congratulations and a long life,' he said to Chuck. 'Fellow Alphane.'

'I wonder,' Chuck said to Hentman, 'if you could do me a favour.'

'Like what? Anything.'

Chuck said. 'Lend me a launch. Let me drop down to the surface.'

'What for? You're a hell of a lot safer up here.'

'I want to look for my wife,' Chuck said.

Raising an eyebrow Hentman said, 'You're sure you want that? Yeah, I can see by the expression on your face. You poor damn guy. Well, maybe you can talk her into staying with you on Alpha III M2. If the clans don't mind. And if the Alphane authorities —'

'Just give him the launch,' Feld interrupted. 'At this moment he's a terribly unhappy man; he doesn't have time to hear what you want to say.'

'Okay,' Hentman said to Chuck, nodding. 'I'll give you the launch; you can drop down there and do anything foolish that appeals to you – I wash my hands of it. Of course I hope you come back, but if not —' He shrugged. 'That's the way these things go.'

'And take your slime mould with you when you leave,' Feld said to Chuck.

Half an hour later he had parked the launch in a thicket of skinny poplar-like trees and stood in the open air, smelling the wind and listening. He heard nothing. It was only a little world, and nothing much was happening on it; a council had voted, a clan maintained a defensive screen, a few people waited in fear and trembling but probably, as for example the Heebs of Gandhitown, most of the inhabitants shuffled through their psychotic daily routine without interruption.

'Am I insane?' he asked Lord Running Clam, who had slithered off a few dozen yards to a damper spot; the slime mould was aquatropic. 'Is this the all-embracing worst thing, of all the possible worst things, that I could do?'

' "Insane," ' the slime mould responded, 'is, strictly speaking, a legal term. I consider you very foolish; I think Mary Rittersdorf will probably commit an act of ferocity and hostility toward you as soon as she sets eyes on you. But maybe you want that. You're tired. It's been a long struggle. Those illegal stimulant drugs which I supplied you; they didn't help. I think they only made you more despairing and weary.' It added, 'Maybe you ought to go to Cotton Mather Estates.'

'What's *that*?' Even the name made him draw back with aversion.

'The settlement of the Deps. Live with them there, in endless dark gloom.' The slime mould's tone was mildly chiding.

'Thanks,' Chuck said ironically.

'Your wife is not near,' the slime mould decided. 'At least I don't pick up her thoughts. Let us move on.'

'Okay.' He plodded back toward the launch.

As the slime mould followed after him, in through the open hatch, it thought, 'There is always the possibility, which you must consider, that Mary is dead.'

'Dead!' He stared at the slime mould, halting. 'How?'

'As you told Mr. Hentman; there is a war being conducted here on this moon. There have been deaths, although fortunately very few as yet. But the potential here for violent death is enormous. The last we saw of Mary Rittersdorf involved the three mystics, the so-called Holy Triumvirate, and their nauseous psychotic projections in the sky. I suggest therefore that we take the launch to Gandhitown, where the prime mover of the triumvirate, Ignatz Ledebur, exists – and that is the proper word – amidst his customary squalor, among his cats, wives and children.'

'But Ledebur would never —'

'Psychosis is psychosis,' the slime mould pointed out.

'And a fanatic can never really be trusted.'

'True,' Chuck said gratingly.

Shortly, they were on their way to Gandhitown.

'I really wonder,' the slime mould pondered, 'what I hope for your sake; in some respects you would be so much better off if it she were —'

'It's my business,' Chuck interrupted.

'Sorry,' the slime mould thought contritely, .but with sombre overtones; it could not eradicate them from its musings.

The launch buzzed on with no further interchange between the two of them.

Ignatz Ledebur, depositing a heap of cooked, ageing spaghetti before his two black-face pet sheep, glanced up to see the launch descend to a landing in the road adjacent to his shack. He finished feeding the sheep, then walked leisurely back to his shack with the pan. Cats of all sorts followed hopefully.

Indoors, he dropped the pan among the encrusted dishes heaped in the sink, paused a moment to glance toward the woman asleep on the wooden planks which made up the dining table. He then picked up a cat, carried it with him outdoors once more. The arrival of the ship did not, of course, come as a surprise; he had already experienced a vision of it. He was not alarmed, but on the other hand he was scarcely complacent.

Two figures, one of them human, the other amorphous and yellow, emerged from the launch. They made their way with difficulty across the discarded trash toward Ledebur.

'You will be gratified to hear,' Ledebur said to them, by way of greeting, 'that almost at this very moment Alphane warships are preparing to land here on our world.' He smiled, but the man facing him did not smile back. The yellow blob, of course, had nothing to smile with. 'So your mission,' Ledebur said, with a shade of perturbation, 'has yielded successful results.' He did not enjoy the hostility which emanated from the man; he saw, with his mystical Psionic insight, the man's anger glow in a red, ominous nimbus about his head.

'Where's Mary Rittersdorf?' the man, Chuck Rittersdorf, said. 'My wife. Do you know?' He turned to the Ganymedean slime mould beside him. 'Does he know?'

The slime mould thought, 'Yes, Mr. Rittersdorf.'

'Your wife,' Ignatz Ledebur said, nodding. 'She was doing injurious things out there. Already she had killed one Mans and was —'

'If you don't show me my wife,' Chuck Rittersdorf said to Ledebur, 'I'm going to hack you to bits.' He took one step toward the saint.

Petting the cat which he held with agitation, Ledebur said, 'I wish you'd come in and have a cup of tea.'

The next he knew he was lying supine on the ground; his ears rang and his head throbbed dully. With difficulty he managed to sit groggily up, wondering what had happened.

'Mr. Rittersdorf hit you,' the slime mould explained. 'A glancing blow slightly above the cheekbone.'

'No more,' Ledebur said thickly. He tasted blood; spitting, he sat massaging his head. No vision had forewarned him of *this*, unfortunately. 'She's inside the house,' he said, then.

Passing by him Chuck Rittersdorf strode to the door, yanked it open, disappeared inside. Ledebur managed at last to drag himself upright; he stood unsteadily and then, dragging a little, followed.

Indoors, in the front room, he halted by the door, while cats, free to come and go, hopped and scampered and quarrelled on all sides of him.

At the bed Chuck Rittersdorf bent over the sleeping woman. 'Mary,' he said, 'wake up.' He reached out, took hold of her bare, dangling arm, joggled her. 'Get your clothes and get out of here. Come on!'

The woman in Ignatz Ledebur's bed, who had replaced Elsie, gradually opened her eyes; she focused on Chuck's face, then all at once blinked, became fully conscious. She sat reflexively up, then caught hold of the tumble of blankets, wound them about her, covering her small, high breasts.

The slime mould, circumspectly, had remained outdoors.

'Chuck,' Mary Rittersdorf said, in a low, steady voice, 'I came to this house voluntarily. So I—'

He grabbed her by the wrist, yanked her from the bed; blankets fell and a coffee mug bounced and rolled, spilling its cold contents. Two cats who had gone under the bed rushed out in fright, bypassed Ignatz Ledebur in their haste to get away.

Smooth and slender and naked, Mary Rittersdorf faced her husband. 'You don't have a thing to say about what I do any more,' she said. She reached for her clothes, picked up her blouse, then rummaged further, as self-possessed as could under the circumstances be expected. She began methodically, garment by garment, to dress; from the expression on her face she might have been entirely alone.

Chuck said, 'Alphane ships control this area, now. The Manses are ready to lift their shield to let them in; it's all been accomplished. While you were asleep in this—' He jerked his head toward Ignatz Ledebur. 'This individual's bed.'

'And you're with them?' Mary asked frigidly, as she buttoned her blouse. 'Why, of course you are. The Alphanes have seized the moon and you're going to live here under them.' She finished dressing, began then to comb her hair at a reasonable, slow rate.

'If you'll stay here,' Chuck said, 'on Alpha III M2 and not return to Terra—'

'I am staying here,' Mary said. 'I've already worked it out.' She indicated Ignatz Ledebur. 'Not with him; this was only for a little while and he knew it. I wouldn't live in Gandhitown – it's not the place for me, not by any stretch of the imagination.'

'Where then?'

Mary said, 'I think Da Vinci Heights.'

'Why?' Incredulous, he stared at her.

'I'm not sure. I haven't even seen it. But I admire the Manses; I even admire the one I killed. He never was afraid, even when he was running for his tank and knowing he wouldn't make it. Never in my life have I seen anything resembling that, not ever.'

'The Manses,' Chuck said, 'will never let you in.'

'Oh yes.' She nodded calmly. 'They certainly will.'

Chuck turned questioningly to Ignatz Ledebur.

'They will,' Ledebur agreed. 'Your wife is right.' Both of us, he realized, you and I; we've lost her. Nobody can claim this woman for long. It's just not in her nature, in her biology. Turning, he mournfully left the shack, stepped outside, walked over to the spot at which the slime mould waited.

'I think you have showed Mr. Rittersdorf,' the slime mould thought to him, 'the impossibility of what he is trying to do.'

'I suppose so,' Ledebur said, without an iota of enthusiasm.

Chuck appeared, pale and grim; he strode past Ledebur toward the launch. 'Let's go,' he said roughly to the slime mould over his shoulder.

The slime mould, as hastily as was physically possible, followed after him. The two of them entered the launch; the hatch shut and the launch zooped up into the mid-morning sky.

For an interval Ignatz Ledebur watched it go, and then he re-entered the shack. He found Mary at the ice box searching for something out of which to fashion breakfast.

Together he and she prepared their morning meal.

'The Manses,' Ledebur pointed out, 'are very brutal, in some ways.'

Mary laughed. 'So what?' she said mockingly.

He had no answer to that. His saintliness and his visions did not help him there, not one bit.

After a long time Chuck said, 'Will this launch take us back to the Sol system and Terra?'

'Absolutely not,' Lord Running Clam said.

'Okay,' Chuck said, 'I'll locate a Terran warship parked in this region. I'm going back to Terra, accept whatever punitive litigation the authorities have in mind, and then work out an arrangement with Joan Trieste.'

The slime mould stated, 'In view of the fact that the punitive litigation will consist of a request for the death penalty, any arrangement with Joan Trieste is unlikely.'

'What do you suggest, then?'

'Something you will baulk at.'

Chuck said, 'Tell me anyhow.' In view of his situation he could not turn anything down.

'You – ahem. This is awkward; I must put it properly. You must entice your wife into giving you a thorough battery of psychological tests.'

After a while he managed to say, 'To find out which settlement I would fit best in?'

'Yes,' the slime mould said, but reluctantly. 'That was the idea. This is not to say you're psychotic; this is merely to determine the drift of your personality in the most general —'

'Suppose the tests show no drift, no neurosis, no latent psychosis, no character deformation, no psychopathic tendencies, in other words nothing? What do I do then?' Without unduly complimenting himself – at this point he was well beyond that – he had an inkling that was precisely what the tests would show. He did not belong in any of the settlements here on Alpha III M2; here he was a loner, an outcast, accompanied by no one even remotely resembling him.

'Your long-held urge to murder your wife,' the slime mould said, 'may well be a symptom of an underlying emotional illness.' It tried to sound hopeful, but none the less it failed. 'I still believe it's worth a try,' it persisted.

Chuck said, 'Suppose I founded one more settlement here.'

'A settlement composed of one person?'

'There must be occasional normals showing up here. People who work their way out of their derangements and possibly children who never developed them. As it stands here you're classified as polymorphous schizophrenic until proved otherwise; that's not right.' He had been giving this considerable thought, ever since it had first appeared that he might be required to remain on the moon. 'They'll come trickling in. Given time.'

'The gingerbread house in the woods of this moon,' the slime mould mused. 'And you inside, waiting stealthily to trap whoever passes by. Especially the children.' It tittered. 'Pardon me. I shouldn't take this lightly; forgive me.'

Chuck said nothing; her merely piloted the launch upward.

'Will you try the tests?' the slime mould asked. 'Before going off and founding your own settlement?'

'Okay,' Chuck said. That did not seem unreasonable to ask.

'Do you imagine, in view of your mutual hostility toward each other, that your wife can properly administer the tests?'

'I suppose so.' Scoring was routine, not interpretive.

The slime mould decided, 'I will act as the intermediary between you and her; you will not have to confront each other again until the results are obtained.'

'Thanks,' Chuck said, with gratitude.

The slime mould said reflectively, 'There is one other possibility which although admittedly farfetched might well be considered. It might yield a great harvest, although of course considerable time would be involved for that to come about.' It plunged through to the summation of its thought. 'Perhaps you can induce Mary to take the tests, too.'

The idea came to Chuck as a complete, shocking surprise. For one thing – his mind moved swiftly, analysing and introspecting – he could not see the advantage in it whatever showed up. Because the inhabitants of the moon would not be receiving therapy; that had already been decided, and by his own actions. If Mary revealed herself in the tests – as well she might – as seriously disturbed, she would simply remain so, would continue as she was; no psychiatrist was about to enter and begin tinkering with her. So what did the slime mould mean by a 'great harvest'?

The slime mould, receiving his rapid thoughts, explained,

'Suppose your wife did disclose by means of the testing process that she includes a severe streak of the manic in her makeup. This would be my lay analysis of her, and it evidently is her own as well. For her to recognize this, that she is, like Howard Straw or those wild tank drivers, a Mans, would be for her to face the fact that —'

'You seriously believe it would make her *humble*? Less sure of herself?' The slime mould patently was no authority on human nature – and in particular Mary Rittersdorf's nature. Not to mention the fact that for a manic, as well as a Pare, self-doubt was beyond conception; their entire emotional structure was predicated on a sense of certitude.

How simple it would be if the slime mould's naïve view were correct, if a severely disturbed person had only to see his test results to comprehend and accept his psychological deformation. Lord, Chuck thought dismally. If there's one thing that contemporary psychiatry has shown, it's that. Merely knowing that you are mentaly sick won't make you well, any more than knowing you have a heart condition provides a suddenly sound heart.

In fact, the opposite would more than likely be the case. Mary, fortified by the companionship of a settlement of those resembling her, would be stabilized forever: her manic tendency would have received social sanction. She would probably wind up as the mistress of Howard Straw, perhaps even eventually replace him as the Mans delegate to the supreme inter-clan council. At Da Vinci Heights she would rise to power – by treading on those around her.

'Never the less,' the slime mould persisted, 'when I ask her to give you the tests I will beg her to do the same for herself. I still believe that some good can arise out of this. *Know thyself*; that was an ancient Terran slogan, is it not? Dating from your highly-praised Greek antiquity. I can't help thinking that to know yourself is to provide yourself with a weapon by which you non-telepathic species may reshape your psyche until —'

'Until just what?'

The slime mould was silent; clearly when it came right down to it the slime mould did not actually know.

'Give her the tests,' Chuck said. 'And we'll see.' We'll see who is right, he thought. He hoped that it would be the slime mould.

That night in Da Vinci Heights, very late, Lord Running Clam after much delicate negotiation managed to persuade Dr. Mary Rittersdorf to take a full spectrum of psychological profile tests and then to administer, in her professional capacity, the same group of tests to her husband.

In the intricately-decorated, convoluted home of the Mans council delegate, Howard Straw, the three of them faced one another; Straw himself lurked in the background, amused by what was taking place, aloof and constitutionally contemptuous. He sat and sketched with pastel crayons, rapidly, a series of portraits of Mary; this was only one of his many artistic and creative pursuits and even at this time of upheaval, with the Alphane warships landing on the moon one behind another, he did not abandon it. Typically Mans, he had countless irons in the fire simultaneously; he was multi-sided.

Mary, with the test results spread out before her on Howard Straw's hand-wrought handsome wood and black-iron table, said, 'This is a dreadful thing for me to have to admit, but it was a good idea. The two of us subjecting ourselves to these standard psych-profile testing procedures. Frankly I'm surprised at the results. Obviously – it goes without saying – I should have been exposing myself at regular intervals to such tests ... in view of the results.' She sat back, willowy and supple in her white turtleneck sweater and Titanian og-metal slacks; getting out a cigarette with trembling fingers she lit up. 'You're without a trace of mental disturbance, dear,' she said to Chuck, who sat across from her. 'Merry Christmas,' she added, and smiled frozenly.

'What about you?' Chuck said, constricted in his throat and heart with tension.

'I'm not Mans at all. In fact I'm just the opposite; I reveal a marked agitated depression. I'm a Dep.' She continued to smile; it was a worthy effort on her part and he took note of it, of her courage. 'My continual pressing of you regarding your income – that was certainly due to my depression, my delusional sense that everything had gone wrong, that something *had* to be done or we were doomed.' She stubbed her cigarette out, all at once, and lit another. To Howard Straw she said, 'What's your reaction to that?'

'Though,' Straw said with his customary lack of empathy, 'you won't be living here after all; you'll be situated over at Cotton Mather Estates. With happy-boy Dino Watters and the rest like him.' He chuckled. 'And some of them are even worse, as you're going to discover. We'll let you hang around here a few days but then you've absolutely got to go. You're just not one of us.' He added, in a little less brutal tone, 'If you could have foreseen this moment when you volunteered to TERPLAN for this job, this *Operation Fifty-minutes* – I'll bet you would have thought twice. Am I right?' He gazed at her penetratingly.

She shrugged without answering. And then all at once, to the surprise of all of them, she began to cry. 'Jesus, I don't want to live with those damn Deps,' she whispered. 'I'm going back to Terra.' To Chuck she said, 'I can, but you can't. I don't have to stay here and find a niche. Like you do.'

The slime mould's thoughts reached Chuck. 'Now that you've received your tests results what do you intend to do, Mr. Rittersdorf?'

'Go ahead and found my own settlement,' Chuck said. 'I'm calling it Thomas Jeffersonburg. Mather was a Dep, Da Vinci was a Mans, Adolf Hitler was a Pare, Gandhi was a Heeb. Jefferson was a —' He hunted for the correct word. 'A Norm. That will be Thomas Jeffersonburg: the Norm settlement. So far containing only one person, but with great anticipations for the future.' At least the problem of picking the delegate to the supreme inter-clan council is automatically solved, he thought to himself.

'You're an absolute fool,' Howard Straw said disparagingly. 'Nobody'll ever show up and live with you in your settlement. You'll spend the rest of your life in isolation – six weeks from now you'll be out of your mind; you'll be ready for every other settlement on the moon, except of course this one.'

'Maybe so.' Chuck nodded. But he was not so positive as Straw. He was thinking once more of Annette Golding, for one. Surely in her case it would not require much; she was so close to rationality, to a balanced outlook. There was virtually nothing separating himself from her. And if there existed one such as this there had to be more. He had a feeling that he would not be the sole inhabitant of Thomas Jeffersonburg for long. But even if he were —

He would wait it out. For however much time it took. And he would get help in building his settlement; already he had established what appeared to be a solid working relationship with the Pare rep, Gabriel Baines, and that portended something. If he could get along with Baines he probably could get along with the several clans as such, with perhaps the possible exception of Manses such as Straw and of course the noxious, deteriorated Heebs like Ignatz Ledebur, who had no sense of inter-personal responsibility.

'I feel sick,' Mary said, her lips trembling. 'Will you come and visit me in Cotton Mather Estates, Chuck? I'm not going to be stuck with just Deps around me the rest of my life, am I?'

'You said —' he began.

'I just *can't* go back to Terra, not if I'm sick; not with what those tests showed.'

'Of course,' he said. 'I'll be glad to visit you.' As a matter of fact he expected to spend a good deal of his time at the other settlements. By this he would forestall Howard Straw's prophecy from coming true. By this – and a great deal else.

'When I next sporify,' the slime mould thought to him, 'there will be a reasonably large number of myselves; some of us will be glad to settle in Thomas Jeffersonburg. And we will stay away from burning autos, this time.'

'Thanks,' Chuck said. 'I'll be grateful to have you. All of you.'

Howard Straw's jeering, manic laugh filled the room; the

idea seemed to awaken his cynical amusement. However, no one paid attention to him. Straw shrugged, returned to his pastel sketching.

Outside the house the retro-rockets of a warship roared as the ship expertly settled to a landing. The Alphane occupation of Da Vinci Heights, long delayed, was about to begin.

Rising to his feet and opening the front door Chuck Rittersdorf stepped out into the night darkness to watch and listen. For a time he stood alone, smoking, hearing the sounds that gradually settled lower and lower to the surface of the moon, came to rest in a silence that seemed permanent. It would be a long time, perhaps after he himself had disappeared from the scene, before they would be taking off again; he felt that keenly as he lounged in the darkness, close by Howard Straw's front door.

All at once the door behind him opened. His wife, or more specifically his former wife, stepped out, shut the door after her and stood beside him, not speaking; together the two of them listened to the racket of the descending Alphane warships and admired the fiery trails in the sky, each enclosed in his own thoughts.

'Chuck,' Mary said abruptly, 'you know we have to do one vital thing ... you probably haven't thought about it but if we're going to settle here we've got to find some way to get our children from Terra.'

'That's right.' Actually he had thought of it; he nodded. 'But would you want to bring the kids up here?' Especially Debby, he thought. She was extremely sensitive; undoubtedly she would, living here, pick up the deranged patterns of belief and conduct from the psychotic majority. It was going to be a difficult problem.

Mary said. 'If I'm sick—' She did not finish; it was unnecessary. Because if she were sick, Debby would already have been exposed to the subtle play of mental illness operating within the close quarters of family life; the harm, if it were to be done, had already been accomplished.

Tossing his cigarette away into the darkness Chuck put his arm around his wife's small waist and drew her against him; he kissed the top of her head, smelling the warm, sweet odour of her hair. 'We'll take the chance, exposing the children to this environment. Maybe they'll supply a model to the other children here ... we can put them into the common school which is maintained here on Alpha III M2; I'd be willing to risk it, if you would. What do you say?'

'Okay,' Mary said remotely. And then more vigorously she said, 'Chuck, do you really think we have a chance, you and I? Of working out a new basis of living ... by which we can be around one another for a prolonged time? Or are we just—' She gestured. 'Just going to drift back into the old ways of hatred and suspicion and all the rest.'

'I don't know,' he said, and that was the truth.

'Lie to me. Tell me we can do it.'

'We can do it.'

'You really think so? Or are you lying?'

'I'm—'

'Say you're not lying.' Her voice was urgent.

'I'm not lying,' he said. 'I know we can do it. We're both young and viable and we're not rigid like the Pares and the Manses. Right?'

'Right.' Mary was silent a moment and then she said, 'You're sure you don't prefer that Poly girl, that Annette Golding, to me? Be honest.'

'I prefer you.' And this time he was not lying.

'What about that girl Alfson took the potent-pics of? You and that Joan whatever-her-name-is ... I mean, you actually went to bed with her.'

'I still prefer you.'

'Tell me *why* you prefer me,' she said. 'Sick and mean as I am.'

'I can't exactly say.' In fact he could not explain it at all; it was in the nature of a mystery. Still, it was the truth; he felt its validity within him.

'I wish you luck in your one-man settlement,' Mary said. 'One man and a dozen slime moulds.' She laughed. 'What a crazy enclave. Yes, I'm sure we should bring our children here. I used to think that I was so – you know. So completely different from my patients. They were sick and I wasn't. Now —' She became silent.

'There's not that much difference,' he finished for her.

'You don't feel that about yourself, do you? That you're basically different from me ... after all, you do test out as being well and I don't.'

'It's just degree,' he said, and meant it. Suicidal impulses had motivated him, and after that hostile, murderous impulses toward her – and yet he tested out satisfactorily on the formal graphs derived from long-accepted testing procedures, while Mary did not. What a slight degree it was. She, as well as he, as well as everyone on Alpha III M2 including the arrogant Mans rep Howard Straw, struggled for balance, for insight; it was a natural tendency for living creatures. Hope always existed, even perhaps – God forbid – for the Heebs. Although unfortunately the hope for those of Gandhitown was slender indeed.

He thought: And the hope is slender enough for us of Terra. We who have just now emigrated to Alpha III M2. Yet – it is there.

'I've decided,' Mary announced huskily, 'that I love you.'

'Okay,' he agreed, pleased.

Abruptly, obliterating his tranquil state, a sharp, highly-articulated rumination by the slime mould reached him. 'As long as it is confession-of-feeling-and-deeds time I suggest that your wife lay on the table the full account of her brief affair with Bunny Hentman.' It corrected itself, 'I retract the expression, "lay on the table," as unbelievably unfortunate. However my basic point remains: so anxious was she that you obtain employment with high financial return —'

'Let me say it,' Mary said.

'Please do,' the slime mould agreed. 'And I will speak up again only if you are remiss as regards completeness of account.'

Mary said, 'I had a very short affair with Bunny Hentman, Chuck. Just prior to my leaving Terra. That's all there is.'

'There is more,' the slime mould contradicted.

'Details?' she said hotly. 'Do I have to tell exactly when

and where we —'

'Not that. Another aspect of your relationship with Hentman.'

'All right.' Resignedly Mary nodded. 'During those four days,' she said to Chuck, 'I told Bunny that as I saw it, using all my experience with marital break-ups, I foresaw – based on my knowledge of your personality – that you'd try to kill me. If you failed in your suicide attempt.' She was silent, then. 'I don't know why I told him. Maybe I was scared. Evidently I had to tell someone and I was with him quite a bit, then.'

So it had not been Joan. He felt a little better about the whole thing, knowing this. And he could hardly blame Mary for what she had done. It was a wonder she hadn't gone to the police; evidently she was telling the truth when she said she loved him. This shed new light on her; she had forfeited a chance to injure him, and at a time of great crisis.

'Maybe we'll have more children while we're here on this moon,' Mary said. 'Like the slime moulds ... we arrived and we'll increase in numbers until we become legion. The majority.' She laughed in an odd, soft way, and, in the darkness, relaxed against him, as she had not done in ages.

In the sky the Alphane ships continued to appear and both he and Mary remained silent, planning out schemes by which to obtain the children. It would be difficult, he realized soberly, perhaps even more tricky than anything they had done so far. But possibly the remains of the Hentman organization could assist them. Or some of the slime mould's countless business contacts among Terrans and non-Terrans. Both were distinct possibilities. And Hentman's agent who had infiltrated the CIA, his former boss Jack Elwood ... but Elwood was now in jail. Anyhow if unhappily enough their efforts failed, as Mary said they would be having more children; this did not make up for the ones lost, but it would be a good omen, one that could not be overlooked.

'Do you love me, too?' Mary asked, her lips close to his ear.

'Yes,' he said truthfully. And then he said, 'Ouch.' Because without warning she had bitten him, nearly severing the lobe of his ear.

That, too, seemed to him an omen.

But of what he could not quite yet tell.

Philip K. Dick

The Divine Invasion

Deep in cryonic suspension, Herb Asher thought he was still happily puttering about in his dome in the star system CY30-CY30B, listening to the latest Linda Fox album.

In only he hadn't been such a nice guy, he'd still have really been there. Instead he married the terminally ill (and pregnant) woman in the next dome and was taken advantage of by an obstreperous local deity (father of his wife's unborn avatar).

And now he had to go through it all again. (The story had been oddly familiar the first time.) Who would have thought that he, Herb Asher, would assist an invasion of his own planet – even an invasion by the Son of God . . . ?

'The funniest sf writer of his time, and perhaps the most terrifying' *Encyclopaedia of Science Fiction*

'This greatest of science fiction writers has control over the idioms of science fiction and demonstrates it in this effortless novel' JOHN CLUTE, *Bookworld*

ISBN 978 0 00 648250 5

Philip K. Dick

The Game-Players of Titan

Roaming the pristine landscape of Earth, cared for by machines and aliens, the few remaining humans alive since the war with Titan play Bluff to maximise the remote chance some pairings will produce a child. When Pete Garden, a particularly suicidal member of the Pretty Blue Fox game-playing group, loses his current wife and his deed to Berkeley, he stumbles upon a far bigger, more sinister version of the game. The telepathic Vugs of Titan are the players and at stake is the Earth itself.

'One of the most original practitioners writing any kind of fiction' *Sunday Times*

'The most brilliant sci-fi mind on any planet' *Rolling Stone*

ISBN 978 0 00 711588 4